THE LOST SISTER

THE LOST SISTER

ANDREA GUNRAJ

Vagrant PRESS

Advance praise for *The Lost Sister*

"With compassion, clarity, and enormous talent, Andrea Gunraj tells an epic story of sisters from Guyana to Canada, from the Nova Scotia Home for Colored Children to the University of Toronto, and from 1938 to the present. This novel exposes losses no one should suffer but all too many bear. Reading it will break your heart and give you hope to heal."

– Julia Phillips, author of *Disappearing Earth*

"Two women, mysteriously connected, pulled me into their stories page by page. I could not stop reading for a minute until the stories became one story beautifully resolved."

– Linda Spalding, author of *The Purchase,* Winner of the 2012 Governor General's Literary Award

"In clear, resonant language, blending present and past, inner turmoil, outer pleasures, and occasional torment, Andrea Gunraj tells the haunting tale of three generations of women. In a skillfully measured dissection of experiences, we see the world, mysterious in its deceit and intrigue, through the eyes of children, and share in their rivalries and remorse. A deeply felt story that balances the realism of its content with the tenderness of its treatment."

–Karim Alrawi, author of *Book Of Sands: A Novel of the Arab Uprising*

"*The Lost Sister* is a carefully crafted collision of loss and family and pain, intertwining history and culture and place through a brilliantly deliberate life dance."

–Wanda Taylor, author of *The Nova Scotia Home for Colored Children: The Hurt, the Hope, and the Healing*

"A finely crafted story about forgiveness and redemption between two sets of sisters, this novel's beating heart is the longing that comes from missing someone you love. *The Lost Sister* is both a mystery and a coming-of-age story that is as compelling as it is empathetic."

–Harriet Alida Lye, author of *The Honey Farm*

Praise for *The Sudden Disappearance of Seetha*

"A sparkling first novel.... A riveting, expertly told tale full of satisfying counterbalances and impeccable narrative timing. This is an exciting, memorable debut."

–***Quill & Quire*, starred review**

"Andrea Gunraj's debut novel, *The Sudden Disappearance of Seetha*, is wonderfully accomplished. It is a riveting, often violent tale of the lives of girls who grow to be women in a fictional, politically corrupt Guyana... This is certainly a novel to relish, and I'm sure—I hope—we will see much more of Gunraj in the future."

–***The Globe and Mail***

"In this impressive Canadian debut, a young Guyanese woman steps out from under the shadow of her brother by running off with the local bad boy. Gunraj isn't afraid of dark subjects—jealousy, violence, regret—but she keeps a grip on her optimism, too."

–***Chatelaine***

"*The Sudden Disappearance of Seetha* announces the arrival of a wonderful storyteller. The dynamics of the relationship between Navi and Neela, a brother and a sister, and how their individual lives play out show that fate is unalterable depending on one's social standing in life. Andrea Gunraj has written a book that once you pick up, you won't be able to put down—a thrilling and excellent read."

–**Musharraf Ali Farooqi, author of *The Story of a Widow***

"Ambitious, rich and wide-ranging.... [Gunraj] will be a writer to watch as she hones her craft."

–***Winnipeg Free Press***

"Andrea Gunraj's debut novel is a tale of innocence and experience...Gunraj's true facility as a storyteller [is] her ability to humanize the freak as well as the villain."

–***The Rover***

Vagrant Press is an imprint of
Nimbus Publishing Limited
3660 Strawberry Hill St, Halifax, NS, B3K 5A9
(902) 455-4286 nimbus.ca

Printed and bound in Canada

Editor: Bethany Gibson
Copy Editor: Kate Juniper
Cover Design: Heather Bryan
Interior Design: Jenn Embree

NB1427

This story is a work of fiction. Names, characters, incidents, and places, including organizations and institutions, either are the product of the author's imagination or are used fictitiously.

Library and Archives Canada Cataloguing in Publication

Title: The lost sister / Andrea Gunraj.
Names: Gunraj, Andrea, 1978- author.
Identifiers: Canadiana (print) 20190154152 | Canadiana (ebook) 20190154160 | ISBN 9781771087650 (softcover) | ISBN 9781771088411 (HTML)
Classification: LCC PS8613.U58 L67 2019 | DDC C813/.6—dc23

Canada

Canada Council for the Arts Conseil des arts du Canada

NOVA SCOTIA

ONTARIO ARTS COUNCIL
CONSEIL DES ARTS DE L'ONTARIO
an Ontario government agency
un organisme du gouvernement de l'Ontario

Nimbus Publishing acknowledges the financial support for its publishing activities from the Government of Canada, the Canada Council for the Arts, and from the Province of Nova Scotia. We are pleased to work in partnership with the Province of Nova Scotia to develop and promote our creative industries for the benefit of all Nova Scotians.

CHAPTER 1

I WAS THE COWARDLY SISTER. BUT THAT DAY IN JUNE OF 1998, I SOMEHOW fooled myself into bravery. I waited outside for hours, wandering through the public library stacks and small streets and parks of my neighbourhood as the sky turned deep blue and settled to darkness, a few feeble star points surfacing above the city's pollution. It was my first real attempt at defiance.

I wanted my older sister Diana to get in trouble.

How could you let your little sister stay outside, alone in the dark? I imagined my father reprimanding her. *You're fifteen. You're supposed to take care of her!*

But as I made my way back home, the pleasure of getting my sister into trouble sieved away and I was skewered by doubt. *Why didn't you stay with Diana like you promised, Alisha? You're hardly thirteen. She's in charge of you.* I could never be sure my parents would choose me over her.

My chest was tight; my heartbeat ricocheted to my throat. The sidewalks were emptied of bikes and strollers and pattering children, and even the few passing cars seemed quieter than usual. It was just me and my wheezing breath, my stinging legs, hurrying past buildings and townhouses that were dark rectangles, past bushes and trees that were billows of black.

Stoplights and orange-yellow street lamps and empty backlit bus shelters glowed. As I turned onto my street and approached my apartment building, I passed some teenage boys. They were crouched at the curb, passing a smouldering blunt between them, their ball cap visors pulled low. The smells of spicy food that always wafted out of the apartment windows at dinnertime had already blown away from the block: the curry and jerk and cardamom and masala.

I jogged over the patch of grass and up the front steps of my building. I shoved through the broken outer door, jammed my key into the inner door, and dashed into the lobby to stab at the chipped elevator button. All I could picture was my mother and her queenly gesticulations. *Off with her head!*

From inside the elevator shaft came distant pings, hollow clangings, humming. An elevator had roused itself from the floors above and was making its way down to the lobby like a metal sloth.

Hurry up, hurry up, I thought as the beat-up doors parted lazily in front of me.

I reached the twenty-third floor and bounded down the brown-carpeted hallway. Light leaked out of the slit between our apartment door and its frame. My mother never left it cracked open like that and would get upset when me and my sister forgot to close the door ourselves. *You want these people to stroll in here?* she would say, flicking a hand to implicate the whole neighbourhood, as if everyone wanted to step on our parquet floors and admire our furniture and our squat television set.

If I'd had the presence of mind I would have been gentler in my entrance. Instead I tumbled into the apartment, battering the door like I was the leader of a police raid. My mother sat on the couch in front of me, her narrow frame curved in on itself and her face contorted. The lamp on the side table glossed her skin. My father stood in the kitchen to my left, braced over the counter with his fingertips on his forehead and the phone to his ear. The stove's blue digits read 10:23 P.M. and the night beyond the living room window was lit up by the high-rises and the headlights and the street lamps that stretched into the distance.

The apartment depressurized and bloated again in a second. My mother rushed to me and wrapped her arms around me, crying and trembling. I felt tugging at my elbows and hands as my father tried to claim me as well.

They talked over each other. *Where were you? We waited and you didn't come.... Your mother, she nearly had a heart attack.... And your father called the police.... It's dark out there, how could you come home so late, how could you do this to us? Mommy waited and Daddy drove around the whole place, up and down the streets.... We thought you died, we thought both of our children had died.... Alisha, baby, oh my baby...where's your sister? Where's your sister?*

I was so astonished by my parents' reactions, so pleased at their concern for me, that I hardly heard their question.

My father stepped back to look out of the apartment doorway. "Why isn't she with you?"

"Where did Diana go?" my mother asked, gripping me at my shoulders.

Relief had hardly had the opportunity to set in before dread was already mounting, threatening to crash over them again.

"I don't know," I answered.

My father clutched my elbow. "What do you mean?"

His brown skin was pale and his neck had developed a sheen. By that point in my life I had already witnessed every emotion my mother possessed. I knew her pretty face better than anyone else's because I had spent my whole childhood adoring it and tracing its lines in my mind. But my father's face had always contained unknowns. I had never been privy to this look of shock and desperation, and his wide frightened eyes struck me.

I felt weak. *Why did I talk to that man at the mall? Why did I lead him to Diana?*

I couldn't tell my parents about the man without revealing my own guilt. I was afraid I'd lose the sliver of a foothold I had achieved with them over the last year by pretending I wanted to study hard like my sister did. *Diana will be a doctor and Alisha will be our little lawyer. Our wonderful girls! Every sacrifice we've made has been for our girls!*

I would preserve myself the only way I knew how. I would lie.

"I waited outside the mall," I said, words assembling in my brain at breakneck speed. "Diana told me I had to stay there so I waited and waited for her to come back but she didn't come and I didn't know what I was supposed to do."

My mother's fingers went to her mouth. She looked to my father and then back to me. "I told you to stay together!"

"I didn't see you," my father said, shaking my elbow so my hand flicked limp like a rag doll's. "I drove everywhere and I didn't see you or Diana."

"But I searched for her, Daddy. I went around the cars and the park and everywhere I could, I promise I did. I kept looking and looking and I didn't see her so I decided to come home...."

As rapidly as these words slipped over my tongue, my mind swallowed and digested them. How easy it was for me to believe my own lies, to accept them as the true facts of what had happened that afternoon. How easy it was to convince myself that I had really waited and watched and searched for my sister—when she was really the one who had to run after me.

"Mommy, I tried to find Diana but I couldn't...." My voice crumbled and the tears began to well. *Dee's our special and ambitious girl and 'Lisha's growing up to be just like her and the two of them are the very best of friends!* My stomach felt like dough being folded in a mixer.

"Oh, 'Lisha," my mother whimpered, hugging me close and propping her chin on top of my head, "why didn't you girls just stay together and come home?"

Her scent, a potent floral perfume mixed with baby powder, consumed my nose and mouth. I had banked on the compassion of a mother for her child and knew it would obscure my culpability. "I didn't want to be late," I said. "I knew I wasn't supposed to be out so late but I didn't know what to do."

My father hadn't let go of my arm. He pulled my elbow toward him as if I was one of those candy machines at the front of the grocery store where we shopped: persist on the crank and bits of information will rattle down.

"I stayed outside the mall...."

Clank, clank.

"...and Diana didn't come back out to get me...."

Click, roll.

"...and I searched for her all afternoon, this whole time...."

My father launched back to the telephone, punching numbers and stretching the cord taut so he could stand outside the kitchen and listen to me as he spoke with the police. My mother nodded and nodded at me like a dipping bird toy, encouraging me to recall every detail.

Before long, my truths had been determined and replicated and we were all choking on them. I was a good girl obeying Mommy and Daddy. I had stood waiting and watching in the mall parking lot for my big sister's return, dutifully searching for her when she didn't come back out. Finally I had had no choice but to find my own way home in the dark without her.

We stayed up all night in the living room in front of a black television screen, staring at the half-open apartment door and studying its locks and chains and dents. We prayed to it, hating and loving it. Hating it because it was closed when we longed for it to open with her arrival; loving it because it was the only portal through which that arrival could come.

Each time one of the elevators dinged down the hall we rushed out with cries on the ledges of our tongues, only to return to our posts with our beating hearts in our hands. My father perched on the armrest of the couch until he could no longer stand waiting for the police to come. He left the apartment with his car keys in his hand to search the streets again. My mother sat against a cushion and brushed her clammy hand over my hair as I lay my head on her lap. I battled sleep and the sickening shame of what I had done.

❀

Six years back, on Christmas Day of 1992, I was seven years old. My parents gave me a stuffed baby seal, all fuzzy and white. Diana was nine and in grade four. They gave her a boxed set of medical books, each volume stamped with gold lettering. *Digestive System. Human Skeleton. Male and Female Reproduction.* They were thick, glossy-paged, and small-printed. She kept them in a special place above her other books, on the top shelf of her bedroom closet.

"I'm going to read every one," she declared, standing in her pyjamas and looking up at their spines.

I pressed my fingertips to my temple. "But they have so many words. That'll take you forever!"

She forbade me to put my sticky hands on them, but she did let me sit beside her on her bed as she read the books aloud before bedtime.

"The duodenum is the beginning of the small intestine," she said, astounding me with her pronunciation of biological terms, "designed to absorb nutrients from partially digested food exiting the stomach."

I rested my chin on her forearm to examine the watercolour diagrams on her lap, the pink spleens and butter-yellow fat with tiny-lettered labels, more delicate than any illustrations in my picture books.

Do your organs get itchy? I wanted to ask. *If you jump around, can they get scrambled out of place?* But I didn't voice my questions, afraid to interrupt the lesson.

She plucked a different volume from the box, flicking through the pages. "I'm going to show you something you're too little to learn about in school," she said. "It's my duty as your doctor to make sure you know. Don't tell Mommy and Daddy." She found a picture of what looked like a school of swarming tadpoles. "Sperms are the *essence* of a man—everything rolled into a tiny animal. Men make sperms in their balls and women make eggs in their bellies, millions of them, everything so small you'd never be able to see it. That's how babies are born."

I looked at the sperms, propelled to the top of the page by their waggling tails. I was dismayed that anyone harboured such nasty creepy crawlies inside of them. I wasn't sure I knew where a man's balls were. "Ew!"

"I'm not allowed to get grossed out by anything, you know," said Diana. "Doctors have to be professional."

"Can I be your nurse?"

"Yeah. You'll help me with my procedures."

I pictured wearing a white dress and a white hat like I had seen on television. I would walk down hospital corridors beside my sister in her lab coat and stethoscope. *Yes doctor, no doctor, this man is dying, doctor!*

When grade two was over and school paused for summer, the asphalt and heat of the city gave way to colossal, run-on thunderstorms. None of the neighbourhood kids played outside when it rained, so Diana and I played doctor on our balcony. I would take on the role of elderly Guyanese patient by lying on our fold-out recliner, its frayed plastic lattice tickling the undersides of my knee joints, and cry, "Doctor-man, this belly *a-bust* me! Paining, ow, mercy! I need an *x-tray*!"

She would rush out with my father's old Polaroid camera, her bare feet slapping the concrete, and snap pictures around my torso as fast as the churning machine would allow. My father had gotten it years back and didn't wanted us touching it, so he hid it on the top shelf of his bedroom closet. All Diana had to do was steady herself with one hand on the clothes rod and stretch up her long arm. I would be behind, poised to catch the camera when she knocked it down, along with one of the bulk film boxes, which we would re-seal and put back in place when we were done. We had no reason to be concerned about our mother as we smuggled the camera out of our parents' room. She would be preoccupied on the couch, reading a recipe, folding laundry, or painting her fingernails. She had little interest in protecting that camera.

"Let's see what's going on in your organs *internally*," my sister would say, retrieving one of the spit-out photos scattered over the balcony. She would peel and toss away the waxy paper covering, letting it get snatched up by the breeze.

I would sit up and follow its wild path beyond our band of apartments at Jane Street and Finch Avenue. It flew over the road and the park and then disappeared entirely.

I would yank at her shirt. "What's wrong with me, doctor-man? I gon' live or die?"

She'd squint and ponder, turn the photo and squint, and ponder some more.

"Ow, tell me, *nah*?"

And it would finally come, the grand diagnosis. *Cream-of-Cornosis*, the result of ingesting too much canned corn. *Watery Uteronious*, a plague of sweat suffered by women who wear too much makeup. *Overblown Spleenocitus*, a common affliction of those who pretend to have more friends than they do.

"*Terminal Gutsotitis*," she once told me. "Sorry to inform you but it's my responsibility as your physician and your sibling. Queen Bea has it too." That was the first time she uttered the nickname she had created for our mother.

"*Eh-eh*, what is that?"

"The woman is so uptight that intestinal gasses can't escape her butt. Like many of the Guyanese, she caught it on the way to this country."

Diana pushed me flat on my back and compressed my stomach with her hands. I would have laughed at the tickling but I was hardly able to breathe as her fingertips dug into my diaphragm.

"Gracious *rice and peas*," I coughed at her, "is it contagious, doctor-man?"

"Yes. And there's no cure. Our mother is completely fartless."

✿

My parents received invitations to summer weekend get-togethers at the homes of cousins and neighbours they had grown up with in Guyana. We would pick up my mother's sister, Auntie Julie, and drive over to the hosts' house in the afternoon. My sister and I would run around and play games with the other kids in the backyard.

"My sister's going to be a doctor!" I blurted to Celia, a girl who was about my age. She wore a pink T-shirt and pink shorts and her hair was tied into two frizzy braids. Guyana-gold jewelry dangled at her neck and ears. We were in the middle of a big game of tag. Everyone screamed amongst the smell of barbeque chicken grilling on the deck where the adults sat together.

"Which one is she?" she asked, panting and flushed.

I pointed to Diana. She was cackling and chasing one of the boys, on a collision course with the fence, one sandal on and the other kicked off onto the lawn somewhere.

Celia twisted her face. "She's smart?"

Annoyance bubbled up in me. "She's the smartest kid here!"

"She don't look it."

Something overtook my limbs, a defensive loyalty I didn't even know I had. I shoved her and she tripped and thumped onto her bottom, braids flicking up on impact.

"Ow!" she cried when she realized what had happened.

I reached out to her but she shrank away from me and began to howl.

"Shhh," I said, "stop it! I'm sorry!"

Diana ran up to us, still missing her shoe. "What'd you do, 'Lisha?" Her hair was all tossed up from the game.

"She just fell."

"She pushed me!" Celia screeched.

"She called you dumb!"

Celia's mother rushed over to her and crouched low, gathering her up to her breasts to hush her and caress her head. "What in the world happened?" she asked me. Her hair was a curly brown bob and she wore pink pants and gold jewelry herself.

"We don't know," Diana responded for me, "she just fell." My sister yanked at my arm and leaned close to my ear. "Let's go."

She hauled me away, hiding us in the clump of other kids.

It was Labour Day. Diana was to start grade five and I was to start grade three at our elementary school that week. She ate fried saltfish and bakes with my parents at the living room table while I sat on the couch watching *Power Rangers* with a soup bowl full of Froot Loops nestled between my folded legs.

I heard Diana tell them something but I didn't pay attention. I took notice only when my father laid his newspaper on the table and removed his glasses. "This child," he said to my mother, "she liked the books we gave her, after all. She's something else, huh?"

My mother went into the kitchen. "Julie," she said into the phone without a greeting, "do you know what Dee just told us? She wants to be a doctor."

My parents perked up and the whole apartment seemed to have freshened itself, alight with gauzy sunshine. Diana pretended to be blasé, chewing her fish and sipping her tea.

"There's a museum of anatomical oddities in France," Diana told me a week later as she sat on her bed next to me with a medical book open on her lap. "My teacher told me about it. They have cut-off heads and diseased eyeballs and lumps they had to dig out of peoples' skin. Everything's in jars for you to look at." She set her fist against the side of her neck as if it were a growth and spit out the tip of her tongue.

"Gross!" I said.

"I want to see it."

"I'll throw up."

"I'll explain everything to you. It's so cool."

I continued to fuss and wretch but I was exhilarated by the thought of flying in a plane with my sister, soaring over the Eiffel Tower I had learned about in French class.

"Dee!" my father called from the couch. "Come watch this with me, come quick!"

I skidded down the hallway in my socks after my sister. She launched onto the cushion beside him in her blue-checkered pyjamas and I hovered at the entrance of the living room.

My father had long changed out of his work suit and was in checkered pyjamas himself. He pointed the remote at the screen and braced his thumb on the volume button, his free arm around Diana's shoulders. "They're going to do an operation on this man's brain."

"They keep them awake so they can poke around and see what moves," she cheeped.

"What a thing!"

"I should be a brain surgeon."

That dashing toothy grin of my father's appeared. "Better than a foot doctor."

My mother approached me from behind. "Donald, won't they show blood?" she asked over my head. Her long hair was unravelled from its bun and she was in a nightgown, just as I was. My nightgown was made of flat cotton and hers was layered, flowing, and shiny, but both were white, hemmed under the knee, and frilled at their cap sleeves. "Dee, you can stand it?"

Neither my father nor Diana responded, already too absorbed in the surgeon's step-by-step. *We're making a surface incision. Soon we'll saw through the skull to get at the grey matter.*

"Ouch," said my father, "that must hurt." He placed a palm on the highest part of Diana's head, just for a moment.

"They don't feel anything," answered my sister. "They use local anesthetic."

My mother's eyes were fixed on Diana and she seemed puzzled, as if she needed to ask a question.

"I'm not afraid of blood," I said, out of place.

My mother smiled at me, combed her fingers through the ends of my loosed tufts and fluffed them. I reached around her waist to play with the end of a lock of her long hair, but my ears were still tuned to the television. *One slip and we'll sentence this patient to an early death.* I wondered if my sister would remember that she had told me we would go to France together.

"Let me brush your hair before you go to sleep," my mother said to me. "I want it to keep growing."

She took my hand, threading it into hers. She led the way to my bedroom and we left my father and my sister there together on the couch: Daddy and Dee, fascinated by brain surgery. It was my sister's bedtime too, but I seemed to be the only one who remembered.

CHAPTER 2

1938

WHEN SHE WAS SEVEN PAULA HEARD NOISES AND THOUGHT HER MOTHER was making them. She got out of bed and felt about in the dark. She reached the front door of the house and opened it. The looming shape of a man in a long black coat stood in front of her. A car rumbled out on the road behind him—a hunk of black metal with headlights that looked like a pair of unblinking eyes. The air was icy. She shivered as the wind shot under her collar and down her nightgown.

Paula feared the man. White people never came by for good reasons. She felt tugs at the hem of her nightgown. Ave stood next to her in cloth diaper and bare chest. She had wobbled out of the bedroom behind Paula. She was two years old and following her big sister as she always did. Her legs were chubby and goosefleshed.

"Go back to bed!" Paula whispered.

Looking up at her sister with her marble eyes, Ave shoved a few fingers in her mouth, her thumb hooked out the side.

Paula heard steps and turned to see her mother coming toward her in her nightdress. Her brow was knitted in shadow as there were no lights, nothing beyond a leaking moon. Paula didn't know why her mother had stopped a few paces behind her and Ave, why she wasn't crouching down to pull them in with her slender, sturdy arms. Her heart began to thump.

"No," her mother said with a cracked voice, "please."

"I have to," the man answered.

Foop. Paula's bare feet left the floor as the man picked her and Ave up, one in each arm. He turned and carried them toward the car with its smoking tailpipe. Paula strained to look back over his shoulder.

Her mother stood frozen. She didn't cry out, didn't so much as whimper. Paula was confused and no words came.

Ave screamed and wriggled in his arm. "No, no, no!" she shrieked. "Mama, don't wanna go, don't wanna go!"

Her mother skidded forward to clutch at the doorframe, as if the wind might tear through and blow her away. Paula tried to make out her mother's face, the most beautiful in the world, with her chestnut skin and pepper-black eyes. But her features were a blur.

Ave reached over the man's chest. "Paw! Paw! Paw!" she wheezed in her baby voice, digging her tiny nails into Paula's arm.

But Paula didn't answer. She felt too far from solid ground in the man's grip, too small and weak. She sealed her hands over her ears and clamped her teeth together as she did when it stormed, when the hulking sky thundered over their clapboard roof.

The car revved on the road. Another man in a black coat sat behind the wheel and he leaned out of the open passenger window. "Two?" His breath billowed in the cold night air.

"Yeah." The man carrying them grunted in a way Paula felt in her belly. "Mama should've kept her legs together."

She turned to look for her mother's reaction to their laughter.

The door of the house was closed.

The man thrust Paula into the back seat of the car and her bottom bounced on the upholstery. She recoiled at the door's slam. He carried Ave to the front, yanked his door open, and struggled to hold her on his lap. Her limbs thrashed.

"Take me!" Paula screamed. "She's just a baby!" She would put herself in Ave's place, the older for the younger, because she had nothing else to offer. Just her arms and hands and legs and head, her whole body for her little sister. She stood on that scratchy car mat on her naked feet; she grabbed the man's sleeve and yanked and hollered. "Leave her alone, take me!"

He twisted back and detached her hands, pushed her into the crook of the seat and grabbed her jaw. "Behave and be quiet," he ordered. "This is for your own good."

Paula and Ave were driven to a large brick house. A white woman in a white dress took them inside and drew musty cotton shifts that were too big over their heads. She led them into a room with many white women and children. Some lay on cots. Others crouched on the plank floor or sat braced against the walls. They were all swaddled in blankets—some clutched them to their necks and others drew them right over their heads. Everybody was unsmiling.

Paula sat with her knees up to her chin in a corner on the floor and gripped a woollen blanket around them both, bracing Ave against her side. Her feet were still bare and numb.

After hours of whimpering, Ave fell asleep. Once in a while, a noise escaped her chest. Paula thought she must have been dreaming about the two men.

Paula had screamed out everything. Her throat felt raw and her stomach ached. She couldn't sleep and kept her eyes on the doorway. "Don't worry," she whispered to the top of her sister's head. "Mommy will be here soon."

Ave didn't stir.

Paula would take care of her sister until their mother came. She had long come to understand Ave's lexicon of cries and whines and squeaks, attuned as she was to her sister's needs. At home, Paula would always wait until Ave fell asleep beside her before allowing herself to fade into a dream. She would insist on feeding her sister her porridge before her own, spooning the excess from the corners of Ave's little mouth.

You're a natural, Paula's mother would tell her. *You look after her so well.*

What a frightening place they had been brought to—huge and infected with every manner of noise and smell! There wasn't a familiar face in sight and strange people paced the room and hallway, cursing each other up and down, scuffing and scratching at the walls.

Ha, ha!

Paula was jolted from her daze by a man's joyless laughter from the floor above her. But what was there to be amused about? Babies bawled and children whined to their mothers for food. Men's voices called out for the Lord and for porridge and for rum like they were the holy trinity.

A young girl with stringy blonde hair and a purple spot on her jaw sat at the edge of the cot beside Paula and Ave. She held her palms under her blanket against a bulging belly, and glared at Paula with muddy eyes and tight lips. No words, no kindness. A drowsy boy who hardly seemed older than Paula sat cross-legged at the girl's feet. He fisted the blanket at his chest with one hand, rocking back and forth and knocking a stick on the floor with his other hand in no particular rhythm.

Paula stared at the bruise on the girl's face. A stretched oval with blue-green flecks.

Frigid hours passed. Yelps and cackles, scraping feet and things smashing echoed from upstairs. Light changed in the window and crossed the room, going from sharp to hazy and then slinking away entirely. Pockets of shadows emerged as the night crept in.

Paula watched a spider at the baseboard where the plank floor met the plaster wall. The spider was black and immobile as a pebble, suspended on a web. She wanted to reach over and nudge it to life with her finger, to give it a perch on her thumb, to cup and bring it under the blanket into the tent of warmth that sustained her and Ave. But the spider eventually roused itself and began a cautious survey—two legs stretching in front, four more venturing to follow, the last two pushing off. It recreated that movement again and again as it crept about in search of something.

"Don't be scared," Paula said to Ave, whose eyes were still closed. "We'll go home soon."

Paula hoped the spider would know how much she cared about it. She had failed Ave so badly by letting the men bring them to this place. By morning, she hoped she and Ave would wake to find themselves under a dome of webbing, strung thick as a basket and stiff as straw.

A woman with grey hair entered the room, followed by a short girl who carried a tray with bread and metal cups and bowls. Both of them wore white dresses and white handkerchiefs on their heads. Everyone gathered, resuscitated back to life. *There's been no food, Miss, please,* said the women, *nothing to eat all day, and my children are hungry, my milk has already dried up and I think my baby is starving, Miss....*

Paula looked to her sister in the crook of her arm. Ave's eyes were open, bright as ever, watching as women and children, hooded in their blankets, closed in around the woman and girl in white dresses.

"All right, we're here now," the old woman said over the protests, swatting away the women's hands. "Patience, ladies, you'll get your due. Good Lord!"

The girl went around the room passing out the bread, bowls, and cups. *Please, Miss,* women said, *there's been no food all day and my children are still so little, they're losing strength....*

The old woman busied her wrinkled hands, lighting lamps that hung from iron hooks in the walls. "Better now, isn't it?" she said, chipper. "Don't be content in the dark like bats in a cave, ladies, the Lord gives light."

Each lamp glowed violent yellow.

When the girl came to Paula and Ave, she squatted down and set a single bowl, cup, and slice of bread at their feet. "Here you go, little ones." She tried to get Paula to smile back at her. "Eat up or it'll disappear." She smelled of sweat and cooked food. Soft wisps of blonde hair grew above her top lip.

Paula's belly felt like a cavern but she couldn't move. Her limbs were leaden and her head slumped to the shoulder, close to her sister's.

Paula could see Ave under her cheek, looking up at her. Ave waited on her sister to show her what to do, unwilling to attempt anything Paula didn't do first. *Remember,* their mother had said to them, *the older always goes before the younger.*

The girl pinched off a hunk of bread and fed it to Paula, holding the cup to her lips to wash the solid down with liquid. She did the same for Ave, who was not nearly as languid. Ave slid close to Paula's hip and pushed her head across her sister's chest, opening her mouth to consent to the food and water.

Paula struggled to chew, even to moisten the morsel enough to swallow it. Ave pressed her ear into the hollow of her sister's neck, chewing noisily.

"You're weak," the girl said to Paula.

Paula's eyelids crept to a close, reopening at the coolness of a spoon holding sweet, lumpy porridge at her mouth. The girl fed her and Ave in turn, one after the other, ignoring the fussing and begging of the women around them.

Oh, Miss, please come here. My babies need your charity too.

"Mommy," Paula finally spoke in a rasp that barely made it out of her throat.

"No, silly," the girl answered, sweeping her index finger over Paula's cheek. "Look at you, black as tar. I couldn't be your mommy."

But Paula was asking a question.

The girl pushed close to Paula. Her lips were dry, a patchy pink. "You won't have to be in the poorhouse much longer," she whispered. "They'll take you where they take the other negro children." She used the edge of her sleeve to wipe away porridge that had dribbled onto Paula's chin. "You'll be with your own kind. You're lucky girls."

Ave breathed, open-mouthed, anticipating the next spoon of porridge.

Paula didn't feel lucky. The girl was telling her that they would not be taken back to their mother. Paula surveyed the floorboards to find her beloved spider, but all she could see was its abandoned webs.

CHAPTER 3

THE NIGHT AFTER DIANA DIDN'T RETURN HOME, WE FORKED A HASTY CHICKEN stew with glutinous rice around our plates. The telephone rang and we all jumped. My father launched out of his chair and rushed to the kitchen.

"Yes?" he answered.

My mother and I stopped our listless chewing. Our eyes met, ricocheted off of each other, and scurried off in opposite directions.

My father's voice was edged with an impatience I wasn't used to. I could tell the police were on the other end, asking us again to consider where my sister might have gone and whom she might have gone with. Maybe she had made an escape from the suburbs into downtown or another nearby city, or maybe even across the border to Detroit or Buffalo.

"My daughter is not a runaway." My father's voice was hoarse. He had always had strong shoulders and a proud chest to match his straight nose and side-parted hair, but today he had developed a hunch. Dark stains painted the skin around his eyes.

I tried to swallow the lump stuck in my throat. It felt as if I had sprouted a man-sized Adam's apple.

My mother's gaze sank to her plate. She wore none of her usual adornments—no eyeliner, lipstick, or powder—and none of her sparkling jewelry. Her face was bare and her bun, usually a blooming black flower at the nape, was tied sloppily, tufts slipping from the frayed clump. She and I had spent the whole day watching the apartment door, waiting for Diana to come home. My father had missed work to search the streets in our silver sedan.

The police told us that teenagers ran away all the time, even fifteen-year-old girls raised by overprotective immigrant parents. Sometimes good girls from hardworking families were influenced by rebellious friends and bad boys, they said. Sometimes they started to skip school, shoplifting and sneaking around and staying out late. *Skipping, shoplifting, sneaking, staying out.* These were the things the police seemed to believe in, right from the start. *Most runaways come back after a couple of days,* they told us. *A little time might straighten it out.*

"But Diana had no reason to run away, can't you see?" my father spoke into the phone, trying to disguise his anger with pleading. "She was a good girl, a well-behaved girl. She did what she was told."

But he didn't know everything. I wondered if my sister really might have run away from us, maybe to see that boy she liked. *Maybe she'll come home soon,* I thought.

I stuck my fork into a scrap of chicken and thought about the fire hydrant across the street.

A week ago, I had looked down from the living room window as a group of kids cracked it open at its armless joints. They hopped and danced in the spray, their shorts clinging to their skinny legs. Some cars even parked at the curb to boom dancehall and bhangra. I wished I were at the spontaneous party too.

"Isn't anybody watching these children?" my mother had asked, coming up behind me. "Do their parents even care?"

I decided against asking her if I could join them. The next day the hydrant was wrapped in black plastic and secured with yellow duct tape.

Wasn't anybody watching Diana? I wondered if people would ask the question of my own family now. *Do her parents even care?* My gut grumbled and my ears became warm with embarrassment. My parents would never admit to feeling ashamed, but I couldn't help taking the burden of worry on for them.

I sipped water from my glass and realized that the lump in my throat had sprouted burrs. I knew my parents weren't the ones to blame. It was me. I had willed Diana away, because she was too talented and ambitious about everything, school and sports and speeches. She didn't need me for anything and I was jealous and angry at her for it. Now that I had made her disappear, I ached for her.

I hope she dies, I had said to myself the last time I saw her.

I looked to my mother across the table. She was blinking at her plate, one and two and three, willing herself not to cry. Maybe she thought that too much crying would mean there wasn't enough hope in our apartment, and hope might be the only thing left to compel my sister back.

✿

In 1996 when Diana started grade eight and I started grade six, she added sports to her list of passions.

"I want to join the track team," she said as my family ate dinner together before September tryouts.

"Work on your studies," replied my mother at the head of the table, focused on her plate of eggplant and chicken stew. "You don't need anything to distract you."

"But I always get the best grades in my class."

Both Diana and I looked to our father at the other end of the table. He set his fork on the rim of his plate and took up his cup of tea, slurping from it. "We'll have to think about it."

If anyone can do it all, I thought, *it's Diana.*

Eventually they allowed her to join the team. My parents insisted we walk to school together, so I had to go with her early so she could make morning practices. I would trip down the sidewalk beside her, yawning in the chilly air, barely able to match her pace.

"Come, on," she'd urge, "I can't be late."

When we got to the schoolyard, Diana's teammates, a pack of tall grade eight girls in sweats and windbreakers, would be waiting under the basketball nets. She would jog to them with the noisy thighs of her track pants, her high ponytail swinging from shoulder blade to shoulder blade. She had the same black *W*-shaped hairline at the nape of her neck as my father.

Bye, Dee! I would imagine calling out to her. I wasn't sure she would hear me so I never said it out loud.

While Diana was at practice, I went to homeroom to meet my teacher, Miss Stewart. She was a short, young white lady with a reddish pixie haircut and a bouncing, stubby walk. Some mornings she would let me do my homework at my desk. Other days she would assign me chores, like scrubbing pencil marks from desks and sponging down blackboards that had become grey with chalk residue.

On a late November morning Miss Stewart had me collate worksheets as she marked quizzes. I stacked papers and listened for patterns in the scraping tip of her marker: three strokes, two long and one short. Was that an A on my paper? *Oh, 'Lisha, finally!* my mother would swoon, sweeping me to her bosom. Scoring top marks was a regular accomplishment for Diana, but it would have been a first for me.

"You're a great help, Alisha," Miss Stewart said from her desk at the back of the room in that voice that was pitched too high to pierce the classroom din.

"Thanks," I answered.

"You've probably figured out what you're going to do yours on by now, huh?" Realizing her fingers were splotched with ink, she stared at the tip of her marker, cross-eyed.

I flipped over one of the packages I had been putting together. *Public Speaking Competition: The Rules.* Beyond the classroom window, I saw the girls' track team doing walk-kicks and jumping jacks on the field.

I spent the rest of the morning pondering the first speech topics that came to my mind. *Mommy, daddy, sister, auntie.* It continued into recess and lunch and had become a rhythm by the walk home. *Mommy, daddy, sister, auntie, mommy, daddy, sister, auntie....*

"Who are you doing your speech on?" I asked Diana breathlessly, my stumpy legs scuttling next to her gliding gazelle strides.

"No one." She pumped her arms like pistons, her hair swinging left to right. She insisted on taking every opportunity to train. "I'm going to do it on what it means to be a doctor."

I felt the too-fast motion of my jeans shimmying my panties out of their proper place. "What should I do mine on?"

She blew a cloud of air from her lips into the chilly air. "Don't know. What are you interested in?"

"Don't know."

"You have to figure it out. What about stickers or something? You like that, right?"

I hadn't played with stickers since grade four. But when I got home and sifted through my bedroom, they certainly appeared central to my life. They were stuck to the frame of the mirror behind my door, clumped in constellations on my lampshade. Those and the dolls on top of my dresser, the battalion of plush toys against my headboard, and the collection of large-print paperbacks on the shelf above my desk were my girly pastel litter. They all signified the growing difference between me and Diana. She was developing a speech about physicians. I was mired in child's play.

Of course, my inclination was to do a speech on the person I admired most, my mother, Beatrice Sookermany. It was her beauty—her long hair, slim figure, light brown skin, and luminous smile—that enamoured me most. I knew that she and my Auntie Julie had been revered for their loveliness ever since they were children growing up in Suddie, a rural Guyanese village at the mouth of the Essequibo River, which flows from the Acarai Mountains to the Atlantic Ocean. *Pretty-pretty coolie girls!* people called them. They became accustomed to double-glances from boys and gifts of pine tarts and tamarind balls from neighbourhood women, and they always had to protect themselves from the cutting murmurs of jealous girls at their school. Even my grandmother guarded her favour for them, taking them out of my grandfather's home to ensure he wouldn't put any more babies in her belly. She couldn't stand the thought of her own split loyalties.

My mother's young life in the South American bush was far removed from my life in high-rises and winter storms, and I was deeply proud of her tropical beauty. I had always assumed Diana felt the same way, since when we were younger she used to be as passionate for our mother's attention as I was. We would both beg my mother to play makeup with us, giggling and pinching our eyes shut when she swept the prickly bristles of a rouge brush over our cheeks.

But when I saw Diana at the living room table with her handsome medical books laid out in a curve, consulting this one and that one as she prepared her speech on medicine, I began to worry about my choice of topic. I suspected she wouldn't approve.

Diana scribbled in her notebook as I lingered in the kitchen on a pretend mission for a particular mug in the cupboard. I wondered how she had learned to concentrate on anything for so long.

✿

My class had our first library period of the school year the next morning, and we stomped in from the waxy hallway onto the matted carpet. Some students, new arrivals from India and Pakistan and Bangladesh, weren't very confident in English. Their legs slowed as they crossed the threshold and they lingered around the checkout counter.

The rest of us, mostly West Indian and a couple of stray white kids, jostled past them to get to the magazines and the paperbacks, yanking things down and brusquely fanning them open. I twirled a rack to find the volume of *Scary Stories to Tell in the Dark* I had favoured since grade five, flipping through to its charcoal drawings of phantoms that still made my heart somersault.

"Don't forget, kids," Miss Stewart tried to squeak over the clamour, "you need to decide on your speech topic today!" She looked like an elf in her yellow cardigan and stocky pumps. "Ask the librarians for help if you need it!"

A girl named Brianna turned to me to kiss her teeth, a side-of-the-cheek sucking West Indian kids had introduced and everyone else was quick to adopt. "My sister told me about this *bumbaclot* speech thing," she said. "We'll have to do it every year from now on. *Cha*. These teachers make you perform for them like you're their minstrel." Her hair was tied in puffs behind each ear and she winced and grabbed at her sweater's collar. Lots of kids at my school didn't know how to dress for cold weather.

I kissed my teeth in agreement, realizing that my sister hadn't warned me about the speeches at all.

The students learning English gathered at a table by the stacks. Standing behind the table was a Black lady with thick-rimmed glasses. She spun the book she was holding so its text would face her audience and skimmed a finger along the sentences as she read them. The kids dipped and bobbed around one another's heads to keep track.

The woman's face was smooth and dotted by freckles. She was older than my parents, and her hair was combed into a compact twist of brown and silver. I had seen her many times before, usually as she restocked library shelves or slid book spines over a strip at the checkout counter. I would have assumed she was a librarian like the others if she didn't always wear a blue vest that read *Volunteer* over a sweatshirt or sports jersey.

When she finished reading, I made my way over to her. Ms. Paula was printed in marker on the left side of her vest, just under her collarbone. Her smile was pinned up politely and this close her glasses seemed to double the size of her eyes.

"Decided on a speech topic?" she asked.

I shook my head.

"No ideas at all?"

"No."

"Okay, where's your family from?"

"Guyana."

"There's a ton of you in this school, yeah?"

She sifted through the books in front of her, cocking her head to read their titles. She selected one and held it out to me. On its cover was a painting of some dark-skinned men, crouching in brush at twilight with rifles and axes. They were muscled and bare-chested, wearing loincloths and headwraps, and only partly visible in the firelight that burned at the apex of a mountain. The title read *The Maroons of the New World.*

"You heard about the Maroon warriors?" she asked.

I shook my head.

"You West Indians really should learn something about them. Where you're from is where they started." She pointed her chin toward me. "What do you go by, Guyana-girl?"

"Alisha." That I was no longer a nameless student turned me shy. I never spoke to strangers. Even my parents hardly seemed to talk to people who weren't family or friends from back home. My eyes slipped to her necklace, a gold leaf pendant with edges that curled as if it were twisting in the wind. It matched the thin gold bangles threaded over the cuffs of her jersey.

"Most people don't know much about the Maroons and hardly anyone knows they were here. Know how I learned about them?"

"No."

"My mother told me and my sister they were in our family, so I read books like this one. You could write a great speech on the Maroons. I'm sure you'll find the topic fascinating, yeah?"

I took the book from her and promptly escaped behind a stack. The cover was rigid from disuse and the paper gave off a chemical odour. I braced it against a shelf and opened it to its first page.

> *In the sixteenth century, contingents of enslaved Africans escaped their captors and formed colonies of their own. They subsisted independently in places such as Jamaica, Brazil, Suriname, Puerto Rico, Haiti, Dominican Republic, and Cuba, and they became known as "Maroons" (from the Spanish cimarrón, meaning "feral animal, fugitive, runaway").*

I was certain none of my classmates would pick a topic like that. I wanted to win the contest as Diana and my classmates were trying to do, and a speech about the Maroons of the New World was not going to grab anyone's interest the way sports stars and singers and the aspiration to become a surgeon would.

I aimed my eyes at a sliver between the shelves, observing Paula, in her loose jeans and jersey and running shoes, from a new angle. She pushed aside her books to reveal the bare table in front of her. She peered over the top of her glasses and wrote something on the surface with her finger. The movement of her hand was careful and smooth and full of curves. When she was finished, she seemed to erase the invisible drawing by sweeping her palm over it.

I didn't dare approach to ask what she was doing.

That night, I placed a sheet of questions from Miss Stewart on the kitchen counter. It was a list of uninspired fill-in-the-blanks that I had filled in: *What is a* paralegal *and when did you become one? What do you do as a* paralegal? *How can students be a* paralegal *just like you?*

I phoned Auntie Julie.

"I can't believe you want to do your assignment on me, babe," my aunt said across the line, her voice polished by delight.

I pictured her pleased expression in the upswung tail of her *babe*—her voice so closely matched my mother's. Our parents had told us that my sister and I couldn't tell the difference between her and our mother's voices when we were little, when Mommy, Daddy, Auntie Julie, and we two babies had just arrived from the West Indies to live on the twenty-third floor of our high-rise tower together. My aunt was the only one who called me *babe*.

Diana would be happy about my topic. She admired our aunt. She was always going on about how she had her own job and car and house. *She's going to be somebody someday, and she's prettier than Queen Bea too!*

I couldn't be convinced that anyone was prettier than my mother.

I moved through the interview script in a pout, scribbling down lazy cues as Auntie Julie answered my questions. I kept thinking about what Paula might have been drawing on that tabletop.

After a few short days Diana started memorizing her speech. As she did her morning track stretches on the living room rug, I heard her whispering through her paragraphs. Even as she ate dinner she double-checked the crib sheets next to her plate, lips contorting. I was still in the process of writing the first draft of mine, struggling to get a half page to bulge into three.

"I'm almost done," Diana told me on the way to track practice. She walked so fast she was almost jogging.

"Me too," I answered, huffing and puffing beside her. "Can I read yours?"

"I'll practice it in front of you tonight."

"Okay."

"You know, I think I might actually win the contest."

I kept quiet.

That night as I worked on my speech in my bedroom, I heard my parents' applause in the living room. My father clapped heavily while my mother sprinkled lighter, faster claps on top.

"Very good, Dee," my father said.

I left the wrinkled pages on my bed and crept to my cracked-open door.

"It wasn't too long?" Diana asked with put-on insecurity. I could hear how pleased she really was.

"Four minutes, fifty seconds," my father answered. "Perfect timing.

You know, none of the boys at the brokerage could do what you just did. Their presentations can put a room to sleep, man."

He often complained about the incompetence of the brokerage boys at the insurance company he worked for as an administrative assistant. It made me believe that those men didn't deserve the jobs they had, that my father was the one with undiscovered gifts.

"That was an excellent speech, Dee," my mother said. But there it was, a question lining her voice, something I noticed now when my mother talked to Diana. *Who is this child?* I thought she might have been thinking, *and how is she the way she is?* I wondered if anyone else had heard it.

"Bea, ain't it something? How'd our daughter know about the Hippopotamus Oath?"

"Daddy," said Diana, "it's Hippocratic. Stop it."

"Just testing you, girl. I know you know what you're talking about."

Left and right together, my lungs deflated in my chest.

CHAPTER 4

1938

O*UR FAMILY IS UNIQUE*, PAULA'S MOTHER HAD TOLD HER. *IT'S THE MAROON* *blood in us.* She told Paula that her great-great-grandmother was Queen Nanny of the Blue Mountain Maroons, an Asante warrior who couldn't be enslaved, elder of a people so sovereign that when they were exiled from Jamaica to Nova Scotia they soon found a way back to their African homeland. Big Turtle Island, with its hatchling flecks of land on every side, could not hope to contain them.

The words of Paula's mother helped her understand that her great-great-grandmother's cunning lived in her. She could feel Queen Nanny and the Maroons inside of her, lighting bonfires and slashing thicket and stalking enemies, protesting and forging their way forward. They were her ancestry, they were her bones, and she wasn't surprised when a dissident fever started to creep through her veins as she and her sister were led to another car by two white people, a woman and a man this time, wearing dark coats and saying nothing. The woman wore stockings and heels. The man wore black pants. Paula and Ave clutched each other in the back seat, still in the cotton shifts they had worn in the poorhouse.

At the end of a curved gravel driveway they arrived at a three-storey shingled home with many windows. The white woman brought them through the front door into a chilly room with chairs. Paula heard the yaps and stomps of other children from rooms she couldn't see.

A Black woman wearing a blue dress with white cuffs and collar came and scooped Ave up without a word and carried her through another door. Ave screamed and flailed and cried and the woman fought to keep hold of her.

"Where are you going?" Paula shouted, reaching up for her sister, who stretched her hands down over the woman's shoulder.

Paula started to follow but the white woman yanked her back by the arm. "No, you stay here with me and behave," she scolded, squeezing Paula's elbow and pointing her finger at her face.

But soon the white woman left and another Black woman in a blue dress led Paula into a big open room bursting with brown-skinned children. Girls wore ragged blue jumpers and boys wore torn pants and shorts. They ignored Paula as they yelped at each other over a couple of roughed-up dolls and chipped wooden blocks. Some of the younger ones crawled under and over a table at the centre of the room. It was the only furniture there. Paula sat on the floor in the corner and hugged her knees to her chest. It was cold but she felt her skin flare with heat. She knew the Maroons inside of her were rebelling, rejecting this place and raging for Ave.

A while later, Paula saw her sister in the arms of a woman who came to stand in the doorway. Another stood beside her, brushing her fingers through Ave's ringlets, cooing into her doughy neck, and play-biting her arm. The women wore the same dresses. Their hair was tied in rolls.

"What a doll this one is!" the one carrying Ave said, bouncing her at her hip.

"She sure is," answered the other. "Who in the world would let you go, honey?"

Ave gaped at the women, bewildered.

Paula jumped to her feet and rushed to her sister.

The second woman bent low and blocked Paula's path with her long arms. "You're not going anywhere, missy." She shoved her back towards the other children with a sharp slap to her bottom.

At dinnertime, Paula sat hip-to-hip on crowded benches in a dining room. All the children protected their bowls with their arms as they slurped a watery stew of gristle and broth, watched over by more stern, nameless women in collared dresses and dark stockings, who shushed them over and over.

Paula kept looking to the doorway, expecting her mother to appear with Ave in her arms. *Where have you been?* her mother would exclaim. *Your sister and I couldn't find you!*

"What are you doing?" asked the girl across the table, frowning at Paula's unguarded meal. She wore the same jumper all the girls wore, and her hair was tied at the side of her head where it sprang out like a shoot. A smear of soup shone on her cheek.

A small hand holding a spoon crept in past Paula's arm and scooped a wad of fat from her bowl, but Paula was too slow to stop the thief. The hunger she had felt for days transformed into nausea and she felt as if a clamp were crushing her temples. She watched the girl across from her fragment into a thousand pieces before she passed out.

The Maroon fever dug into Paula's flesh that night, tossing her into the itchy margin between sleep and consciousness. She dreamed vividly, haunted by the men who had kidnapped her and her sister. Her breath thickened like beeswax. She was trapped in a replaying nightmare, a skipping and lurching film that starred Ave, helpless in a strange man's arms.

Paula was five years old when the group of women came to her house. She trembled at the terrible screaming coming from her mother's bedroom and watched the women scurry about, carrying soiled cloths and bowls of water in their damp hands. A good time later, one of the women led Paula into her mother's room to meet a crying newborn in her mother's arms. Paula reached up and poked her thumb into the baby's ear, causing her to shriek even louder.

Bad girl! her mother had scolded. She rubbed her hand over the baby's gummy, matted hair. *You're supposed to help me take care of her.*

But Paula felt nothing for the baby, even if Ave was beautiful with a round caramel face and long eyelashes. She bawled too much; her throaty gurgle rose to the rafters day and night. *Make her quiet!* Paula griped to her mother. She had no sympathy for the crybaby who had overstayed her welcome.

Some time later Paula and Ave lay on a blanket on the floor, Paula in her nightgown and Ave in her diaper, while their mother went outside to warm porridge over a small fire. Paula watched the baby's perfect pink mouth open and close, and her bare chest lifted and fell in peaceful sleep. She stroked the silk of the baby's elbows and knees. *Little girl,* she whispered, *don't got nobody.*

Ave gifted her sister a slight sleep-smile and Paula realized that it had been the sound of her own voice that had moved the baby to do it. She realized that this creature, new and defenseless, needed her, and something changed. She decided to care for her sister. She felt Queen Nanny and the warriors rallying with their rifles and machetes to protect this child.

Paw! Paw! Paw! Ave screamed to Paula in her fever dreams as she had in real life. The man's stilt-legs swung out in eerie formations as he reared and jerked and swept Ave away. Paula tried to shout but only froth came to her tongue.

No, she heard her mother plead, *please.*

Paula opened her eyes. The room, its curtains and drawers and sheets, shuffled around before settling on a layout. Her torso felt like an overfilled hot water bottle. She lifted her head to see she was wearing a burlap nightgown she couldn't remember putting on.

Suddenly aware of a wet swatch on her forehead, she shrieked, snapped upright, and pelted the cloth to the floor. She moved her legs under the blanket and it bruised her skin, but she forced herself out of bed. Her feet touched the planks and she shivered and made her way to the window at the other end of the room. She stretched her chin over the ledge.

Acres of fields stretched beyond a little house that stood below the window, and a spring-yellow sun radiated over the budding bushes and tangled horizon of alder and pine. Paula had never seen such a majestic vista and looked to see if she could locate her home beyond the trees.

Paula! She imagined her mother waving and calling out to her from a distance. *I've been looking for you and Ave everywhere! Come back home!*

A head poked up from the foliage, disrupting Paula's daydream. It snapped around, small and brown, and was soon sucked back into the green. It happened in another spot and then again and again in other places, all these children popping up and peeping out of the bush. Paula tried to make sense of the game they were playing and wondered if she would be allowed to play with them.

A thought reached her sideways, wringing her like a sponge. *What if we have to stay here for good?* Her skin tingled and hot-cold sweat broke out at her neck.

"Why are you out of bed?" a voice blared from behind her.

Paula whirled around. Two women, one older and one younger, stood over her, white aprons over their blue dresses.

"You're anxious to run with the others but you have to get better," the young one told her. Her hair was set in a high poof at her forehead.

Paula opened her mouth. *Where's my mother? How will she find us?* The words wouldn't swim out of the swamp of her chest, let alone reach her lips. *Why can't I see my sister? I'm the only one who can look after her.* Her voice box seemed to collapse on the second try and she smacked her hand against her throat at the roasting oven that had taken its place.

The young woman pulled Paula's arm down to her side. "Stop it. You're too sick to speak."

The older woman was bigger and taller and looked at Paula through thick glasses. "She's had nothing to eat for three days."

Paula was transfixed by her hair, those dark waves pressed against her head like a helmet. It was nothing like her mother's. When her mother combed her hair from the clip, it was kinky and soft and flyaway like it couldn't wait to break free. She loved getting her fingers jumbled in her mother's hair.

"You need to do as you're told," the older woman explained. "If you're good, you'll get better."

Paula's stomach capsized. Now a mute lamb, the only response she could manage was a nod.

The older woman took Paula's hand in her own frigid hand, and she led Paula back to the bed. It took no effort for her to raise Paula by her armpits and place her on the mattress. She lay her flat, pulled the blanket over her, and adjusted the pillow under her head. Paula gazed at the woman as she pressed the top of her arm as if testing the ripeness of a pear.

"You're strong for—how old are you? Six? Seven?"

Paula nodded. She hadn't met a kind face or heard a gentle word amongst these strangers; the women and children in this house didn't even seem to know her name. Was this the merciful grown-up she'd been searching for? The one who would help her and Ave get back home?

"Weeding'll come easy to you," the older woman concluded, pinching Paula's nose between her thumb and curled index. "Know my name?"

Paula's nostrils stung. She shook her head.

"Call me Granny. I'm in charge of the home. Did you know that? I take care of you kiddies when your families can't handle you and the government brings you here."

My mother couldn't handle us? Paula thought. She wondered if her sister had already learned to call this woman Granny.

Paula, she tried to tell Granny in return, *my name is Paula and my sister's name is Ave and we need to go home*. But her voice still wouldn't cooperate and Granny walked away.

CHAPTER 5

ON THE THIRD DAY AFTER DIANA DIDN'T COME HOME, WE WENT TO THE POLICE station to meet a detective. He sat on the important side of the desk. He was tall and had curly blonde hair and a mud-brown suit jacket. The three of us were on the other side, my parents sitting on chairs and me on my mother's lap.

"Any chance she might've have left on her own?" the detective said, pen in hand. He didn't look up from the papers in front of him. "I hate to ask again."

"No," answered my father stiffly. "She's a good girl." A manila folder he had begun carrying everywhere lay open on his lap, some madly scribbled notes splayed on top. We each had our own loads to carry: my father had his folder of notes, my mother had me, and I had a leaking, stinking sack of guilt.

"We need to consider every possibility. You understand." The detective's lips were flat and as pale as the skin of his face. Perhaps he had gone through this routine with other families, the same scene with enraged father, suffering mother, and trembling sibling.

"You don't know my daughter," said my father.

The twinge of anger on my father's face, the sense that my family was being ignored by the police, infected me. *They don't care about brown girls,* he had said to my mother, slamming down the phone receiver after another call.

But I punched my feelings right back into my gut. I felt sweat tingle at my hairline. *Don't you dare get mad,* I told myself. *Not after what you did.*

"Mr. Sookermany, how were things at home? Did she hang around with the wrong crowd? Drugs, boys, sneaking out? Things can go off in high school."

"None of those things," my mother said. "She's only fifteen." She'd put on a strong-woman voice and I could hear her constricted breathing behind my head. "She wants to be a doctor. She's not like the other girls around here."

"And she didn't take anything with her, not even a jacket," my father continued, black pupils flaring over the rim of his reading glasses. "Wouldn't she have packed? Wouldn't she have taken food?" In his mind, Diana would have excelled even at running away.

The policeman locked his icy green eyes on me. My stomach lurched.

"Can I speak with her?" he asked my father, his mouth curled up at a corner in an attempt to smile. "Alisha, right?"

My gaze drooped to the place where his creased shirt collar should have been bound by the knot of a tie.

I felt my mother's legs stiffen under my bottom. "Why?"

"Girls talk to each other. I've got two of my own."

I waited, I watched, I searched. Surely he would slice through the lies that had tumbled from my mouth the day Diana disappeared.

"You can have a seat right outside," said the detective, pointing my parents to the door with his pen. "We won't be long."

My father looked to my mother. Fluorescent light flickered against his lenses. I could tell he didn't trust this man, but we needed him to believe that we were as we presented, a cheerful healthy family, pretty mommy and handsome daddy, two innocent girls deserving of pity and help.

I sat in my mother's chair and gripped my hands together in my lap, wetness collecting in the pockets of my palms. I focused on the items on the desk, the business card holder and coffee mug, the fat grey computer monitor, the smiling white lady in one picture frame and the two smiling white girls in another.

"Want a drink, Alisha? A Coke?"

I shook my head. Cup of pens with police crests. Framed certificates. Filing cabinet behind his chair.

"You're thirteen, right? I'm going to take notes as we talk."

His attention lingered on me too long, ruminating on something I couldn't make out. I looked to the lady in the photograph, his pretty wife. Not as pretty as my mother, but her smile was bright and she sat, reclining against a lake-and-trees backdrop, in a sheer cotton dress. There was no special pose or new outfit to show off, no makeup or straightened shoulders as my mother would have done it.

The girls in the other photograph were copies of each other with their identical faces and identical pink sundresses. Their hair was curly blonde like the detective's only it cascaded past their shoulders. They hugged each other, laughing at the camera, and behind them was a table with an iced cake surrounded by balloons that looked ready to roll to the floor.

"Was Diana happy at home?"

"Yes," I croaked. It was the first time I had spoken since the meeting began.

"How about you? Get along with your parents?"

"Yes."

My heart almost vaulted out of my chest when the computer fan clacked into a rattling whir under the desk. One of his brown dress shoes shifted to rest on a jumble of cables.

"You ever lie to them?"

The rapid and uncomplicated *no* I'd intended to supply didn't come. He pulled a napkin from his pocket to swipe under his nostrils.

Coffee mug with dried drip of coffee down the side.

"I don't know," I managed to sputter. There was a prickling at the root of my tongue. The lump in my throat had returned.

"And your sister? Did she? Not because she's bad. Maybe she wanted that summer job and they weren't happy. They're not permissive, right? It's part of your culture for girls to do what they're told."

"No." This man and the other police officers didn't know my sister or my family. That was why I had hidden Diana's diary before the police clomped into our apartment to look through her bedroom and canvass the building and neighbourhood. I was the only one who knew about the diary and I knew it said too much about everything: the boy she'd met, the tattoo she wanted to get, her desire to leave home and start a real life. Her words would have only confirmed the police's assessment of her as a bad girl and made my parents look worse. Hiding Diana's diary was the only way I could protect her.

The detective shuffled through the papers on his desk, frowning. "Maybe your father gets mad? Maybe drinking and yelling at you girls, maybe giving your mom a little push? Good dads are like that sometimes. It could be that your sister took off to prove a point. She just wanted him to notice."

Is that what happened? I wondered. Did she leave to prove something? Maybe it had nothing to do with the strange man I had talked to at the mall, the one who followed us. Maybe Diana had left on her own. Maybe we would go back to the apartment to meet her standing in the living room, waiting on us.

Where were you? my parents would scream, livid and relieved, hugging her. *It's been three whole days! Do you know what you did to us?*

The detective found the paper he was searching for and wrote something on it, thin mouth squeezed thinner in the process. "You waited for your sister and when she didn't come, you went to look for her yourself around the Jane Finch Mall, the side streets, your school, and the park? Is that correct?"

I nodded weakly, still unable to admit to anything, even as the detective prepared to smother me in the truth. A shiver undulated through my body, a mixed rumble of fear and anticipated reprieve. *I waited. I watched. I searched.* I longed for the myth of my bravery to be over. I was grateful that my parents weren't in the room. A small mercy.

Dark blue carpet with flecks of purple and white. Light beige walls.

"Why do you think you couldn't find her?"

I gave a slow shrug.

He looked at me again but didn't attempt to smile as he had done before.

"I'm sorry," I said softly.

Pen gliding, dot, dot, cross, cross. The detective scratched more marks on the page before he put his pen down. "Do you think she might've been abducted?"

Abducted. That word was the reason why my father meditated so deeply on his notes, why my mother tiptoed about the apartment like an intruder in her own home, too frightened to move. They would never have used such a brutal word in my presence, but it must have echoed in their guts. *Diana was abducted.* It was too horrible a possibility and I didn't want to acknowledge it either. I had been trying instead to convince myself that I was a child capable of noble things, and that I hadn't done anything wrong. *I waited, I watched, I searched.*

"I don't know," I responded, a warble in my voice. I felt as if shadows were spiralling about my feet, opening a pit under me. Unavoidable questions were upon me, along with the disgrace that always seemed to lurk behind the truth. *You didn't wait, you didn't watch, you didn't search for your sister,* the detective would say to me. *You lied and you've always been a liar.*

And a sorrowful peace would wash through me. Even if they were to hate me, my beautiful mother and handsome father, even if I crumbled like dry earth, at least it would be over. *I'm not brave and I'm not what you want,* I would tell them. *I'm not like Diana and I never will be.*

"Don't worry, honey," the detective said instead.

He smiled at me sadly, just like my mother had smiled at me the night we became watchmen in our living room, waiting on my sister's return. Each time my mother had passed her hand over my hair, she had smiled down, silently begging for her absent daughter. Making me want to die.

"That was a terrible thing to ask." He stood and manoeuvred around his messy desk. He placed a hand on the backrest of my chair and I noticed the bulge of a potbelly under his shirt and the lines at the corners of his eyes. Up close, he wasn't as young as I had thought he was. "Let's get your parents back in here, okay?"

I glanced again at his wife and the blonde sisters. The accusations I had awaited, the terrifying and freeing revelations, simply never came. I felt sure that the pit of swirling shadows that yawned under my feet would stay, antagonizing me but never quite sucking me in. I was caught in some kind of in-between life, and it seemed I would stay there.

The speech I wrote about Auntie Julie placed me second in my class. I accepted a wall plaque and a coupon for a free slice of pizza. Diana won first place in hers. Along with winning students from all the homerooms, she would have to recite her speech in front of the entire school to win the big prize.

Competitors sat on a line of chairs onstage, facing the open gymnasium that doubled as our auditorium as the rest of the school streamed in. Screams and laughter magnified into an echoing racket. Junior grade students sat cross-legged on the hardwood floor, snug to the stage and squirming. Middle grade students like me sat on folding chairs, kissing teeth and play-arguing with each other. Teachers sat as sentinels along the walls, and three teacher-judges wearing suit jackets folded themselves into child-sized desks at the centre of the room.

My sister's hair was combed down and she wore a skirt, pantyhose, and dress shoes, just as my mother had insisted. She appeared unperturbed by the burden of public performance, turning to gab with her fellow orators. Her cue cards lay bound under her chair. I wondered when she would begin sifting through them, anxiously twirling her fingers through her hair, like the other girls beside her.

But Diana didn't touch her hair and she abandoned her cards entirely when they called her name. She stepped toward the microphone with nothing in her hands, shoes clacking. The room was quiet as she moved to stand under a light that gave her a halo, and the fear that should have seized her shot through me instead, making my chest thump, my muscles quiver, and my neck burn like a bonfire.

"There is no more sacred oath than the one physicians take," she began, "and it is to that oath that we all entrust our lives."

She sounded nothing like the speakers who had gone before her. Their words were swallowed in fog. Her voice made the microphone squeal and pop. Otherworldly silence descended over the audience, the cinder-block walls catching her words and reverberating them back.

I can't recall the speech itself. I just remember her regal gestures—one arm and then the other used for emphasis—and her gaze, oscillating where mine would have jumped and skittered into a corner. Alternating strokes of pride and longing swept through me as I watched her. That was the day my mother lost her place as the person I wanted to become.

Applause poured in my ears. The kids around me got up from their seats and hooted. The younger students smacked their palms and feet on the floor. I scrambled to join the standing ovation and looked to the adults at the wall. Paula was among them, pressing forward in her chair. She stuck her thumb and index finger into her mouth and whistled at a piercing pitch. There was no question that Diana would win the contest that afternoon.

We filed down the side aisle when it was over. I was the last in a line of my classmates. Paula's eyes caught mine when I got close.

"Alisha, yeah?" She was still squatting in a student's chair. She straightened her back and smoothed the front of her vest over her jersey. "How'd you do on your speech, Guyana-girl?"

Teacher and fellow classmates, my Aunt Julie was born in the village of Suddie in the country of Guyana. Her first word was "Bea" because she looked up to her older sister, my mother, Beatrice. They are best friends to this day. I had completely forgotten about the plaque I had won, a piece of plywood with my name printed in magic marker by my elfin teacher, a heart replacing the dot of the *i*.

"Second place," I answered, "but my sister won the whole thing today." I wasn't certain why I had felt so obliged to say it.

"That's your sister?" She scrunched her lips, pushing them to the side of her face. "I can see the resemblance. You must come from a long line of orators, yeah?"

Diana had my father's proud posture, my mother's graceful arms, and my aunt's independence, but it was clear to me that she stood above us all, a flashing firelight orbiting above our heads. "Thank you," I responded, unable to fish out a more suitable reply. I could feel the flatness of my face.

She leaned in, her spectacles coming close enough for me to see that the lenses were thicker than the frames. Her freckles were all layered over each other, some darker and some lighter, across her cheeks and nose. "Don't worry," she said, "I know what it's like. It might be hard to measure up now, but you'll get there."

I managed a peep of a goodbye before rushing out of the gymnasium, catching up to my classmates in the hall.

That Saturday, my mother put on pantyhose and a fancy flowered dress. She curled her hair while my father, in undershirt and trousers, unfolded the ironing board. He rarely did housework, but when he did, he was meticulous about it. He unwrapped a new collared shirt and studied the fabric, flipping and smoothing it with his hand. By the time we left the apartment, the creases of his shirt traced his arms perfectly, and the whole place smelled of his cologne mixed with my mother's perfume.

My father drove our old sedan. My mother sat to his right and Diana and I were in the back seat. The neighbourhood swept by. We cleared our group of apartment buildings, passing women walking down the sidewalk whose strides were slowed by children and grocery bags. People congregated at the bus shelters and squinted in the gusty October wind. High-rises turned to low-rises and townhouses before transforming themselves into duplexes and detached houses buffered by fences and evergreen hedges.

"Dad, the kids on my team come around here to train on Sunday mornings," said Diana, pressing up to his backrest. "Can I go with them tomorrow?"

My mother kept looking straight out of the windshield.

My father played with the knob that controlled the fan. "You train at school every morning. That's enough for you."

Diana flopped back into her seat and scowled out of her window. "You never let me do anything," I heard her murmur to herself.

We slowed at the light next to a plaza. The strip of grass in front of it was covered by signs advertising stay-at-home careers and church-tent revivals. Dozens of seagulls stood on the grass too, squawking so persistently that I could hear them through my rolled up window. When the stoplight flicked to green, a bass-rattling, low-riding sports car zoomed past us and claimed the roadway.

Auntie Julie was waiting for us at our table at Captain Johnny's Family Seafood Shack, my sister's favourite restaurant. Diana and my father both ordered lobster and my mother and Auntie Julie shared a shrimp platter. I selected my meal from the thirteen-and-under menu: oily fish and chips, a cup of Pepsi, and a quaking bowl of green Jell-O, the same thing Diana used to order when she had been young enough for it.

They were still chattering about the details of Diana's speech when Auntie Julie turned to me, dabbing the corners of her mouth with a napkin. "You didn't even let me read what you wrote about me, 'Lisha-babe. What if you made up crazy things?"

I was accustomed to seeing her in pants and shirts, but tonight my aunt was a near copy of my mother in a white blouse, long flowered skirt, and high heels. She even wore the same shade of pink lipstick and her hair was combed into the kind of bun my mother usually had.

"It was all true," I answered.

"Your mother told me you got second place. You and Dee should be so proud of yourselves. How many other siblings at your school can say they achieved what you two did?"

I wished everyone would stop talking about those damned speeches. I slurped a whole cube of Jell-O, letting it inflate my cheek. "Thank you," I blubbered back.

My mother had ordered a glass of cola but she favoured her water, so my father reached behind Diana to claim it, eating and drinking for his wife as he often did. He sipped, then replaced the fizzing glass on the ring of condensation it had sweated onto the table and returned his suit-jacketed arm to the back of Diana's chair. I couldn't recall a single instance when my father's arm had found a place so naturally around me.

My vision loosened from my family and sank to the tablecloth. "I won a coupon for pizza," I said to my aunt.

"Oh, that's good."

I used my fork to pierce another piece of Jell-O and a hasty decision clacked together in my mind. *My Aunt Julie is a paralegal,* I had written in my speech. *Her dream is to become a lawyer to help children in need.* "I want to be a lawyer when I grow up, Auntie Julie, just like you."

"Really?" She lay a hand over the pendent she wore on special occasions, a loop of two Pisces fish made of pounded Guyana-gold the colour of a sunset, each fish's puckered mouth attached to the other's tail fin. "But you know I won't finish my studies for a while, right?"

My father stretched his hand from the back of Diana's chair and rubbed my mother's shoulder. The three of them formed a closed tableau, a family of mommy and daddy and daughter that didn't need a fourth person. I felt like gunpowder caps were snapping off in my brain.

"And I'll go to the same school as you," I said to my aunt, wiggling my bottom to sit straighter, "and I can even work with delinquents like you're going to."

She tapped my mother's flower-print leg beside her, slim under the skirt. "You hear that, Bea? Your daughter wants to become a lawyer."

"Since when?" My mother smiled at me. Her curling iron ringlets had slackened so they jangled around her jaw like black springs. She touched my father's arm. "Did you hear that, Don? 'Lisha's going to be a lawyer like her auntie."

A wash of peace, however contrived, foamed around me. I was going to win them over.

Groomed as the rest of him, my father's eyebrows peaked in unison. A toothy smile came to his lips. He gave a throaty laugh that sounded like a drawn-out cough. I knew it as my father's truest laugh, deep and satisfying, a rare sound in our apartment during the workweek. I was certain the brokerage boys in his office had never even heard it. "I didn't think you thought about these things, 'Lisha."

"I do," I answered.

"What a thing. A doctor and lawyer, together in one house! What about you and your auntie? What if you have to go up against her in court?"

"Brother Don," my aunt replied, "'Lisha would win. Our girls are so smart."

"You'd give a good fight."

Waiting for her to prance in with her praises, I turned to my mother, but all I found was the dregs of a fading smile. Worry jolted through me. Could she so easily see through my fabrications?

Diana stretched to steal a shrimp from my mother's plate and a sphere of oil splat onto the tablecloth in the process. "You guys had the best grades in school, right mom?" she asked. She bit to detach the meat from the tail with her front teeth, her eyes ping-ponging between mother and aunt.

"Top of the class," my mother answered, "one week me, one week Julie, back and forth. Remember, this was Anna Regina School. It was harder than schools over here. We had high standards to live up to. We had to wear uniforms and memorize Shakespeare, you know." She looked to me. "Can you keep up with Dee's grades like Julie had to keep up with mine?"

I grinned and nodded broadly, and the three adults flapped around the table. I didn't know how long their excitement would last, but it didn't matter, not in the moment. *'Lisha and Dee, our smart girls, top of the class!*

I glanced at my sister as she used her fork to prod the hunk of lobster flesh on her plate. Her eyes lassoed mine. She hadn't perked up the way my other family members had, expectant as graduates tossing their mortarboards into the sky. I turned away from her and hoped Auntie Julie would ask me more questions.

A few nights later, my father returned from work with a handsome edition of *The Criminal Code of Canada*. It was a thick book, printed on tissue-thin paper and bound in royal blue hardcover. I revelled in the gift and carried it to my bedroom, certain that my father would soon be calling me to watch legal dramas with him.

But the book remained on my dresser. It didn't find its way to the top shelf of my closet and I didn't reject sleep to browse its pages. I didn't read it beyond my father's cursive writing on the inner cover: *Best of success in your legal studies. Don't quit! Love, Mommy and Daddy.* That book was the only thing I owned that was decorated with his handwriting, those distinct British West Indies *g*'s and *q*'s I had always attempted to imitate.

A few days later, Diana came into my bedroom and shut the door behind her. She was wearing her track team's uniform shorts and T-shirt. She leaned her bottom against the edge of my dresser, resting one foot on top of the other, and I noticed the bristle of thousands of black prickles on her shins. I was surprised that my mother had allowed her to shave her legs.

"What do you really know about all this lawyer stuff?" she asked.

Sitting on the bed with my homework, I gave her the casual shrug she would have given me. "Lots of things."

I focused on my notebook though I felt her watching the top of my head, waiting for me to relent. I flipped through the pages, pretending to search for something I had written before. I could only breathe again when I heard leg against leg and the sound of the door closing as she left.

How does she always know the truth about me, I wondered, *no matter what I do?*

I avoided Diana that evening and I didn't say anything to her on the way to school the next day. She and I parted when the school grounds opened before us, two pairs of shoes drawing a widening *V* over the crispy, frost-coated field. I walked toward my homeroom, and Diana walked toward the other grade eight girls waiting for practice to begin.

"You think this is the way things should be?" I heard my father say in the living room that night. He was answered by a silence that felt angry.

I was on my bed. My bedside lamp illuminated the open binder on my lap. When my parents fought, my father would develop a barrel chest and clomp around as if he had muscles to tear the place apart. My mother would become more imperious than ever, her spine lengthened and her proud nose pointed. As much as I wanted to slink away and shut it out, I would find my ears straining for a nicety between them, a sigh, even a cleared throat as a sign that it was going to end.

"I make a secretary's salary," said my father, "and don't expect no promotion either. I'll never become one of their little *pets*."

"You want the girls to come to an empty home like every other child in this building? We left Guyana for that?"

Every time they fought, one of them would evoke their children. I hated to be incorporated into their arguments against each other. I struggled through my math homework, lost in a cascade of long-division errors. I erased, and pink particles sprinkled over the page.

"Beatrice, I can't do it alone."

There was a pause. I imagined my mother's scandalized scoff and fast-blinking eyes. "Fine, I'll get a job, then. We'll move to a big house and the girls won't get to see their parents no more."

"You spoil them. They need to learn more independence."

I couldn't imagine my classmates' parents being so competitive with each other about how they raised their children. I shoved the binder off my lap and pushed my textbook to the end of the bed with my heel, bending my knees up under my chin. I slapped my hands over my ears. Even as my own booming pulse filled my brain, I still listened out for them, reserving a gritty black corner of my mind to log their charges against each other.

"You don't know what I do," my mother said, her voice sounding like it had been stuffed into a sock, "you don't dedicate your life—"

"They're mine too!" the muffled bass replied.

"You don't understand what a mother feels."

"And a father doesn't count?"

I sucked in my lips, clamping them between my teeth. Tears poured down my cheeks.

"Beatrice, you want to live in this shithole forever?"

"The man is cursing me! He goes out all day and does heaven knows what with who knows who and he's cursing *me*—"

"How the hell can you say that?"

Vague as my mother's insinuations were, I could tell they were unique to a man's obligations to his wife. Resentment of her crystallized under my ribs. Couldn't she see my father adored her?

Something brushed my elbow and I almost screamed. Diana stood beside my bed.

"Don't cry," she said.

I buried my forehead in her belly, her baggy sports jersey voluminous all around me, and I felt her arms encircle my neck.

"They won't split up. I feel kind of sorry for them, really. For Auntie Julie, too. They didn't think it would be like this when they came here. I don't even think they got the chance to do the things they really wanted to do."

But splitting up wasn't a concept I could apply to my parents, the Beauty Queen and her King, together since they had lived amongst the green canopies and silty waters of Guyana, fated to stand above the other couples in Jane and Finch. Those parents had no crackle between them, no shared secrets to smile at each other about, and a good number were women on their own, besieged by children. My parents were a different sort entirely.

"I shouldn't have told them I wanted to become a lawyer," I spoke in a craggy sob. "I don't know what I want to be."

"That's why you're crying?"

I spread tears on her jersey as I sniffed and sniffed. "Please don't tell them. I don't know what I should be and I'm still trying to figure it out. I'm really trying."

I felt her hand caress the back of my hair. "Why can't we both be doctors?"

I considered again what it might be like to be my sister, the one everybody invested themselves in, the real reason my parents left Guyana to live in this city, this half of the globe. A quiver shimmied up and down the rungs of my spine. The knowledge that I would never be like her didn't douse an inch of my desire to become her. My bones were made of it.

I wiped my nose with my knuckles. "It's okay. You're the smart one. You be a doctor and I'll be a lawyer. Then everybody'll be happy. After all, you did the speech on the Hippopotamus Oath."

She clapped a hand over her laugh, hoping our parents wouldn't hear.

We stayed shielded in my bedroom until the argument blew over our parents, travelled down the hallway, went out the window, and flew across the towers, searching unit to unit for another family to disturb.

CHAPTER 6

1939

PAULA LAY ON HER SIDE OF THE STIFF MATTRESS. SHE FELT THE SWEAT AT her temples but she kept the blanket up, clamped to her chin.

Step, step, step. She listened to Granny's slow footfalls, each one making the floorboards creak.

Paula shut her eyes and held her breath, battling her trembling muscles. She could hear Granny's breathing and knew she had come to stand over her bed. Paula was convinced it was only a matter of seconds before Granny would rip her blankets away and plant a switch up and down her legs. In the months she had been there, she had seen matrons lash many of the other boys and girls, who numbered about sixty in total. The children always begged and cried and pleaded innocence, but it made no difference. Welts bloomed on their scrawny limbs.

Paula imagined Granny raising the switch over her bed. *Dreaming of escape, were you? I'll teach you good!* Granny was the meanest of the adults and she ordered the others around all day. *Yes, ma'am, No ma'am, Sorry ma'am,* the matrons and farmhands answered to her nervously. She was the one who decreed the children's waking and working hours, and their eating and sleeping and stripping for bucket baths. The children cowered at her unsmiling mouth and fell silent when she came near them with her thick glasses, her helmet-waved hair, and her glaring eyes.

Behaving like a good girl today? She would lean close to ask in Paula's face. *Or are you a troublemaker who wasn't raised right? Hmmm?* Paula, smelling cigarettes on Granny's breath, would give a tight shake of her head and look down to her feet.

Agitated whispers emerged a few beds from Paula's in the crowded girls' dormitory. She opened her eyes and saw Granny whirl around.

"Which one of you is talking now?" she shouted across the room.

No one dared to answer.

"Didn't I tell you that when lights go off, mouths shut up?"

Paula squeezed her eyes shut again, still feeling Granny looming at her bedside, shifting her weight from one leg to another under her dress. *Today's the day,* Paula told herself, *she's gonna get you good.* Granny's perfume was a cloud of smoky flowers that overtook her brain.

Step, step, step. Paula listened to Granny's footsteps leave the dormitory, echo in the hallway, and descend the staircase. Her pulse still throbbed in her neck. The pungent perfume still lingered in her nostrils.

"Hey," she whispered to the girl in the bed closest to hers. She still didn't know most people's names. "You awake?"

The girl was maybe ten or eleven, and she was the tallest of all the girls. She lay on her side facing Paula every night, but she rarely spoke and never smiled. Moonlight broke through the slit in the curtains above the girl's bed. It sliced across her forehead, isolating a nostril and curling over her stern, pursed lips.

"Hey, answer me!"

The girl's eyes snapped open. "You're going to get us beat! Go to sleep!"

"Where's the baby room?"

"Shut up!"

"But I need to find it."

"You can't, so just be quiet and go to sleep." The girl flipped over, yanking her blanket over her head. Her heels, two nubs, poked out from the bottom of the covers.

Paula slid out of bed anyway. She pushed down the front of her nightdress, cut from gunny sack burlap. It reached the middle of her thighs and grazed her skin wherever it touched. She took careful steps toward the door, shivering and feeling the other girls' eyes on her.

"*Where are you going?*" another girl whispered over her blanket, only to be shushed by the others nearby.

"You're gonna get us in trouble!" said another.

Paula left the room and tiptoed toward the yellow light where the hallway intersected with the staircase. Each floorboard squawked and her heart pounded, but she fought the urge to scamper back to bed. *Queen Nanny wasn't scared of anybody,* she said to herself. *Queen Nanny could do anything.*

Radio music—the sound of horns and piano and drums in a riotous melody—drifted up the stairs from the floor below. A burst of laughter rolled up too, along with men's and women's mingling voices. Paula inhaled the scent of onions frying with fish and seasoning. Her empty stomach curled to a lump. All she had eaten for dinner was the same watery broth the children always ate. Even as she pined for the taste of real food, the milk and bread her mother would sometimes give to her at home, she found herself sickened by the smell of the cooking downstairs.

Paula turned a corner and pushed through a weighty door. She entered a room with a large window that looked out to the treetops. It sounded like Granny and the other adults were right under the place where she stood. Light bounced through leaves tossed about by roughhousing winds and strange, shifting shapes were cast over rows of bars. About a dozen cribs were lined flush against the walls the way the beds were arranged in the girls' room. But in this room, the scent of cooking fish had transformed into the sour-sweet odour of piss.

"Ave?" she whispered. "You here?"

A scattered reply came from more than one crib—scuffles and noisy *aahs* and thumps. She cringed and stopped, listening to the voices under the peppy music, and she continued to tiptoe over the icy planks.

She peered between the bars, crib after crib. Some contained tiny infants and others had toddlers. Some children were asleep and others were awake in a hodgepodge of blankets. A few sat up with pillow-messed heads.

She found Ave at the very end of the room, kneeling at the foot of her crib. Ave pushed her face against the bars and poked her arms through to feel Paula's forehead, ears, eyes.

"You're here."

Ave pressed a few chubby digits into Paula's mouth and Paula gently bit on them.

"You don't miss me," Paula said, "do you?"

Ave dug at both of Paula's cheeks and opened her mouth to shout nonsense as she used to when they would lie in bed together at home. *Paw,* her sounds implied, *there are so many things I've been dying to tell you!*

Paula scrambled to press her palm over Ave's mouth. "No, don't do that, they'll take me away."

Ave's eyes welled, glossy in the dark. Paula knew the truth, that her little sister had been waiting for her this whole time, convinced that she would come to her as she had always done. *What took you so long?* Ave's eyes seemed to say.

"Don't cry," Paula said. "I'm sorry I couldn't be with you. They won't tell me why we have to be here." Paula felt hot, breathy vibrations rumbling under her palm and she pulled her hand away from Ave's lips. "What'd you say?"

"Paw," Ave answered. "Paaaw." It was guttural, and her mouth hung open after the sound left. Feeble light from the window fell soft and blue on her smooth cheek, and her eyelashes, glistening black, slid low, doused in quiet tears.

Paula brushed her sister's chin. She decided she would sneak to her crib the next night and the night after that—as many nights as she could, no matter the scolding and the lashes she risked from Granny and the matrons. At least then Ave wouldn't have to cry in that crib for her big sister, as they waited for their mother to bring them back home.

CHAPTER 7

THE TELEPHONE KEPT RINGING BECAUSE MY PARENTS' FRIENDS AND COUSINS called non-stop for updates. Some came by the apartment with food, trays of lasagna and chow mein, roti wrapped in foil and curry spooned into margarine and yogurt containers. Even people in our building came offering red-red and pilau and biryani.

The police, they all asked, *did they find anything yet?*

When I was at the dining table and my parents and aunt were in the living room talking to an officer, I overheard the other officer on his phone in the kitchen. "Over four days now," he mumbled into the receiver. "Don't know. Not good."

That night, Auntie Julie came to our apartment with a duffel bag, which she placed in the corner of Diana's bedroom along with a plastic grocery bag stretched by shoes. I knew those black and tan and grey chunky-heeled pumps from her townhouse's coat closet.

My aunt unfurled my sister's bedcovers tucked tight between the mattress and box spring. My mother had made sure everything was crisp and ready, and she chose the sheets my sister preferred, the ones with rambling brown vines and tiny blue flowers. The bedside lamp glowed hazy yellow against the wall and my aunt's hair, which rolled down her back in rivulets. She wore flannel pyjamas with a block pattern, like my sister would have worn.

I was in my girly short-sleeved nightgown, slouching in the doorway. Her face was youthful and lovely as always. She looked to me.

"You okay, babe?" she asked in the same near whisper she had used when she arrived at our door with three sad kisses for mother, father, and niece.

No, Auntie Julie, I thought, I'm not okay. Can't you see? "Yeah."

She sat on the bed and stretched her hand toward me. "Come here."

I padded toward her on bare feet and she pulled me onto her lap, the back of my head against her face.

"Tell me," she said.

"Nothing."

"Not nothing. You can tell me anything."

I smelled her citrusy perfume. Her fingers raked through my hair, which was only half as long as hers and my mother's. I let my eyes climb to the top of Diana's closet. Its door was open as it was the day she disappeared. Her medical books stood together. There had been so many nights that I had wanted to sneak into her bedroom and snatch her books and trace my finger over the diagrams without her bother or fuss. Had I won the opportunity in this unthinkable way? I shuddered, feeling a surge of shame in my bones. It was between two of those books that Diana had hidden her diary, the one I had read without her permission and kept buried in my closet since she'd been gone. How trivial it seemed now, her writing about the boy with the black sun tattoo and her desire to start a new life away from her family, away from her little sister. Her betrayals paled against my own.

"When is Dee coming home?" I asked.

I felt my aunt's breath shuffle amongst the strands of my hair. "I don't know, love. I wish I did." Her voice had gotten even quieter.

I could hear my mother in the kitchen, taking her time going through the cupboards and drawers, meticulously drying each plate and fork from dinner. My father was at the table, still in his suit because he had just come in from driving around in search of Diana. He pored over the newspaper, his notes in his manila folder, hunting for strings of information, because strings might lead to other strings, and other strings might lead to Diana's whereabouts. My parents lingered near the apartment door, waiting for her knock.

"But where'd she go, Auntie Julie?"

"I don't know."

To visit the boy she had met when we went camping? Or did she get *abducted*? I was too afraid to summon the word. Surely saying it out loud would only make it true. *There was a man,* I was tempted to tell my aunt. *I don't know why he was following us and why I left Diana with him and now she's gone.*

But I knew why I had done what I did. I had wanted my sister to suffer.

"I wish she'd come back," I said, the words tucked close to my hot mouth. I was a sad child and knew that sad children are rarely expected to say meaningful things, rarely asked to explain hard things. *Did you really wait, watch, and search for your sister, Alisha? Or did you leave her when she needed you and wish her dead?*

My aunt squeezed her arms tighter around my body. "Oh, babe, this is so hard for you." She rested her forehead on the back of my head and I nudged my head backward to prop hers up. "I want her to come back too."

I knew she would say that.

I looked up to the closet's top shelf again. I waited for the edges of the image of my sister's precious medical books to darken and melt inward like a reverse Polaroid, undeveloping before me.

My father squinted into his camera's viewfinder. "Smile, girls. Say *rice and peas.*"

My mother stood in front of the tree with her arms around my sister and me. Every spring, she insisted that my father take a picture of us under the crabapple tree across from our building's lobby, during the short window when all the crabapple trees around the apartments bloomed into a fluffy pink backdrop. Today, her hair was combed over her shoulder to brush against her hip, and she angled one of her feet in front of the other to show off the lilac pumps that matched her swishing lilac skirt, neither of which I had seen before that morning.

It was April 1998. I was twelve, almost thirteen, and in grade seven. Diana was fifteen and in the grade nine gifted program at William Lyon Mackenzie Collegiate Institute. Diana kept up her honour roll marks and even though my parents told her they didn't want her doing high school sports she went to track tryouts anyway. She told them about it when she had already made the team, arguing back at them when they ordered her to quit. Somehow she convinced them to let her stay on the team. I went to the same elementary school as usual and came home at the regular times. I did nothing extracurricular. It seemed like Diana was always busy at her school or at the library or inside her bedroom, studying for exams and working on assignments so our parents would let her stay on the track team.

"Smile, Alisha," said my father. "What's wrong with you?"

I grimaced, hoping he'd interpret it as a grin. I had sunken into a bad mood since early that morning because Diana had told me I couldn't go with her to her downtown track meet. Several city high schools were going to compete and each team member was only allowed to bring one guest with them. Diana chose my father.

"Don?" asked my mother through grinning teeth.

"Stay where you are." He inspected his Polaroid camera, flicking and snapping the latches.

Immersed in preparations for her meet, my sister tapped her sneaker on the grass. When we were younger, my mother would dress me and Diana up and dab lipstick and eyeshadow on us for the photo, and we would feel that we were imbued with her glamour. Now that we were older, the crabapple portrait had lost its thrill. Diana was already in her tracksuit. I wore one of her old sweatshirts.

As we waited, I noticed the activity at the fifth building down from ours, the high-rise with the largest yard out front. People were setting up for something, carrying tables and boxes and milling about and talking.

My father aimed the camera at us again. "Okay, now, *rice and peas*!"

In that photograph, my head is turned away from the lens. My sleep-tousled hair makes me look like a straggler yanked into the frame at the last second.

My father and sister drove off to the track meet at noon. He wore suit pants, a button-up shirt, and barely worn white sneakers. My mother stayed in the kitchen to prepare lamb curry and rice. We were going to pick up Auntie Julie that evening for a potluck at the house of one of my father's cousins. I told my mother that I was going to play across the street with some of the neighbourhood kids, but I had no intention of doing so. I only ever hung out with them if Diana was with me.

I walked five buildings over, still mopey and scuffing my feet. By then, a residents' yard sale was bustling. Cars clogged the front driveway, and double-parked along the road. A big boombox with scratchy speakers played a dub reggae medley overlaid with siren and machine-gun sound effects. Little girls clustered on the grassy island at the centre of the driveway, giggling in their unzipped winter jackets, taking turns doing the bogle and the butterfly. Two industrial grills hissed with hamburgers; flipping patties between them was a squat black man in a white *babariga* that reached his ankles. A couple of small boys in kente cloth *kufi* hats and Ninja Turtle sweatshirts skipped around him, frolicking in the smoke as if it were summertime.

I pushed my way through the makeshift aisles of folding tables on the grass, following other people as they scrutinized the treasures set out.

Toys and strollers, mismatched plates and mugs and serving dishes, videotapes with handwritten cases—*The Karate Kid* and *Coming to America* and *Salaam Bombay!* There were children's snow pants and boots, and pots of every kind, some for cooking or steeping tea, others for percolating coffee.

Paula was at a table, sitting in a lawn chair in a puffy sports jacket that was too heavy for the weather and a fitted wool cap over her bun. Her table had towers of books, some oven mitts, and a row of bushy potted plants. An easel with a stack of plastic-wrapped paintings was positioned beside her chair.

In my silent sulk, I almost turned the other way. But I rambled over to her and when I saw her look my way, I gave a little wave and tucked some loose hair behind my ear. I shoved my hand into my jacket pocket, unsure she would even recognize me outside of school.

She clapped her palms together at her chest. "Well hello there, Guyana-girl," she said. She pressed toward me in her chair. "Which building's yours?"

"Twenty-nine forty-seven."

"Good one."

"This one's nice too."

"I like it."

I picked up one of her books. Its cover was made of shredded, peeling purple cloth. I opened it to the first page and found a faded ink stamp with ornate lettering. *This text belongs to Paula Benton.*

She dipped her chin to watch me over the rims of her glasses. "Wore that book right out. It's still a great story."

The embossed gold lettering had almost entirely chipped away and all that remained of *The Bluest Eye* was the oversized capital *E*. I looked to the top of another book tower, this one made up of creased paperbacks. "*Robinson Crusoe*," I read. "I heard of that."

"That was one of the first stories I ever read, you know. I thought it made sense for me to start at the first English novel and go from there. What do you read?"

My thoughts flew to the shelf in my sister's closet, those heavy medical textbooks she still flipped through all the time with their serious diagrams and fine print. My cheeks flushed at the thought of them. The few books I had ever read were for children, thinner and floppier than anything on Paula's table. "Baby-Sitter's Club."

"Oh, yeah, those get checked out of the library a lot. Girls love 'em."

The top of my ears warmed. I pointed to her easel. "What are those?"

Now it was her turn to blush, a faint tint under her freckles, come and gone in a flash. I wouldn't have noticed it if we had been under the school's fluorescent library lights. "Oh, they're my paintings." She got to her feet. "I've got a knack."

The one at the front was a watercolour of a fuzzy baby chick perched on a ledge. On the bottom right, calligraphic letters had been brushed in an upward curl. *Ave's Friend.*

"You like birds?" I asked.

"I'm not fussy. But I knew someone who loved to play with baby chicks."

"Is the person's name Ave?"

She nodded. "We both used to work on a farm down east. Chicks hatched by the dozens there."

"Where?"

"Nova Scotia. You know where that is, don't you?"

I nodded, remembering the description I had read in my geography textbook. *The Maritime province of Nova Scotia, Mi'kmaq Nation territory, Halifax its capital.* I had never met a Nova Scotian before, but the coil of Paula's words had already signalled that she wasn't from Toronto, and her manner wasn't anything like the other adults in the neighbourhood. Most of them didn't wear sneakers and sports jerseys and jeans the way Paula did, and most didn't talk to the children of strangers. Certainly none of them spent their afternoons assisting librarians at the local elementary school.

We both stood there, admiring her painting, and then my eyes drifted over to her. I saw her blink down to the grass. New streaks of pink coloured her face. I felt heat graze my own cheeks too.

"Can I see the other ones?" I asked.

She tipped the chick painting forward and I could hear her bracelets tinkling under her jacket sleeves as she revealed the pieces underneath. *Ave's Lily, Ave's Hands, Ave's Heart.* So many canvases about someone named Ave.

She slid a painting from under the bunch and placed it at the front. "How about this one?"

Jeanette's Hibiscuses. Two flowers, one big and one small, with stems that had little beads at their ends. The tangerine petals lapped out with flouncy edges that reminded me of the hems of some of my mother's skirts.

"Hibiscuses are my girlfriend Jeanette's favourite," she said. "I did a tropical flower series for her. She's Guyanese like you, yeah? I had to look at her photographs to get them just right."

Hibiscuses grew in the pages of my parents' wedding album too. They were bright red and fuchsia and orange and they dotted the bushes around my mother and father, posing in gown and tuxedo, a landscape of palm trees and ocean water behind them.

I drew my shoulders up to my ears. "I wish I could paint like you."

"Why couldn't you learn?"

"I can't see pictures in my mind."

"Well, I always make sure to plan my pieces out first." She dragged her finger over the tabletop and I realized what I had seen her do months ago in the library. She had been mapping a painting.

"I'm not good at anything," I said.

"What's all this here? You have to be good at something."

"My sister's really good at sports."

"But what about you?"

"I'm going to be a lawyer. I'm reading the criminal code."

"Well, look at that."

A ball of irritation popped up in my throat. I knew I hadn't given her a real answer.

She lifted *Jeanette's Hibiscuses* from the easel and held it out to me. The plastic wrap caught the piercing reflection of the sun. "Why don't you take this one home?"

I hesitated and she nudged it closer to me.

"It doesn't seem like anyone's going to invest in books and art today, and I'm not carrying them back upstairs."

I grabbed the painting, hugging it, hibiscuses to heart. Paula's grin made her freckles slip up her cheeks.

When the beat-up elevator doors dinged open at my floor, I bolted down the hall to get to the apartment and go straight into my bedroom. I unhooked the cardboard-backed poster of Dalmatian puppies from its spot above my headboard and slid it under my bed, sneezing at the disturbed dust. After ripping the plastic off the painting, I hung my twin hibiscuses in its place.

I jumped off the bed and stepped back until I hit my desk. Stuffed toys and stickers were still strewn across my room, but a sunbeam passed through my window and glowed on the beautiful new tangerine flowers on my wall.

A few days passed before my mother mentioned the painting. We were in the living room, sitting over a heap of clean laundry on the coffee table, the tail end of the four o'clock news on the television. In preparation for track finals, Diana's team had stayed late after school for extra practice. So I took her place, pulling apart staticky towels and pillowcases, as my mother sat beside me reuniting socks and laying her silk-and-lace panties on her lap.

"Your hibiscuses are pretty, 'Lisha," she said. "When we move, you could paint your new bedroom the same colour. Where'd you get them?"

"It was a present."

I could feel her eyes on the side of my face. I concentrated on the snapping electricity as I pulled cotton from terrycloth.

"Who gave it to you?"

"My friend."

"Which one?"

"A lady who works in the library. She can paint by looking at a picture."

"What's her name? Jeanette? Have I met her?"

"Her name's Miss Paula."

The only people my parents ever really wanted to talk to were the cousins and neighbours they had brought with them from back home. That had become clear to me the time an Indian girl who went to my school, wore bindi, and lived in my building invited me and my mother to her family's Diwali dinner. The girl's mother, a stocky woman with a thick braid, always offered bashful nods in the elevator while her daughter gaped at my mother like she was in the presence of a Bollywood star. *My father was a Hindu,* my mother answered when I had relayed the girl's request, *and my mother said she'd never trust a Hindu again.* Soon enough, the girl and her mother moved out of our building. We didn't visit them to say goodbye, and I understood that the space to befriend anybody new was narrow.

"Where's she from?" my mother asked. "She's Black?"

"She's from Nova Scotia and she's really nice. She helps the teachers."

My mother added another pair of panties to the collection on her thighs, this one scarlet satin. "She gives gifts to other children too?"

"Uh-huh." I aligned the corners of a tea towel, overshooting the third fold, pinching the hems and letting the whole thing drop open. Nervousness was escaping through my fingers.

"I don't want you taking things from strangers. Who's this Black lady? I don't know her. You have to be careful. There are a lot of bad people around here. Ask Mommy next time."

"Okay," I responded, convinced my mother would make me return it.

Her shoulders finally relaxed. "Good. You're my good baby girl, you know that?"

She offered me a generous Queen Bea smile, shiny and flawless. I tried to stop myself from smiling back but I couldn't seem to wrestle it down. I could never deny my mother's smiles.

"Are you reading the law book Daddy bought for you?"

"Yes."

She clacked her tongue softly against the back of her top teeth. "My little lawyer. You two are no ordinary girls." She raised an index finger, twirling it in the air. "None of these people have children like you."

My Little Lawyer. I hoped the offhand name would stick. I saw myself carrying a briefcase like my father and wearing heels like my aunt, riding the train downtown to ascend a glass building that looked like it was spray-painted gold.

I watched my mother fish a pair of my father's boxers from the pile, snap them in the air, and place them on the coffee table. She lined up the seams and I realized her meticulousness was the result of a growing jungle of thoughts that had nothing to do with my future career. "Remember how we used to be last summer, how me, you, and Diana used to talk and stay together?"

I reached for a wad of my father's ribbed undershirts. "Yeah."

"Dee's in high school and this time it might just be you and me. Soon Daddy will find a big house for us to move into, but he doesn't know what's going to happen. Both you and Dee will move on, busy with your studies and teams and school and friends, no time to waste on your mommy or daddy anymore. That's what always happens. Julie and I did it to our mommy and you girls will do the same to me. You won't be here forever." She plucked another pair of boxers and treated them with the same care. "Your father doesn't know about those things."

I didn't want to tell her that I didn't believe the issue to be sports or studies, a house or friends, and I didn't want to tell her that the problem had little to do with me. It was a matter of my sister transcending us all. I worried I was losing Diana as much as my parents were. I knew I would have to do something to get close to her again. I just didn't have any idea about what that could be.

I continued separating my family's laundry in silence and awaited orders about what I would have to do with my hibiscuses, but my mother didn't mention the painting again.

CHAPTER 8

1941

IT WAS FEBRUARY. THE SKY HAD BECOME A MILDEWED WOOL BLANKET THAT couldn't be shaken out. In the pits, where the snow was deep, children drove their feet down like spikes, puncturing the top crust of ice and burying their legs past their knees. The older children pelted snowballs at each other while the younger ones sat in the shallow areas, crafting snow dolls and snow animals with their numb fingers to dine on snow food and snow drink. *Yum, yum, yum, kiss, kiss, kiss.*

Paula hooked her arm into Ave's. The two of them hopped around the front yard to keep warm and distract themselves from their hunger. Their boots kicked a rough circle in the snow. *Ring around the rosy, pocketful of posies....*

They were let in to have their lunch and when they were put back outside, the bracing winds had picked up. Instead of playing, the children gathered around the trees at the edges of the yard. On her way to a tree, Paula squinted around and realized that Ave had slipped away from her side. Her heart drummed heavy in her chest. She flipped her coat collar around her ears and curled her fingers into fists inside her pockets. Cold air cuffed both wrists because she was ten years old and had outgrown her coat two winters ago.

Paula hunched into the wind with faltering, stiff steps, walking up the slope toward the home. Water pooled in her eyes and clouded her vision. The other children didn't notice her because they were glaring at the front door, attempting to compel it open. They knew hours would pass before they would be allowed back inside for dinner.

Paula's toes felt like ten stones trapped in her boots. By the time she reached the brown shingles at the side of the building, the top of her skull burned like hell. It wasn't the first time she had experienced freezing to the point of burning, and she pressed her knuckle against the middle of her forehead to offset the sting. Her skin felt like taut leather.

A muffled slap and a sharp cry came out of the basement window by her boot. Her body stopped in place.

"No," she heard a boy whimper down there, "I didn't do nothing!"

The sound of another strike came all the same, followed by a few pairs of skittering feet.

"Bend over and hold your legs. Take it like a man," a woman's smoky voice barked. It was Granny. "Get him again."

Paula heard the sound of a buckle smacking against bare skin, over and over again. "No more," begged the boy between heaves of breath. "I swear it wasn't me!"

"Who said it was all right to lie like that? Your mother? You won't be going anywhere until you do better. Get him again!"

Paula swallowed the wind, fighting the instinct urging her to flee. Granny always told them that their parents didn't teach them right, that they would have to stay in the home until they learned how to behave. Paula lifted her feet high and pushed them cautiously back into the snow, turning the corner towards the back of the building.

She found Ave, in her black coat and red mittens, crouched with her hands pressed against the concrete foundation. She was peering into the basement through another window's shutters. Like her sister's, her hair was tied in two braids that started at her forehead and traced her scalp to the back of her neck. Paula knew Ave had snuck off to find the barn to rub her fingers through the fluffy feathers of baby chicks.

So soft! Ave had said the last time they were there with some of the other girls, collecting unhatched eggs to be graded and sold. Ave caressed a cheeping yellow pompom against her cheek. *Paula, feel how soft he is!*

Paula's weak shadow spilled onto the snow beside her sister's boot. Ave drew back with a jump and looked up at her sister, fear spread across her face. Paula held her finger to her lips and grabbed Ave's sleeve, yanking her to stand by the armpits and hugging her to her chest. They hurried off, a skinny ten-year-old lugging a five-year-old, boots scraping through the snow. She made it just far enough into the wooded area behind the home before Ave's mouth ripped into an all-out howl.

"Shhh," Paula said, planting Ave in the snow and crouching to rub both of her arms, "stop it or they'll hear you, okay?" She wrapped her arms around Paula's neck.

"The boy was down there," Ave sobbed into her ear, her breath still smelling of breakfast porridge. "They hit him and hit him and they wouldn't stop...."

Paula could hear that her sister was battling her tears, stomaching them, trying to choke them away entirely. "Good, good. You have to stop." The sound of Ave's gulps made her belly feel like a big bruise.

Ave pushed her head to the side of Paula's face, resting her icy cheek against her neck. Soon they would go back inside and return to their separate chores, their faraway spots at the dinner table, and their beds at opposite ends of the dormitory.

Ave, come sweetie, come over here to me, Granny would say when she noticed the two of them together. *Paula, you go do your chores. Go on.* Granny and the other matrons always wanted Ave to themselves.

Ave tugged one of Paula's braids. "When is mommy sposed to come for us?" she asked, repeating the old question. It had become a game.

"Soon. Probably tomorrow."

"And we'll live in a big house together?"

"A palace. Biggest in the world."

"How many rooms?"

"One hundred. You get fifty, I get fifty. We'll go 'round and count them together."

"Okay."

But Paula knew Ave didn't remember their mother. She had come to rely on her sister to define the story of their past, as well as their present and future. Paula closed her eyes against the winds, which was making them water again. "Mommy's still out there looking for us. The bad men came to our house and stole us away and hid us from her. 'Where is my Ave? Where is my Paula,' she says, crying, crying every day. 'Where are my girls?' She's going around, house to house, asking everyone where we are, but she'll find us here soon. We just have to wait. You know what else?"

"What?"

"Mommy loved you best and made me promise to take care of you. She told me, 'If anything bad happens, you have to take care of my baby girl.'"

"Yeah?"

"Um-hm. She said you were special and you have to be brave. Remember what I told you. Queen Nanny never let her warriors cry. They couldn't win the battle against the evil white man if they sat around crying. She taught them to show no fear and slay the enemy with no mercy. You, me, and Mommy take after her, so we can't be afraid of anything, okay?"

Paula felt Ave's chin sink into the dip of her collarbone and make a single nod.

The ache of the cold pierced Paula's knees and elbows. It radiated through every muscle and bone, but still she wouldn't let go of Ave. She had to keep telling her these stories or Ave might not understand she had a real home and mother to go back to, that they were descendants of the Maroons and not of Granny and the matrons in this place. Without that, Paula worried they would be locked inside forever like the other children. Maybe she and Ave would never be able to leave.

Paula wove her pain into the words she spoke and knotted them into a silent promise. She would be everything to Ave and keep her close. She would make sure that they would stay ready for their mother's return. She would never allow herself or Ave to be deceived into thinking they belonged in this place.

CHAPTER 9

THE SUMMER OF OUR MISSING DIANA CONTINUED. THE LOCAL NEIGHBOURHOOD association organized sweeps of nearby parks and wooded areas and put up flyers on lampposts and telephone polls. At the same time, my father began to buy half-page ads in the community newspaper. Diana's grade nine school portrait smiled demurely from the newsprint, next to the rental listings and used car ads. *Missing child,* the print read, *fifteen years of age. Call immediately with information. Cash reward by family.*

The amount was fifteen thousand dollars. I wondered if people would think that we valued each year at a thousand.

Our extended family and friends continued to call the apartment. Along with neighbours in our building, they kept bringing their containers of food.

Everyone needs to eat, they told us, *even at a time like this.*

My parents and aunt would accept the parcels but every inch of the refrigerator was packed. Almost every night Aunt Julie would have to throw something away: rancid fried rice, slimy chicken, browning salads. We couldn't eat fast enough.

"When Dee comes back," my aunt said as she scraped mouldy pasta from a container into the garbage bag I held open for her, "we're going to wish we had so much nice food all the time, right?"

I held my breath and knotted the handles.

Labour Day came around and Diana remained a missing girl. No one talked. My mother stayed in bed and my father stayed in the living room. I sat in my bedroom, listening to my aunt clean the kitchen, do the laundry, and vacuum and tidy for hours. I didn't know what it meant that Diana hadn't come home, that she would miss the first day of her grade ten school year. Would she fall behind in her classes? Would she lose out on track tryouts too?

You always hated missing school, I imagined my parents reprimanding her when she returned, my mother tossing her hands up and my father storming around the living room. *How do you think you'll ever become a doctor now?* Diana would be hunched on the couch, Auntie Julie on one side of her, hugging her in, and I on her other side.

'Lisha, my sister would say to me with tears in her eyes, *I'm so sorry I left you.*

That's okay, I would say.

Or *I'm just glad you're back.*

Or *I was worried you had been abducted....*

I couldn't decide on what I would say.

I started grade eight. Every morning my aunt would make tea and toast for breakfast and walk me to school, waiting for the metal double doors to fold me in before returning to the apartment to carpool to the subway and slip downtown through underground tubes with my father.

My mother stayed at home, only leaving to collect me at the end of the school day, always straining her ears for the ring of the telephone, the ping of the elevator, the click of the door lock. The police didn't commit to labelling Diana an *abductee* or *runaway*, so she simply became a lost teenager in the *Toronto Sun*, tucked into a running list of missing minors.

The neighbourhood caved into a soggy fall. Crabapple trees shed leaves that had blackened like diseased tongues. Rain dragged the severed tongues to the gutters and wedged them under car tires. They clogged the storm drains and rotted in clumps, unleashing a stink of flatulence across the street.

"A loan," I heard my father say beyond my bedroom door one morning, well before it was time for me to wake up for school. His gravelly words came through the walls, even though he was trying to speak under his breath. "Because fifteen thousand don't seem like nothing. That's why no one is saying anything."

"I don't think they'll give it to you, Brother Don."

"You have any more?" my mother's flustered voice replied. She didn't bother to whisper the way she used to when my sister and I were in our rooms and she and my father were in their bed. "Retirement? Stocks?"

"I wish I did," answered my aunt.

"We'll tell the bank it's for something else, then. A business or college."

"They check those things. They'll want proof."

"Home improvement," my father said. "We'll replace your roof or redo the patio. Maybe finish the basement."

"The bank will see the difference—"

"You always say no," my mother cut in. "You don't care."

"I care, Sister Bea," came the soft reply. "Very much."

There were no more words. That was often the end to their three-pronged early morning and late-night conversations. My mother would plunk an accusation into the middle of the room and they would then slot themselves back into their silent duties: bathing and dressing for work, stacking dishes and pots in the cupboards, going to the table to write more notes and read through folders, making my tea and toast.

My mother's and aunt's attentions were directed towards me. Their hands were on my arms and back and their fingers were in my hair. When they weren't pulling me onto one of their laps, they were tugging me so close that my knees would rest against their knees and my thighs would rest against their thighs. I always seemed to be touching a woman.

My father, eyes narrowed and lips locked, fixed his energies elsewhere. As soon as he came home every night he would leave again to spend hours driving in the diminishing light, scanning the sidewalks for long-limbed, black-haired brown girls. He would return after my mother, aunt, and I had already finished dinner, and sit at the living room table with his papers, circling and scribbling and rereading the pages. His manila folder now bulged with notes and clippings. It became two and three folders, and then a plastic case that held several folders.

I wondered what was in his case, but the thought of reading the papers made my muscles slacken and go weak. *Dee was abducted,* I imagined he had written, *and someone's to blame....* I couldn't tolerate the thought of looking at Diana's diary either, though it remained stashed in my closet. Reading it was what had made me hate her—made me wish her dead in the first place.

My father stayed in his work pants, dress shirt, and tie even after I went to bed. One night I awoke in the dark and couldn't force myself back to sleep. I had left my curtains open and the moon was a bleached dot far up in the corner of the sky.

I shimmied out of the covers and went to the kitchen for a glass of water. I found my father in the unlit living room, his forehead collapsed onto his folded arms on the table and his suit jacket slung over the backrest of his chair. I could see the soft, slow rise and fall of his breath, the heaving of his dress shirt.

The microwave clock read 02:37 A.M. Until then I had assumed that he changed into his pyjamas and went to sleep next to my mother after I went to bed.

He was always ready to answer an urgent call or dart out the door and pick up his daughter. But no one called with tips or news, and Diana didn't call to ask for a ride. The apartment's silence muffled us, and when the phone did ring we all jerked at its metallic jangle as if a bullet had blasted past our heads. It was hard to imagine that we had ever made real noise in that place, that we had ever been eager to leave our apartment.

✿

The trip my father planned for the end of June 1998, right after the end of my grade seven year, might have been because of the brokerage boys. My father would complain about how they left work early on summer weekends to visit their cottages, but their tales and tans might have been the influence that caused him to explore camping himself. My family had rarely left the city for long. The furthest we ventured from our neighbourhood were occasional summer day trips to Niagara Falls or the parks within an hour's driving distance.

"What are you planning over there?" my mother asked my father from across the table one evening when he brought out travel brochures and set them beside his dinner plate. They had pictures of lakes and trees and rivers, and they were marked up by his circles and scribbles.

"Don't worry," he replied over his reading glasses, "everyone loves the great outdoors over here. You will too. The fresh air will make you even lovelier."

Diana snorted under her breath and I did the same to copy her, but the truth was I savoured my parents' affections for each other, every compliment, back-of-the-hand brush, and small-of-the-back tickle.

"But how long are we going to have to live outside?" asked my mother.

My sister stopped chewing her fried rice. "We can't be away when they do the job fair at the mall."

My mother frowned. "Why not?"

"I have to get a summer job. All high school kids are supposed to."

"Who says?"

"My teachers. They told us we should get our first job before we go to driver's ed. I'm getting my license in seven months."

"Which parents let their children get a job at fifteen years old?"

"Normal people," my sister murmured, scraping her fork about her plate to create a hill of rice.

"What was that, Diana?"

Diana rolled her eyes at me. I rolled my eyes in return, though I didn't understand why she wasn't as excited as I was about going away.

A week later, my father rented a boxy eight-seat minivan and we drove out of the city, my parents in front, Auntie Julie in the middle, and Diana and me at the back. Once we cleared the big highways, the roads got straight and almost empty and the landscape transformed into fields and forest. Once in a while, we would turn into a small town where the lineup of shops, gas stations, and houses were never much longer than our street of apartment buildings.

"Dee, would you live out here?" Auntie Julie turned to ask. "They say they need doctors in the country."

Diana lifted one end of her foam headphones from her ear. "I'm a city girl," she answered and snapped it back into place.

"'Lisha?"

"City." But I wasn't sure. All I knew was my school, my building, my apartment, my bedroom.

We drove under overpasses that crossed the mounded layers of rock on both sides of the road. Above and beyond them were what seemed like miles of evergreen trees. I imagined I was travelling further than any of the kids in my class ever had, even though I knew many of them had flown in planes to come and live in my neighbourhood.

"Bea," I heard my father say as he pointed a finger at the windshield, "you could buy a plot and build a house out here for almost nothing. Compare it to where we are. No buildings or people in your way." On his head he wore a floppy camouflage hat he had bought especially for the trip.

In her flipped-down visor mirror I could see half of my mother's face. Her eye skidded over to him for a few seconds and then settled right back onto the open road.

When we arrived at Algonquin Provincial Park, other families were unhooking upside-down canoes from their car roofs and dragging bags and chairs and tarp bundles out of their trunks. A bunch of teenagers who wore the same yellow T-shirt carried pylons and beach balls, preparing for some kind of game. I saw the start of footpaths beyond the parking lot and arrow signs pointing toward bathrooms, woods, and water. At every turn, groups of children zigzagged about, pulling dirt bikes, kicking balls, and wrapping towels over their soggy swimsuits.

"Popular place," my father mumbled to himself as he inched the van's crunching tires forward in search of a parking spot.

Queen Bea pouted into her visor mirror, refreshing her lipstick. Only then did I realize she had applied full makeup at some point along the ride. A pair of Guyana-gold earrings dangled from her ears.

"Are you going to swim?" I asked my sister.

"What else are we supposed to do here?"

She extended her long legs, resting her heels on the mat between Auntie Julie's seat and the sliding door. She stretched her arms in front of her, her palms together and her fingers out straight.

We settled on a camping spot at the far side of the plots, a bushy, grassy pocket where we couldn't see the other families around us. Auntie Julie helped my father put up our big blue tent while Diana carried our luggage out of the trunk. My mother and I sorted through the jerky, canned beans, dried fruit, and granola we had packed. She hardly spoke a word, though she sent glaring glances at my father the whole time.

"Isn't this nice?" he asked after lighting the kindling and fanning our messy pile of wood and crumpled newspaper to flame. We sat around the firepit in lawn chairs, passing a bag of potato chips between us as heat radiated against our legs. The sky had turned murky grey over the treetops.

"Very relaxing," answered my aunt. "Girls?"

"Fun," answered Diana. She unzipped her tracksuit jacket and fanned the open collars at her neck.

My mother only clenched a blanket around her shoulders and stared at the fire.

That first night, I lay awake in my sleeping bag and listened to the patter of light rain on the tent as my family slept around me. The view beyond the plastic window square was utterly black. I scratched my left calf with the toes of my right foot and wriggled about in my sleeping bag. I couldn't find a comfortable position on the bumpy ground and I barely slept, attending to the smell of pine and dirt all night.

❀

Within a couple of days, the other teenagers in the camp seemed to know who Diana was. I followed her down the paths as they waved and called out to her. There amongst the trees and lakes and hills, she didn't have to beg my parents for permission to do anything. She played all the sports and participated in any games she wanted to.

I tried to keep up with her, wheezing as I shadowed her through Frisbee tournaments and water polo competitions in the chilly shallows of the lake, running after her as she sprinted around the other kids with her ponytail swinging. The side-to-side motion of her ponytail became my only focus. All I had to do was stay in step with that ponytail, that pendulum of energy, and battle the burning in my chest.

When she joined the boys-against-girls dodgeball challenge, I had to go along to keep proving myself. The whistle blew and I leaped about the field like a flailing puppet with no one to control my strings. I was taken out of the game within the first minute. Diana lasted right to the end and stood alone on one side with four teenage boys on the other.

"You're so dead," called the boy with the red ball. He looked like he was sixteen or seventeen and his short blonde hair shone with sweat. He wore a sleeveless basketball jersey and high-top sneakers and his shorts were long and baggy, barely hanging on to his hips.

He whipped the ball and Diana jumped off to the side, tumbling to the grass. She caught the ball before it rolled too far and bounded back to her feet. She swung her arm and we expected the rubber bullet to shoot out—even the boy thrust himself away from its imagined path—but she dropped it behind her back. It bounced and she scooped it with her other hand to spin it out at a surprise angle.

The ball pinged against the boy's chest. The girls hollered and even boys across the field *ooed*.

"Go, Diana!" I shouted to her. "You can do it!"

It was no trouble for her to defeat the other three boys. She hit the last of them with a hollow *pang* and threw both fists in the air, hooting with the rest of us. She jumped up and down and that ponytail of hers twirled about. I clapped so hard that my palms went numb.

Walking back to our tent, I felt giddy next to my sister. Her track pants swished down the path beside me as she strode along. She seemed taller that morning somehow.

"Hey!" The blonde boy hustled up beside her and bent his left elbow around her neck. He was bigger than her and his high-tops were untied and loose around his ankles. "You're Diana, right? Where'd you learn that move you used on me?" A sheen of blonde whiskers grew on his chin.

"Call me Dee." She gave him a hotshot smile. "And I don't give away my secrets."

He raised his eyebrows. "What would it take for you to teach me?"

She folded her arms and tipped her head so the end of her ponytail brushed his shoulder. "You couldn't handle my lessons."

He laughed and tugged her closer to his side. "So, you're funny and cute, too."

My ears got hot. I looked at my canvas sneakers, the rainbow flower print now crusted with forest mud.

He raised his right hand to rub the back of his head and I saw the shape of a sun tattooed on the inside of his bicep, sharp and black against his pale skin.

"We're going down to the lake tonight," he said. "Bring your little friend if you want."

I'm her sister, I wanted to correct him.

She shrugged. "I'll see if I can drop by, if I have time."

He pulled his arm away, making sure his hand swiped across the top of her back and brushed the edge of her ponytail. "Well, you owe me after beating me in front of everybody, Doctor Dee." He jogged down the path in front of us, shorts bobbing low, high-tops scattering the dirt.

"Dee," I said, all breathless, "you can't go, Mom and Dad will—"

"Chill out." Her cheeks were flushed.

"But you told him you would and you're not even supposed to be talking to boys."

"Oh please, you don't know anything about boys."

"But Mom and Dad said—"

"Relax. I'm not going to *do it* with him or anything."

That night, Diana and I sat next to each other in fold-out chairs under a tree at the edge of our site. She held her Thermos of black tea and I held its cap, turned over and filled with sweet milky tea my mother had prepared for me. A crane fly had snuck into my cup and drowned, its tangled legs sticking up. I swatted the mosquitoes that flew in slow motion around my head, drunk on my blood.

My parents and aunt encircled a small charcoal barbeque they had positioned inside the firepit. They were a mismatched trio, my father in khakis, my mother in a long skirt and blouse, and my aunt in shorts and a T-shirt. A billow of smoke blew from the grill into my mother's face. She fanned and coughed and my aunt giggled at her. Unlike some of the other vacationers who had come to this camp to fish, we had purchased our trout at a nearby supermarket where a teenage boy had deboned and quartered it for us.

Anxiety had clung to my ribs ever since my sister had flirted with that boy. I couldn't understand why Diana would even bother with him. She was smarter and faster than he was and our parents would never allow her to hang around him and his friends. *I'm not going to* do it *with him.* How did he know my sister wanted to be a doctor? Had Diana told the other kids? Had my family been bragging about her all over the camp?

"Dad was right about coming here," my sister said, breaking me out of my thoughts. "It's pretty fun."

"There's a lot of sports."

"You've been doing a good job keeping up."

The compliment bounced around my head, softening my apprehension. During the school year, my sister and I lived in different worlds, but at that camp, surrounded by water, bark, and bush, my solution to the problem was simple: follow the pendulum ponytail and win her back.

The sound of laughter caught my attention. My mother's arms were around Auntie Julie and the two of them had collapsed against each other, shoulder to shoulder and hip to hip.

"Don, you said you knew how to do it," said my mother.

"Girl, you know better than to believe me when I talk!" Grinning, my father smacked his hat to the ground and kneeled over the grill. He used tongs to peel away chunks of charred fish, tossing them into the coals. Plumes of black smoke consumed our corner of the campground and floated off into the trees and sky.

Beatrice, Julie, and Donald. In that moment, they were happy together, and I was happy with Diana. How I would try, and fail, to remember that feeling in the future.

❀

We drove into a tourist town on the way back home, parking in front of a store with an outdoor display of clay pots, glazed and gleaming in the sun. I was relieved to be free of the competitions, biting insects, and the tattooed boy and the troubles he could cause if my parents found out about him.

My sister's earphones were back on her head, spilling clicks and staticky pulses. She had been quiet since we rolled up our tent and packed the trunk. I worried she was reverting to the high school girl who was too preoccupied to care about me. She jumped out of the van and I stepped onto the street behind her to drag the sliding door shut, wincing at the smouldering aches in my muscles from all the sports I'd had to play.

We all followed my mother as she walked amongst the small town's boutiques. In one store, she pressed a necktie to the dip of my father's collarbone and smoothed the material down. "Don't you think it suits him?" she asked.

"Very nice," Auntie Julie replied.

"Isn't it too bright for work, Julie?" my father said, eyes on the silk. "Orange might be too much."

I didn't know why my mother's eyes narrowed as she watched my father, but my ears got hot and I looked to see Diana's reaction. She hadn't noticed a thing. She was too busy fiddling with the buttons of her Discman.

Diana asked my parents if she could go across the street to a second-hand bookstore and I went with her. We were greeted by a jangling bell above the door. I had to angle my shoulders to push through the collapsing aisles of books, stacked on shelves that went right to the ceiling.

She spotted her section, *Medicine and Science*, and went over to read the spines and reach for the high volumes with her long arms. I carried on through the maze of aisles, feeling like I should look for the sections that might have books about the law. *English Language. Literary Analysis. Award-Winners. Western Classics.*

Moby Dick. A Tale of Two Cities. 1984. Pride and Prejudice. Hamlet.

I spotted Daniel Defoe's *The Life and Strange Surprising Adventures of Robinson Crusoe, of York, Mariner*, bound in green cloth. I pulled it out, sifted through its yellowing pages, and noticed it contained drawings. *Robinson Crusoe rescues Friday*: a white man in a cone hat and ragged coat stood over a naked, pleading, dark-skinned man. I thought of the image of the Maroons of the New World with their rifles on the cover of the library book, how Paula drew her painting on a table.

An insert was tucked into the back: *1881 edition. Poor condition. $50.*

We approached the clerk, a short, white-haired man with half-lens glasses. Diana pulled out her wallet and used some of her saved birthday and Christmas money to pay him for *Abnormal Physiology* and *Diseases and Disorders of the Brain*.

I placed *Robinson Crusoe* on the counter.

The man frowned. "I've got more affordable copies."

"Get a cheaper one," Diana murmured into my ear.

"It's antique," I whispered back. "And it's not for me."

"Mommy doesn't like books."

"It's not for Mommy and I need it." But my stomach cartwheeled when I counted the saved gift money in my wallet. I only had thirty-two dollars. I had given too much to the ice cream boy who pedalled his front-heavy bicycle though the grounds every afternoon.

Diana peeked into my wallet. "Will you take thirty?" she asked the clerk with a put-on sweet voice. "My sister can't count. The doctors told us she's a bit retarded."

"I can't go that low."

She blinked in an innocent way. My mother did the same to my father when she wanted something. "Who else is gonna buy it? It's old and it smells. Thirty-five."

Fighting for a forgotten novel had awakened the clerk's wilted features. "It's an antique, my dear. You can't find it just anywhere. Give me forty-five."

"Forty. It's the best we can do."

I was in awe. Where did she learn these things?

He smiled. "Fine. Forty."

She claimed my wallet and placed my natty bills on the counter. "Here's thirty-two." She sifted through her own pocket. "And here's eight more."

"Dee," I whispered to her as the man click-clacked the buttons of his old-timey cash register to get the money tray to pop out, "thanks for helping me."

She put my book in the shopping bag with her books, but not before using a rough hand to jam the insert into the front pocket of my jeans. "Hide that," she ordered. "They'll flip if they see what you paid." She passed the bag to me to hold.

When we were back on the road, I pulled *Robinson Crusoe* out. My father and I were the only ones awake in the van as I flipped through the pages. Diana shifted her body and rolled her head close to my shoulder. "Who'd you buy it for?" she asked groggily.

"My friend."

"Who?" But her mouth stretched into a giant yawn and her lids drifted low and then she was snoozing again. I braced my neck on the backrest and let my cheek press upon the crown of her head. Short hairs that had worked their way out of her ponytail tickled my nose.

✿

Without glasses, Paula's face seemed naked and her pupils glistened like two black beads. She put them back on and pressed her fingertips to the book's cover.

"It's antique," I said, standing in her apartment doorway, "from the eighteen hundreds. I got it in a bookstore far away from here."

She inspected it front to back, the first and last pages. "Oh, it's beautiful."

She had answered my knock, perplexed to see me at her door. I knew it was strange for me to come to her building and ask the first old person I saw which unit she lived in, but I just couldn't wait for the start of school to give it to her.

Paula folded the novel to her chest and fingered her gold leaf pendant. "What an amazing gift," she said. "It's the best any kid has ever given to me."

Handing her the book had also won me a glimpse of her mysterious life. Her apartment smelled of nutmeg. The windowsill was covered with potted herbs and her rich turquoise-painted walls were crowded with watercolour paintings of flowers and birds and leaves and plants. She had three oversized shelves crammed with books and, brightened by window light, a single unfinished canvas sat on her easel. It was a head study, a partial side profile. Facial features were still sketched in pencil, but the hair, short waves set close to the scalp, were painted in milky brown. Lettering was already set on a slant to mimic the curve at the top of the spine.

Ave.

As I walked back home, the afternoon sun cast massive high-rise shadows over the pavement. It was easy for Diana to accumulate friends and admirers wherever she went, something I had never learned to do, but I wondered if she had ever received the kind of compliment Paula had just offered to me.

That evening my family ate my favourite dinner, curried goat and potato roti with a side of spicy dhal. As my mother boiled tea, my father retrieved his deck of Caesar's Palace playing cards. Diana had been moping in front of the television since we got back from our vacation, but my father convinced her to come back to the table for a game. He dealt to both of us and in no time she and he were smack-talking one another and slapping their cards down, always keen to get into a feisty play-brawl.

I giggled at them and tried to play as well as they did.

"You see?" Diana said to him, fanning out her cards after we had both lost a round. "My sister thinks you're a cheat. Right, 'Lisha?"

I grinned. "Yeah, I think he's been cheating the whole time."

"Bea," my father called, "come here and play with us, girl. These children are ganging up on me."

For him, Crazy Eights and Go Fish were only tolerable as warm-ups. I knew he would soon want to play Troefcall, the four-person game he played with other men at gatherings of family and friends, in which partners schemed across the table from each other through sniffs and shifty glances. Before we had gone camping, my father had never played it with us.

But my mother wasn't ready to sit down. She stood by the kitchen telephone with her back against the counter, her skirt hem sweeping her bare calves. She was talking with Auntie Julie about their plans to host a barbeque at her townhouse in a few weeks. She chatted away with her sister as effortlessly as she had done when we all lived together in a tent in the woods, amongst the wailing birds holding vigil in the trees across the lake.

CHAPTER 10

1942

PAULA DASHED UP THE FIELD; UP THE SLOPE OF CLOVER, CRABGRASS, AND weeds that led to the home's steep front steps and the covered porch rimmed by white railing and pillars. She wove through the other boys and girls who were chasing each other and screaming. Her sandals pinched her toes and she kicked a squall of dust and dandelion puffs into the air. The sky above looked like cheesecloth with its streaky, overlapping clouds.

She arrived at the stubby lone maple that always served as jail in their games of Cops and Robbers. Ave stood there with the others who had been tagged, all of them waiting under patchy afternoon shade. The other girls were dressed in their worn-out blue jumpers or old skirts, but Ave wore a pretty yellow sundress that Granny had given to her. It had red piping and tie-up shoulder straps and not a single tear.

"You're gonna win again!" Ave exclaimed.

"I know," answered Paula, "you just keep watching." She was eleven and sprightly in the boys's slacks and T-shirts she would sneak out of the laundry.

"She's a tomboy," Granny had said, tipping her nose to eye Paula over her spectacles. A pair of matrons had reprimanded Paula and dragged her to the office by her collar. "What'd you think? Her mother had babies out of wedlock and couldn't teach her how to be a lady. It's too late now."

You don't know a thing about my mother! Paula wanted to holler at her. But she kept her mouth shut.

"Hey, Jeremiah!" Amelia called out from under the tree to a cop boy at the bottom of the slope. She waved an arm and tugged at the sagging side of her pleated skirt that was too big for her narrow hips. "You're gonna let Paula get away again?" Her hair was tied in the same two braids along her scalp as most of the girls' at the home.

He paused then started in a lazy jog toward the maple. He was gangly, his arms and legs too long for his shirt and pants. A couple of the boys under the tree clapped along with Amelia. "Yeah, come and put her in her place!"

"Be quiet!" Ave said to them, grinning. "Don't let that copper get you, Paula!"

Paula stuck her tongue out at Jeremiah.

A girl named Lucy giggled at Ave. She was skinny and short, her face all cheeks. Her faded blue jumper was coming apart at its seams. She kneeled in a little circle with some other girls around Ave's age, all of them plucking long blades of grass to twist in their fingers. "You're not supposed to encourage the robbers!"

"But she's faster than them!"

"You're only sticking up for her because she's your sister."

"So?"

The flock of prisoners began to argue, laughing and debating their allegiances. Most of the girls had grievances with Paula. Her talking back to Granny and the other matrons often got them all in trouble.

As for the boys, Paula weeded and picked faster than most of them and the farmhands had started to draw comparisons. *You mean to tell me that this girl can do a better job than you boys? A weak little girl?*

"I'm gonna finish you!" Jeremiah shouted, pointing at Paula and picking up speed.

Paula cackled and hopped away from the tree. None of the other children ever cheered for her but she didn't care. She had to win to prove to her sister that she stood separate—even with the twinge in her muscles and the thirst parching her mouth, even though she was scrawny compared to the older boys and the faster girls. She had to win so that Ave could rush up to Paula after a game and act the victory out, waving her arms and legs. *You went* zoom *and Jackie went* whoa! *And you kept running and running, and Terrance couldn't catch you, and I screamed, 'Go, Paula, go!' And Sharon got mad at me for yelling, but you heard me and you ran! You just kept going, and all the girls said, 'Oh my goodness, she's so fast!'*

Paula bolted, forcing Jeremiah to tail her in a lopsided spiral, up and down the slope, between the other children, over and over again.

"Go, go!" she heard Ave cry to her.

Grass scratched her ankles and her knees ached, but she felt untouchable. The dank, jam-packed orphanage, her endless hunger and missing mother fell away. The summer breeze stroked her face and she felt like she could tear past the tree, grab onto her sister's hand, and launch into the atmosphere. She pictured them flying over Granny and the matrons and the children, swooping back down to earth to snatch up their mother and yank her into the air too. Paula imagined holding Ave's hand in her right and her mother's hand in her left, leading them both to skip amongst the clouds.

Jeremiah puffed and coughed and lagged behind her. "Slow down!"

She pivoted to face him, jogging backward. "No fair! You have to try to catch me, that's the rule!"

His shaved head glistened with sweat and his legs lost momentum. He put his hands to his sides and slowed, his ankles peeking from his pants with each step. "I give up," he panted, "you win."

Paula looked to the maple to make sure her sister was watching, but all she saw was a yellow blur tumbling to the dirt. Amelia stood over Ave with a scowl and the other children watching on.

Paula sprinted back up the slope. She wedged herself between Ave and Amelia and shoved Amelia hard with the heels of her hands, clenching her jaw.

Thwump.

Amelia skidded backwards on her bottom, one side of her too-big skirt dragging down past her hip. She lay there blinking as Lucy and the other girls in the circle skittered to their feet.

"Leave us alone," Paula said with a voice that came from deep inside her belly. She felt a scorching sensation at the base of her throat, the flashing and slashing of Maroon blades in her breast.

Tears pooled in Amelia's eyes. "I was just joking!"

Every mouth under the tree that had been snickering and plotting jailbreak had become silent, revealing the squeals of the other children in the distance, the sputters of a passing pickup on the road, and the faraway squeeing of finches in the trees.

Paula pulled Ave to her feet. She bent to brush the dirt from the back of her sundress, straightening its red-piped hems about her knobby knees. She inspected the top of Ave's head, pressing her fingertips along each twist of braid, ensuring everything was where it should be. Ave accepted her sister's care, holding her hands in front of her and watching on with her pretty almond eyes.

"You okay?" Paula asked her.

"Um-hm," she answered.

"Did she hurt you?"

"No."

"Good." Paula smiled.

Ave smiled at her sister for a moment but her cheeks flushed pink. She dropped her head, forcing herself to avoid the gawps of the girls and the sniffles that came from Amelia as she picked herself up.

"Don't be too mad," Ave whispered to Paula.

"We're not playing with them anymore. Come on."

Paula grasped Ave's hand and dragged her away.

Lucy and the other younger ones watched Paula and Ave go. The bigger ones shrank into themselves and didn't say a word. The game was over.

CHAPTER 11

IT WAS OCTOBER AND MY AUNT CONTINUED TO WALK ME TO SCHOOL. I WOULD slip behind my desk and focus on a spot on the chalkboard above everyone's heads, ignoring my classmates as I waited on the national anthem and morning announcements. I could feel their eyes on my skin, roaming my cheeks and neck and arms for clues.

Fatima, the girl who had sat next to me since the start of grade eight, leaned in close. She wore a bright purple hijab that was kept in place by pearl-tipped pins. "What happened to your sister? My mom told me that she went missing. Is she gonna be okay?"

I didn't want to talk to anyone at my school anymore. "I can see your hair," I responded. "Everyone can."

She gasped. She patted the fabric around her head and fingered the pins, pouting when she felt nothing out of the ordinary.

I pointed to the ceiling. "Allah will hate you."

"You shouldn't say things like that."

"What can you do about it?" I hunched and doodled a wide-open eye on my desk, willing myself to forget how Fatima and I used to partner up in gym class, missing baskets and soccer balls together. *My sister can do this easy,* I had once boasted to her from the balance beam, my arms in a *T* as I stepped and dipped, one foot after the other. She walked on the ground alongside me because I was steadier when I had a perfectly folded hijab to concentrate on.

During class, I would watch the clock on the right-hand wall and look to the windows on the left, seeing the field surrounding the school and the brick faces of apartments beyond it. A Ferris wheel would sometimes materialize out there, a memory from the day Diana disappeared, moving in a slow red-yellow spin. It was one of the rides that would get trucked into the neighbourhood during the summer, set up in a little fair in a plaza's parking lot. It would attract families for a few weeks, then be brusquely disassembled and driven off.

I'm sorry I left you in the parking lot that day, I imagined Diana would say to me when she got back home, *and I'm so sorry I made you think I got abducted by that man.*

My attention would only be pulled back when my homeroom teacher, Mrs. Wilson, a woman with tissue-thin white skin and a blunt brown shoulder-length haircut, had finished explaining our homework.

I'd failed three quizzes in a row, so when my mother came to collect me after school she had to stay behind to speak with Mrs. Wilson. I waited out in the hallway and watched the two of them through the wire-reinforced window in the classroom door. They stood by the blackboard with smeared chalk numbers above their heads.

Mrs. Wilson cupped her hand around my mother's forearm and said something. My mother responded, adjusting her necklace, coat clasps, bun, and earrings. Pretty as she was, she reminded me of the old Russian lady who scuffled around our block pulling a grocery cart and wearing an orange parka, zipper up in winter, zipper down in summer, who had woolly hair that looked like white cotton candy. She never stopped her scraping one-two walk, even when little kids would dare each other to run up and tap her arm. *Cyka blyat!* she would screech, making them yowl with laughter. Like my mother with my teacher, she didn't look them in the eye.

I knew what I had to do. *You will not behave like this,* I told myself, *and you will not draw any more attention.* I hugged my textbook to my chest so hard that my budding breasts ached. I wondered if I would have to soon trade my training bra, the one Diana used to wear, for real ones. Diana had started wearing real bras when she was in grade seven. Back then, I snuck into her room to study the lace and satin brassiere my mother had bought for her and my stomach was so scooped out by jealousy that I carried it to my mother and begged her to buy me one too.

You always need so much attention all the time, I thought. *You'll make them find out what you did to Diana.*

I decided I would become the overachieving student I had never been. There would be no failed tests for anyone—not my mother, father, aunt, or teacher—to talk about anymore.

❀

Only a few weeks after we returned from Algonquin Park, the July heat began to bake the streets and made the air buckle over the pavement. The crabapple trees lost their blossoms, the petals browning and frittering away to make way for rubbery leaves and dense, ruddy fruit. Children fought each other to shake them down, but when the crabapples eventually dropped on their own they left mush and stains as sordid as blood splatter on sidewalks and car hoods.

After cereal and cartoons, I peered down from the living room window and saw neighbourhood kids zigzagging about, chasing each other over the grassy patch on the other side of the street from my building. It was the same every summer. Diana and I would spend hours playing games with those kids, everyone squealing when she was It because she was the only person who could catch everybody.

On the way out of the apartment that morning in July my sister walked in a casual, careless stride next to me, finger-combing her hair into a ponytail. We took the elevator down to the lobby and pushed through the front doors of the building. Some of Diana's friends were outside, sitting on the concrete stairs.

Those front steps were where the teenage girls from our building would always gather in the summertime, whispering and laughing and listening to their Discmans. Teenage boys would pass them by, exaggerating their gaits with lower scoops and higher pops. I didn't understand how anyone could spend all day on those steps, but now that Diana was going into grade ten, she had turned into one of them.

"Go away, Alisha," she said when I lingered at the stoop, "go play." She put one foot on a high step and kept the other on a low step, elongating her front leg as if she were stretching for a meet.

Her comment triggered a rolling snicker across the six stoop girls. "Aw, leave your sis alone, Dee," one girl replied. She had short dreadlocks and purple eyeshadow laid on as thick as icing. I didn't recognize her and I didn't know when she and Diana had become friends.

Diana spun and dropped her bottom onto the stairs, her tracksuit swishing. "I always have to take care of her. I don't want to waste my summer."

"You don't have to take care of me!" I yapped, immediately regretting my own snivelling and feeling sticky sweat in my armpits.

The eyeshadow girl pinched her upper eyelashes between her thumb and index finger, carefully pulling dust or fluff caught in her mascara. "My mom should've gotten her tubes tied after I was born. Two little clips and no more stupid little brother and sister to babysit."

Another girl, this one with a gel-slicked ponytail tied so tight that it pulled her whole face, scissored the air with her fingers. The girls snickered again.

"Clip, clip!" laughed Diana.

I retreated from them, kicking my feet past the driveway and crabapple tree, waiting at the curb for a few slow-rolling cars to pass. The kids my age were on the other side of the road, shoving each other in a disorderly game of Red Rover. I never used to have to play with them without my sister. Diana had always been my only real friend.

Murmurs from the stoop girls snaked up to me from behind. I could still hear my sister's chuckles with the rest of them. I wondered if things would ever go back to the way they had been when we were camping, when Diana had seemed to like me again.

The argument Diana and my mother got into a few days later crept up like slowly gathering clouds before a downpour. It started during a noontime talk show. Diana was stretching in front of the screen to keep herself limber over the summer. She spread her legs on the rug, the bottoms of her feet in line together, and pushed her knees down with her elbows.

"This is ridiculous," she commented to the television. "I need a job."

A loyal subject, I turned to Queen Bea beside me, both of us on the couch behind my sister. Her eyes didn't even move to the back of Diana's head. She felt for flyaway strands around her bun and said nothing.

A spark of apprehension burned in my throat.

"I need to go the job fair at the mall," Diana said at three o'clock teatime, a ritual my mother sometimes insisted on when school was out. "It's this Thursday. They're doing student internships and you can get paid at some places. My teacher said we need experience for our university applications and I want to get in somewhere with a good medical program."

Queen Bea remained silent, reaching for a digestive biscuit on the serving plate.

Diana sloshed black tea around in her cup. "Did you hear?"

"I heard."

"So?"

"It sounds like you know what you want to do." My mother crunched testily, her attention on the pearlized teapot that looked like the inside of an oyster shell.

"It's okay, then?" Diana asked.

"You're fifteen years old. That's too young for a girl to work."

"No, it's not."

"You're not poor. You don't need a job." My mother tried to slacken her tight face but her regal shoulders were pushing back and her neck was lengthening. "There will come a time for working and that's when you'll wish you had a summer vacation to relax."

Diana looked into her cup, teeth locked together.

"The kids were playing badminton today," I announced. "They had their own rackets and everything, and Dee taught me how to play when we were camping so I was really good and I almost won."

"Good, 'Lisha," my mother acknowledged, only mildly interested.

"Those kids don't know how to serve, but Dee—"

"I'll babysit," interrupted my sister. "There are lots of little kids in the building."

Queen Bea chinked her cup on its saucer. "It's not safe."

"I can volunteer to help Auntie Julie at her office, then. They probably take students. Can you ask?"

"I don't want to bother her with this."

"What about Dad?"

"They don't do that at his company."

"So I'll go to the job fair, then."

"You're too young! Why can't you spend your summer with me and your sister instead of running around the place?"

My gaze veered to the half-moon print of lipstick on my mother's cup, a bright red stamp on white.

"You never let me do what I want!" Diana cried.

"I let you do your sports and I let you go out and be with your friends any time your heart desires."

"That's nothing!"

I locked my knuckles into fists, my fingernails digging into my palms.

"It's enough for you!" My mother's wrist did a loop and a flick. "Or are those girls you sit around with outside not raised right and becoming a bad influence? Is that what's going on?"

"You don't even know them! And you never let me do anything!" My sister jumped to her feet and shoved her chair back. She pounded toward her bedroom, ranting. "Everyone lets their kids get summer jobs but I can't get one because *you've* never had a real job in your entire life and that means I'm not allowed to have one either, and what is that? Staying at home and letting a man have his career and you have *nothing*? I'll never waste my life like that!"

Diana's bedroom door banged shut.

My mother's eyes fired lasers at no one. "I do have a job, I take care of you!"

I wished Diana would just do what our mother wanted, the way we had both done when we were young. I held my breath, listening for my sister's retort, but I only heard my own blood beating in my ears.

"Why is she like that?" my mother asked quietly. Her cheeks had reddened and her forehead was cut by lines.

She waited for my response but I was the one least capable of answering. Why did my sister always have to have her own way? Why could she invigorate and befuddle everyone around her? I could only swallow against my constricted throat and think about how my mother's face could never disguise her feelings about anything. It was the price of her beauty.

"I can't win, 'Lisha. No matter what."

Diana didn't have dinner that evening and barely left her bedroom the next day. My father parted the fog when he arrived home from the office that night.

"How long are we going to let this go on?" I heard him say to my mother as he put the kettle on the burner and flicked the knob while my mother gathered plates from the dish rack. He was still in his grey suit jacket and pants. His feet were in black socks.

I was at the dining table, scribbling a pen to colour in the empty spaces of the newspaper's crossword puzzle. I raised my eyes to look at my parents without lifting my head.

My father stood with his back against the sink. "She only wants a little work experience over the summer. Let the girl go, *nah*."

"Oh Lord help me," my mother replied, clacking the plates into a pile on the counter. "I should've known you'd be in cahoots. How is fifteen a proper age for getting a job, Don? She'll be out there by herself. She's just a girl and she's taken care of. She doesn't need money like the girls in her class."

"Their teachers are telling them to do it."

"I don't want her to. Aren't I more important?"

My eyes returned to the blue-inked squares. *Is there anything Diana doesn't get to have?* I wondered. *What am I supposed to do the whole summer without her?* I kept my head down until I heard the sound of rustling fabric. My father had enclosed my mother in his arms. Her body was as rigid as an icicle.

"Bea, we need to let her do things. She's growing up and she's a smart girl. I know it's hard."

She was already melting into his frame. I had seen them play out the same scene many times. She would quarrel and withdraw and wait on him to repair the peace.

Some time passed before my mother spoke again. "All right, fine. But you talk to your daughter about it. She doesn't like to listen to me. I'm just a homemaker."

She turned her head and lay her temple on his shoulder so that her face was entirely hidden from my view. He kissed the top of her spine, which showed from under the collar of her blouse. Bumps of neck bones under skin.

She's growing up and she's a smart girl.

My father's voice replayed in my ear as the boiling kettle began to shriek.

CHAPTER 12

1943

SNOW FELL FAST AND ICE TURNED THE ROAD INTO A MIRROR. ICY CHUNKS stuck to the window and melted down in streaks.

Sweeek! The bus ground to a halt and skidded forward on its tires. Paula had to kick out her foot to brace herself against the seat in front of her. The other children squealed and laughed, already overexcited.

"Pipe down back there!" the driver barked.

At fundraising season, the children were given shiny dress shoes, collared dresses, and black suits to wear. They were bussed around Dartmouth, Halifax, and beyond, even up to Moncton and other parts of the Maritimes, to perform their variety shows across a circuit of churches, theatres, and community halls. They did radio telethons too. *You're listening to CHNS,* the announcer would say, *the busiest station in the Maritimes!*

Stuffed into the back of the bus, the boys were a chattering, jumpy mass. The girls were close to the front with the matrons, and they practiced their choruses. *'Tis the season to be jolly, fa la la la la, la la la la!*

Paula stood up from her seat in the middle of the bus, scratching and picking at the pantyhose around her thighs. She was twelve and the matrons wouldn't allow her to wear boys' slacks for these events. If she hadn't obeyed they would have left her behind, but she needed to stay close to Ave. Paula peered over the backrests to see the top of Granny's head in the front row, her pressed waves and pillbox hat brightening and fading in the passing lights. She wasn't tall enough to see Ave's head but she knew Granny had had her sit next to her.

The bus stopped in front of a church that was decorated as prettily as the cover of a Christmas card with wreaths and garlands. The children bumbled off the bus behind the matrons, babbling as they carried their mandolins and banjos up the walkway. Paula watched Granny lead Ave by the hand at the front of the line, and felt the descending snow collect on the top of her head, heavy and wet.

They walked into a sanctuary with holly draped in waves along the windowsills. A pine tree adorned with red and white ornaments and a blinking electric star stood next to a gigantic cross and almost brushed the ceiling. Paula was most impressed by the burnished gold organ pipes lined against the front wall in three big peaks. This was not the sparse playroom where they knelt for prayers before eating their soup. This was the real and true house of the Lord. The pews were soon packed with white congregants celebrating Christmas Eve in their finest dresses and hats, suits, and furs.

"Suffer the little children to come unto me," spoke the priest from the pulpit. The children sat in the choir stalls, watching the back of his grey head and his long black cassock. "Our Lord Jesus took pity and, tonight, the day before the most important celebration of Christendom, the fatherless orphan is where our charity lies. The Nova Scotia Home for Colored Children instills belief in God, obedience to the law, and respect for the rights of others into neglected and abused children of the negro race. It is our duty to make certain it can continue its ministry to these unfortunate youngsters."

Sitting with the boys, Paula cradled her mandolin like it was a doll. Ave sat amongst the singers with her hands folded in her lap.

"Which one of you has that perfect pitch, now?" Granny had asked the girls after they had rehearsed a song together. *Daniel in the lion's den, oh, Daniel in the lion's den....*

Everyone turned to Ave and she blushed.

Granny held Ave's chin between her thumb and curled index finger and inspected her face. "You, sweetheart? You're the one with the pipes? I should've guessed, how pretty and fair you are."

Ave shrugged and couldn't help but smile.

The Christmas program began with the recitation of scripture.

The Lord is my shepherd; I shall not want.

He maketh me to lie down in green pastures: he leadeth me beside the still waters.

He restoreth my soul....

The congregants *awww*'d and bobbed their heads, encouraging the littlest ones at the front of the stage who had been trained to stand with chests puffed out and arms stiff at their sides. Granny sat in the first row with the other women in their Sunday garb, every one of their faces severely powdered and rouged.

Granny *Amen*'d the fastest and applauded the loudest when the children finished their Bible verses. She smoothed her palm over the satin sash of her red dress and cued the girls' chorale. They squeezed to centre stage and Paula and the boys fell behind with their mandolins and guitars, strumming the introductory chords: *Chri—ist, our Saviour is born!*

Next they did "God Rest Ye Merry Gentlemen" and "We Three Kings," followed by one of the folk songs audiences always seemed to like best and wanted to clap along to.

I woke up this morning with my mind stayed on Jesus.
Hallelu,
Hallelu,
Hallelujah!

❀

"Did you hear what happened?" Ave had run, winded, to her sister in her bare feet and nightgown as Paula was changing into her own burlap nightdress. "Granny gave me a solo!"

The chorale girls had been prattling about it all day, wondering if they'd be lucky enough to solo too. Paula yanked the nightdress over her head, adjusting it about her collarbone and wincing at its scratch on her skin.

Ave clutched her sister's elbow and put those almond eyes on her, her pupils glossy. "What do think she'll give me? Nothing too low, right?"

Paula felt the crawly panic growing inside of her—a million tiny legs climbing up the walls of her stomach. "She'll give you something nice. You're the only girl who can reach the high notes."

"You proud of me, Paula?"

Her sister would sing for Granny with her faultless voice, Paula thought, she would sing and forget about her real home, the real life they'd both had outside of this place with their mother. How could she stop it from happening now?

"Of course I am."

❀

Just as Granny had coached her, Ave stood at the front of the church's platform with an arrow-straight spine and her fingers hooked together at her chest, her elbows out in points to the sides of her body. "Oh, holy night," she began, stretching the vowels between her lips like an opera singer, "the stars are brightly shining...."

Paula thought of the praise Ave had received from everyone as the new lead vocalist. Paula worked with the boys in the fields. She trimmed grass, cleared snow, and tended to barn pigs, inhaling the farm's fetid muck. Granny kept Ave inside the house, mending sheets and clothes, doing laundry, and scrubbing floors.

Paula strummed with her eyes on the two braids that came out from under her sister's beret and followed the curve of her scalp. The creepy crawling feeling returned to her belly and she found she didn't have the strength to battle it. Christmas was nothing like it used to be. There were no sweet aromas, no stockings or nuts or fruits. There was nothing to look forward to. Now the day only brought the same chilly, swarming corridors of the home. The same churning gears of hunger, unabated by meatless soup the colour and consistency of slime. Ave couldn't remember what real Christmas had been like back home.

O night, divine! O night when Christ was born! Ave's tone was sharp and smooth like melted diamonds in the ears and the audience gazed at her, enraptured.

Granny was mesmerized in the front pew. Her mouth remained open and she pressed her palm to her crimson bosom. Paula realized that their mother knew nothing of Ave's splendid voice. She wondered what her mother would do if she had the chance to hear it, if she herself would want to fall on her knees.

CHAPTER 13

"TAKE YOUR SISTER TO THE JOB FAIR WITH YOU TOMORROW," MY FATHER said to Diana, standing in the doorway of her bedroom in his suit. I cowered behind him, watching Diana beyond his elbow.

She sat at the edge of her bed in her track clothes, one of her medical books open on her lap. "But what if they want to interview me?"

"*I* don't want to go with *her*," I piped in, petty and false.

"Your mother wants the two of you to go together and come straight home after," he said, "and you better be thankful we're letting you go."

"I always have to watch her! The whole time we were camping, and now this! It's not fair."

"You're the older one. You should want to be a good girl and take care of your sister."

She crossed her arms and moped, and he shook his head. I followed my father as he walked away from her door and felt a fresh wash of offence pour over me.

When she finally left her room that night to eat the plate of dinner our mother had wrapped for her and left in the fridge, I snuck in and stretched up on my tiptoes to reach the top shelf of her closet. I decided I wouldn't stay away from her medical books anymore, that I didn't need to respect them if she detested me anyway. Feeling my way through the volumes in the box, I discovered a thin notebook nestled between them and pulled it down. *Diana's Diary,* read the cover in black marker. *Don't Touch!*

I opened it to find an entry dated a few days after the end of our vacation.

> *I don't really like the name Mark, but I love his ink. I can't believe his parents let him get a tattoo! I'm going to have to move out before I get mine. I wonder what Mark would think if I got one just like his?*

At the bottom of the page were careful doodles: a sun design that matched the crewcut boy's tattoo and a staff with wings and two coiled snakes. Below the drawings was a phone number circled with wiggly lines and the name *Mark Barrington.*

I couldn't imagine when Diana could have gotten the boy's phone number at the campground—I thought we had been together the whole time. Did she sneak out of the tent to meet him and his friends by the lake after all? Confusion tumbled about in my belly. I thought my sister would understand that she shouldn't waste her time with him, that she was better than him.

I flipped to the last entry in her notebook.

> *I can't help but wonder if Auntie Julie might be my real mom. Queen Bea doesn't like me and never did. Things like that happen all the time, and in this family, there's a lot to wonder about.*
>
> *Maybe I'm Auntie Julie's daughter and Alisha is Mom's daughter. Alisha's just like Mom. She freaks out*

about every little thing and can't handle the real world. She's thirteen years old but she still acts like a little kid, pretending she wants to be a lawyer so mommy and daddy will like her.

No one in my family cares about the things I care about. I'm different than them all. I can't wait to finish high school and get out of this house and go to university. I can't wait to get a real life.

The next day Diana wore a black skirt and a white shirt. She brushed out her hair and pulled it back from her forehead with a pink satin ribbon from my mother's dresser. She even drew eyeliner on her eyelids and dabbed on a bit of my mother's peach lipstick. Folded job fair flier in hand, she hurried out of the elevator and through the lobby door. None of her girlfriends were on the stoop that afternoon as she stepped down to rush along the sidewalk. The sky was bright blue with large fluffy clouds that blew fast across it.

I ambled behind her lazily.

We reunited at the stoplight. Two cars had gotten into a crash and blocked the intersection, which was crowded by cars that honked and revved and tried to pass each other. The headlights of the cars that had crashed were shattered and their hoods gaped and steamed. When the light changed, Diana and I followed the crowd of pedestrians weaving through the cars in the crosswalk, everybody shimmying through the gaps like ants.

Diana only half turned her head to me, squinting in the sun. "Hurry up, you're making me late."

I scuffed my feet behind her, feeling the wound of the criticism she had written about me in her diary, her rejection of me altogether. I hadn't bothered putting on the dress pants I had wanted to wear and instead wore ratty shorts and a faded T-shirt more suited to formless summer days spent around our building.

From the mall's parking lot, we saw the job fair sign set out in front of the sliding doors. The sign had fluorescent letters. Sagging balloons were taped to either side. There were no students hanging around outside the mall, just old women with carts and young women with strollers, waiting on taxis.

"You're not coming in with me," Diana said. "Everyone I know will be there."

"I don't want to go with you," I huffed back.

"Stay, then."

"In the parking lot? No way."

She sighed. "Alisha, just wait, okay? I'll come get you when I'm done. I won't be long."

I fell into a sulk and squatted onto the concrete parking barrier at my feet.

Diana jogged toward the mall in her flats, her straight raven hair swishing across her shoulders as she steered through the women and children, zipping by so close to the job fair sign that a balloon flapped and bounced. The automatic doors parted and slid shut behind her, the glass too shiny for me to see her any longer.

I poked at one of the mosquito bites I had gotten while we were camping. What was once a red, nickel-sized bump on my shin had turned into a glossy brown pimple. I waited until the temptation to scratch it was unbearable before I dragged my fingernails across it. I did it over and over again, wondering how long it would take before the bite oozed blood.

The sound of running shoes on the pavement grew closer. They slowed and stopped in front of me, so that I was covered in shadow.

"What's wrong?"

The words came from the shape of a man. The sun had pushed its way out of the clouds and burned so white behind his head that I couldn't make out his face. He stood, hands in the pockets of his jeans, awaiting a response.

My eyes finally adjusted to his pink skin and white T-shirt. He wasn't old but he wasn't a teenager either. His clothes were baggy and I could tell he didn't wear them that way as a matter of style. They just didn't fit. His chin and elbows and wrists were prominent bumps of bone and the tops of his ears poked out from under the rim of his baseball cap.

"That was your sister?" he said, his voice a nasal burble. "You two look alike. Did she come for the job fair?"

I didn't say anything but he waited until I felt like I had to reply. I nodded and stood up, realizing he was only a little taller than me.

He smiled and crinkles formed at the corners of his eyes. His neck had a tinge of sunburn and the bridge of his nose was peeling. "I was just in there. Lots of kids are looking for a job. Don't you want one too?"

"I'm only thirteen," I replied.

"But you couldn't go in and check it out with her?"

He put his lips in an empathetic pucker and I couldn't think of an answer to give to him.

Even a stranger can see what's wrong with me and Diana, I thought. I swallowed against the threat of tears and I looked down at my shoes, the same flower-print canvas sneakers I always wore because I had no reason to ask my parents for a new pair. I wasn't going to join the track and field team at my school.

He chuckled and shook his head. "My brother hated me, too. He'd knock me around and swear at me and my parents wouldn't do a damn thing. To him, I was just a scrawny brat. But he didn't have to be mean like that. I looked up to him, you know?" He pulled a hand out of his pocket and scratched where the visor met his forehead. His fingernails were bitten down half-moons.

I had the urge to disagree with him, but perhaps my sister was just like his brother, and perhaps she wasn't as exceptional as I had always believed. Maybe she was like every other high-schooler out there. I knew my parents and aunt wouldn't be able to fathom that Diana might be a typical girl because they were all too eager to assume the best of their own. Make-believe was the reason they had flown over the ocean in the first place. *Our children are superior to them all! Dee the surgeon and 'Lisha the lawyer, and leaving Guyana was worth it!*

I didn't know who Diana was becoming and I had probably been mistaken about knowing her at all.

He twisted his arm to read his watch, its ragged black Velcro strap fastened over the bony ridge of his wrist. He lifted his head and more light slipped under his visor. His eyes were a muddy brown. "Does she hang out with guys?"

"Huh?"

"Does your sister have a boyfriend or something?"

I thought of the boy at camp, the black sun on the flesh of his underarm.

"I bet she does. A lot of girls like her do, sneaking around with guys all the time to do God knows what. I see it in this neighbourhood all the time. Why do you think so many of them get pregnant? Their parents are clueless about what they get up to, if they even care in the first place."

My heart started to beat faster. I realized how uncomfortable I was, how I wanted the man to go away, but I couldn't deny the truth of what he was saying. Diana had the tattoo boy's phone number. She had to be calling him, and no one knew about it except me. I imagined she wanted to visit him and might actually find some way to do it. I felt my frown sag deeper at the thought. *I bet she would* do it *with him if she could, too.* I curled my toes and they made little peaks in the canvas of my shoes. I hung onto the pleasure of thinking something sullying about my sister.

The man continued to stand there, watching me as I bashed at that rock-hard structure of Diana I had cultivated and protected over the years. *She's just another stupid girl,* I thought, *flirting and running after boys. Why should I want to be like her?* It was time to stop looking up to her. Maybe I would end up being my parents' favourite, after all.

I felt heat on my body as the man backed away, his shadow easing off of me.

He adjusted his hat by tugging at the visor. "Don't worry. Everything'll work out. Sisters as pretty as you should get along, okay? Just smile. Come on, let me see it."

His words made me want to cry all over again. I managed a shaky smile in response.

His smile lingered on me. Confusion and uneasiness swept through me. What was he waiting for me to say? That his brother didn't actually hate him either?

The man finally turned and walked toward the mall. His jeans were light denim, their hems shredded around his sneakers. He quickened his pace when he stepped over the curb's yellow line onto the sidewalk, past the place where the women and children waited on their transportation. None of them bothered to look at him, but oh, how I would meditate on the details of that man.

I scanned the rows and rows of cars, the busy street beyond the parking lot, and the people passing the mall on foot. Dozens of crows were perched along the telephone wires, their feathers fanned by breeze. Seagulls with potbellies paced and picked at the strip of grass that demarcated the mall from the rest of the world. Once in a while a single seagull would screech and the others would turn their beaks away and pretend they had heard nothing.

A couple of bare-chested boys whizzed past on their bicycles, legs pumping purposefully. "*¡Más despacio!*" shouted the one pedalling behind to the one in front. They sped toward the street lights at the end of the parking lot, beyond which a slow-moving yellow and red Ferris wheel with flashing lights churned on. It was the tallest ride in the trucked-in amusement park that came to the plaza next door to the mall.

The last time we had gone to it was a few years ago. My father and mother had shared strawberry soft serve; my father licked and held the cone out for my mother to do the same. My sister forced me to waste my quarters on a water gun game and we won an ugly pink bunny with creepy red eyes. We brought it home and forgot all about it until Dee rediscovered it and decided to do an autopsy like the ones described in her books. She lay it on her bed, cut the stitching on its belly with a pair of scissors, and yanked the fleece panels open to see what was inside.

The bunny bled Styrofoam pellets all over the carpet, and Queen Bea fretted with us to clean it up until she gave up and vacuumed the innards away herself.

Standing outside the mall as my sister looked for a job, I knew things between me and Diana would only worsen as she moved into grade ten. I missed the way we used to play, the way she used to speak to me, how she wanted to become a doctor and have me as her nurse. It seemed like we would never be that way with each other again. I started walking through the parked cars toward the Ferris wheel in the distance.

✿

"'Lisha!" my sister shouted at me from behind.

I pretended not to hear her.

The Ferris wheel had only been turned on for show. The fair was locked up and empty save for a few teenagers leaning against the plaza wall and sharing a cigarette between them, and a young mother with a frayed up-do pushing a crying baby in a stroller. It seemed hardly anyone was excited about going to the fold-up carnival.

I walked between the booths, their doors secured with padlocks and covered with graffiti. It had gotten windier and I gulped against the smells of urine and fried oils emanating from a caravan of falafel, Tex-Mex, and Thai food trucks at the curb.

Diana brushed my forearm as she caught up. "Why won't you answer me?"

I wrenched my arm away from her and swung around. "Leave me alone!"

Beside us, the unattended basketball-toss game came to life, its sirens clanging and flashing.

"I've been looking for you everywhere! We're late and mom's going to kill us!" She was panting and her satin hairband sagged towards her forehead. Her blouse was crinkled and untucked from her skirt. She reached out to me.

I stepped back. "Don't touch me!"

An old man straggled by in tattered jogging pants and sandals. He looked at us and then looked away, hardly interested in our argument.

"Would you stop?" she pressed. "I'm sorry I made you wait outside, okay?"

"I know you hate me!" I choked on tears and turned toward the grounded whirligig ride, squat and doubled down on itself, to hide them.

"I don't hate you."

She said it so simply that I knew it was true. But I was impassioned by the sense of betrayal and couldn't accept it.

"I'm getting out of here," I grunted at the pavement covered in gum spots and gasoline stains.

"Where?"

"I don't know."

"Mom said we have to go home together."

"I'm not going anywhere with you! I saw your stupid diary and I know you're talking to that stupid boy!"

"What?" Her shoulders shrank under her shirt. "That was private."

"So what? Just wait till I tell mom and dad what you're doing. I bet they'll tell Auntie Julie too. You think you're so smart but I know everything."

"You don't." She shook her head to the sky and tucked her hair behind both ears against the wind.

"I'm not listening to you and you can't trick me anymore. You're just another dumb *girl* like all the other dumb girls trying to get boys to like them. You'll never become a doctor chasing after boys like that. Just wait till I tell them what you've done. They'll never trust you again."

"Don't tell them anything!"

"Just try to stop me!" I whipped around and marched away from her. I expected to hear her dress shoes clacking up behind me, but the only sound was rushing traffic on the road and the scratchy disco-calypso wafting over the parking lot from the plaza's loudspeakers.

I slowed, stopped, and turned around. My sister was in the same spot, her eyes cast to her shoes. The basketball game beside her was flashing and screeching again. She didn't notice the person walking toward her from the other direction, the man with the sunburned nose who I had met at the mall, the loose front of his T-shirt undulating like a flag.

He was fixated on the back of her head, focused to a point. The back of Diana's hair rose in the breeze and bandied about in all directions.

With my sister between us, the man's gaze shot to me. I saw the hint of a new smile.

A vacuum opened in my brain and an idea swelled in. *Who cares about that guy?* I thought. *I never want to see my sister again. I hope she dies.*

I always tried to make my parents happy, always tried to impress my sister and make her care for me. What if I gave up and walked away? What if I wandered the sidewalks, went to my school and stayed out on the playground until the sky turned dark, leaving Princess Dee to explain why I wasn't with her? She would have to deal with Queen Bea's fury over abandoning me. She would finally be the one everyone was disappointed in.

I turned from Diana and walked away.

CHAPTER 14

1944

THE TEACHER HAD WIRY LIMBS AND A SHARP CHIN AND SHARP ELBOWS. SHE stood at the front of the schoolroom and held a card over the front of her crisp white blouse. "Read this, please." She looked to Paula through her wire-framed spectacles. Her hair was pinned in a bun that made her protruding cheekbones even more prominent.

In a peach dress, Granny blocked the doorway by bracing her shoulder on the doorframe. She folded her arms. "What do you say when your teacher asks you a question?"

"Yes," Paula mumbled.

"Yes what?"

"Yes, ma'am."

Granny and the teacher glanced at one other. Paula felt as if a flare had ignited under her skin and her ears began to prickle. She felt everyone in the packed schoolroom watching her, from the kindergarteners at the front desks to the teenagers at the back. Paula was thirteen and lodged in the middle. Ave, at eight, sat a few benches away.

"You have to look at the sentence to read it," the teacher said, "don't you?"

Paula squinted at the card but the letters didn't do a jig and reorder themselves to enable her to understand them. The only school she and the other children had experienced were the isolated classes between house chores and farm- and fieldwork. She tried to clear her narrow throat. "The…the…l-…lit-…little…."

Chuckles and coughs crackled around her.

Numbskull! some of the older boys scoffed behind her head. *Ninny!*

Paula saw Granny touch her fingertips to her smiling mouth. She could see Ave looking at her, just a smudge of a face in the corner of her eye. "The little…b-…boy…and…."

The teacher pursed her lips. "Good Lord, you're a stammering fool. Don't guess at the words. Read them."

Paula set her spine straight and dragged a big breath in. "The little boy…and his…his…ex-…ex-…."

Laughter whipped about the room.

Paula's a numbskull!

The teacher rolled her eyes up to the ceiling behind her spectacles. When they came back down, they settled on Ave. "How about you, honey?" she asked. "Can you show us how to do it?"

Ave offered a tiny nod. "The little boy and…his…excited puppy play a g-…game of…go…go…f-…."

"Fetch, sweetheart," Granny said with her voice buffed of its edges, "*go fetch.*"

"Go fetch."

"Very good."

Ave's shoulders drooped in relief before she turned a concerned look to Paula. Paula only blinked back and Ave stared down at her skirt, folding her bottom lip under the top.

"Paula," she had asked last week when the two of them had found an opportunity to be alone in the girl's dormitory, "can you tell me something?"

She sat on the bed with her back to her big sister, who kneeled on the mattress to work a broad-handled, soft-bristled brush through Ave's curls. Granny had given it to Ave as she had given her many other gifts—little barrettes and clips for her hair and pins to wear on her collars.

"What?" said Paula. Light flooded in through the window and made her fingertips glow red.

"I was thinking about what would happen if they took me away."

Paula had heard Granny talk about it to Ave. *You're so sweet and fair! Well, a new family might come by and snap you up any minute. Won't you like that, sweetheart? A whole new family to make up for the bad one you used to have?* Paula angled her head to see Ave's heart-shaped lips trembling.

"What if it happens before Mommy comes back?" asked Ave. "And what if they don't take you too?"

Paula put the brush by her knee and hugged Ave to her chest. She kissed her round cheek. "Silly talk."

"But what if it happens?"

"I'll visit your house every day."

"What about at night?"

"I'll sneak in and if they find out, I'll kidnap you. They'll never find you again."

Ave giggled and gripped Paula's arms from under her chin. She pressed herself back so the warmth of her skinny body would meld with the warmth of her sister's, and they had sat that way, bathed in the aura of the sun.

The little boy and his excited puppy play a game of go fetch.

Paula sat at her desk with her ears burning, wondering why she couldn't have figured it out too, why the teacher would have assumed her capable of reading when they had never taught her how to do it.

"See?" the teacher spoke over the classroom's bubbling amusement, her chin pointed out at them. "What did I tell you children? You won't get anywhere in life if you don't know how to read a simple sentence."

"Some have it and some don't," Granny remarked with a shrug, "and you can't save them all. No cure for the dunce."

A sob swelled in Paula's throat but she swallowed it down. She told herself that she didn't care about what Granny or the teacher or anyone thought of her, that she would never let herself cry in front of them.

Lucy, the little girl who always sat beside her sister, leaned over to hold her curved palm to Ave's ear. She whispered something and she and Ave both crouched forward in their seats, giggling into their hands. Another wave of chortles ran through the room.

Paula is a numbskull and always will be a numbskull!

Paula felt as if her body was spinning. She had been trying so hard to keep her and Ave loyal to each other. Ave pushed her shoulder to her ear, trying to disguise her lingering laughter, and Paula's belly thudded to the floorboards. The rejection blistered her.

CHAPTER 15

I PRESSED MY MECHANICAL PENCIL HARD ONTO THE PAGE OF MY NOTEBOOK, copying the math problem from the blackboard. Mrs. Wilson had just taught us about adding and subtracting fractions and, save for the sounds of scribbling hands and a few exasperated huffs, my grade eight classroom was silent.

The pencil tip snapped and left behind a tiny explosion of dots on the paper. I broke the lead constantly.

I heard voices murmuring outside the classroom and a faint, familiar tinkling of gold bracelets sliding over a wrist. In jeans and a volunteer vest, Paula stood in the hallway speaking with Mrs. Wilson beyond the open door. I had presented the antique copy of *Robinson Crusoe* to her three months ago, but the episode felt like a scene from an entirely different life.

I looked back down. At the edge of the page my sister's black ponytail materialized, swinging side to side as it always did when she ran. But this time it moved in a slow, steady rhythm, as if it were counting the seconds. I squeezed my eyelids together to will the hallucination away.

I felt a palm on my backbone. "Alisha," Mrs. Wilson whispered near my cheek, "do you have a minute? Somebody would like to speak with you."

I slipped off of my chair and walked out into the hallway.

Paula's fingers were woven together in front of her. "We haven't seen each other for a while, yeah? I know I'll see you next week when your class starts library periods, but I wanted to see you before that to tell you that I heard what happened to your sister. How are you doing?"

The gold leaf pendant with its ripples and etched lines sat on the collar of her jersey. "I'm okay," I answered, my words coming out weaker than I had intended.

"If you need any help…."

I nodded, biting my teeth together and tasting the memory of the jelly my aunt had spread on my toast that morning.

A door unlocked at the end of the hall. The school's white-haired janitor dragged his clomping boots in our direction.

She untangled her hands and dropped them to her sides. "Listen, I don't want to keep you from your class. I guess I'm just sorry to hear what happened. Okay?"

"Okay." My voice shrivelled in my throat. I didn't wait for her to turn from me before I hustled back to my desk and the math problem I had been working on.

When the first library period of the year arrived the following week, my classmates skulked around the racks at the front as they always did. I walked directly to the stacks where they kept the dusty blue *Encyclopedia Brittanicas* and peered through the space above the books to watch the trio of Trinidadian girls in my class at the magazine racks. The one in the middle held up an open *Cosmo Girl* and they pressed their heads together behind the pages to make fun of another girl in my class: *fresh-off-the-boat-smells-like-curry-dipshit*. The three of them wore clingy tops, sneakers, and lip gloss, and tied their hair in ponytails and braids. The new girl wore an oversized grey sweater and combed her hair down to cloak her cheeks. It was a straggly cover for angry red acne. Her back was to them and she pretended to read a softcover mystery but I could tell she knew what they were saying about her. She bit her lips.

Don't even think about crying, I thought, and felt the blood pulsing in my neck. *Turn around and scratch those girls' eyes out of their sockets and they'll never think about you the same way again—*

I heard a soft exhale and turned to see Paula standing beside me, holding out a book. "I just thought you might be looking for something new to read."

She held out *Roll of Thunder, Hear My Cry* by Mildred D. Taylor. "It's one of the better books in the library, at least in my opinion."

I was confused and felt my eyebrows furrow, but I took the book from her anyway. "Thanks."

As she walked away, the heel of her runners scraped the carpet and I noticed a slight stiffness in her right leg. I thought of the orange hibiscus flowers she had painted that hung over my headboard, which I hardly even noticed anymore, and I remembered the half-completed canvas of a woman's pressed curls I had seen on her easel.

Roll of Thunder, Hear My Cry stayed crushed at the bottom of my knapsack for several days. I rediscovered it when I shook my bag out over my bed and the novel plopped out, battered and dog-eared, along with my gym shorts and some stray pens.

I could hear that a game show was on in the living room but I knew nobody was there to watch it. My father hadn't returned from work and my mother and Auntie Julie were in the kitchen, silently preparing dinner.

On the cover of the book were three Black children, a girl in overalls hugging two little boys to her sides. They were huddled and frightened in the night, and flames burned close behind them, different than the point of firelight I remembered from the cover of *The Maroons of the New World*. These flames were close and violent.

I stayed up most of the night to read it. I needed to know what happened to those little children. I returned the book to the library the next day, slotting it into the return bin, my tired eyelids prickling with every blink. I was supposed to be in the lunchroom along with the other students, eating at the tables and waiting for some kind of scuffle or argument to cheer for before the teachers stepped in to break it up. But the toast I'd had for breakfast had turned into an immovable lump in my belly and I couldn't imagine eating. I put my elbows on the checkout counter and rested my chin on the heel of my hands, waiting for Paula to emerge from the stacks wheeling a cart of misshelved books.

When I used to go to class early while Diana was at track, everyone knew I had no choice but to be there. My new good grades had caused Mrs. Wilson to assume that I was taking school seriously and cared about extracurriculars, so she agreed to let me volunteer at the library at lunchtime.

"Most children at this school don't care for books very much, do they?" the head librarian said with her Italian accent and cigarette-coffee breath as she showed me how things were shelved. We stood in the stacks at the very end of the room where no students went.

I didn't answer.

"Their parents don't know a thing about education. They don't know anything but entitlement. Handout, handout, handout, all day, all night. It's not right."

She assigned me tasks like taping rips in pages, folding new cellophane over old dust jackets, and identifying books that were too ragged to stay on the shelves. Many of the picture books' pages were marked by crayons, and the young adult novels had a lot of curses and dirty drawings in them. The longer those bad books remained in circulation, the more obscenities they seemed to collect, doodles of breasts and butts that began in the margins and gravitated over to the text.

I would sit at the table by the large window and sort through boxes of defiled books. The maple tree right outside spread its orange-red leaves, and when it was sunny enough, shifting points of light would pass through and fall on the pages in front of me. I worked slowly, because I didn't want to leave.

After Paula had finished her shelving she would sit across from me, crouching to hand-print labels, glue on sign-out cards, and browse through new book catalogues. Sometimes I would catch her as she set her pen down to plan out another painting on the bare table.

"Did you eat?" she asked, looking at me over her glasses, her marker still in hand.

"Um-hm." But the plastic bag at the bottom of my locker where I would hide the sandwiches Auntie Julie prepared for me had developed an odour. I would have to get it to the garbage in the girls' washroom to avoid Mrs. Wilson's attention.

"Hmm." Paula raised an eyebrow at me and her freckles glowed in the light from the window.

I put my head down and focused on the Harlequin Teen novel in my hands, its cover defaced by a doodled penis.

❀

A few days later, Paula placed a paperback on the table. It had a bright red cover with two hands that stretched to touch each other. She pushed it my way and her bracelets rattled against the wood. "You like science fiction?"

I didn't, but I nodded anyway. *Kindred.* There was something troubling about the silhouetted hands on that red background.

"Try reading this one. You won't forget it."

She presented new books to me all the time, some with and some without catalogue stickers on their spines. *The Color Purple. A House for Mr Biswas. A Raisin in the Sun.* I would finish each of them promptly, reading late into the night after I finished my homework and even in the early mornings before getting ready for school. At night I would crush a pair of pants across the bottom of my bedroom door to block my lamplight.

One Hundred Years of Solitude. I Know Why the Caged Bird Sings. The God of Small Things. I had never read anything like these books before. I wasn't sure I understood all of what was in them, but I discovered I could escape in their pages.

I continued reading Paula's books as the leaves of the maple tree outside the library window dropped. On the day of a surprise mid-November winter storm, the falling ice and snow became so heavy that I could hardly make out the tree's branches.

"How could they do that to him?" I asked Paula across the table.

"They couldn't communicate. They couldn't even be sure Gregor was still human anymore, you know?" Paula wore her knitted toque and she pulled it down, patting it over her ears.

I flipped *The Metamorphosis* from front to back. I didn't like looking at the creeping cockroach legs on its cover. "It's only when they got sick of taking care of him that they stopped believing."

"That could be true, but you have to sympathize. He wasn't the son they knew."

"But what they did was so *shitty*." I had never cursed before—my mother would have never allowed such a thing and the sound of the word in my mouth shocked me.

Paula didn't seem to notice. She shook her head. "No, no. His parents were so depressed by what happened to him and his sister didn't get the chance to grow up the way she wanted to, for goodness's sake. Nobody plans on turning into vermin. That's the whole point of the book, yeah?"

I glowered at the words on the back cover. "No. His family treated him like *shit* and gave up on him. It's not fair."

Ice pellets tapped the window. First a few isolated jabs, then quickly turning into an onslaught. I picked at the smarting hangnail on my baby finger as guilt surged through me. *I'm the one who should say sorry,* I would tell my sister when she came back home. *I was the one who rejected you.*

Paula cleared her throat. "I wonder if they'll let you guys go home early. It's getting bad out there. Jeeze. Imagine how January'll be if it's like this now."

"I don't want to go early."

"I guess you could come back here until it's normal time to go."

In the classroom, my hand was first to shoot up in response to my teacher's questions. I didn't allow myself a slip on even one test or assignment, if only to crowd out the vision of my sister's ponytail. That black pendulum.

At the end of the school day, I would rush to pack up my things and jog down the hallway, spotting my mother right outside the window of the school's front double doors. She would be peering in for me in rain and sleet against a bleak sky, her black bun and red lips and eyes ringed with liner. I would push the door open, she would grip my hand in hers, and without a word we would rush down the street, straight for our apartment, side by side. We couldn't leave it unattended for too long.

In the evenings, I would stay in my bedroom doing my assignments, anesthetized by homework. I would hear the neighbours and Guyana friends and family still dropping off food in a steady stream. *Make sure you all take the time to eat,* they said to my aunt and mother, *you need your strength.* They would ask for an update on the investigation, but there was never news to pass onto them.

We would congregate at the table, mother, aunt, and daughter, while father drove the streets, and I would long to retreat into one of Paula's novels. But my aunt would bring out our dinner and her overeager interrogation would begin. *How was school, 'Lisha-babe? What did you do?*

I would invent the details when I couldn't think of anything to say. *My French teacher said I'm good at conjugating and I should go to Montreal and practice making my accent like a real Francophone....*

My mother and aunt would let themselves get swept up in it, but when my father returned home he couldn't stay away from his folders beside the plate my aunt set out for him. He would read through his articles and clippings and scribble down notes, taking a stray bite here and there but leaving most of his food untouched. He was a flame burning up information at the table, and it was clear to me that he had been sparking and flaring the entire working day, waiting to come home to his archives.

When I finally got to go to bed, my book balanced on my bent knees and my lamp shining next to me, I could hear their conversation from the dining table. I thought of the three of them, connected in the shape of a triangle, my mother and father and aunt, one at each point, and I pictured the triangle bouncing down a hill from point to point as they talked.

"Call again." My mother's whisper. *Bounce.*

"I did." My father's whisper. *Bounce.* "He has no news. He never has news. He said I should wait on them to call me."

Bounce. My aunt's whisper. "So what do the police do? They can't talk to people?"

Bounce. My mother's whisper. "They don't treat white children like this, I'm telling you, I've seen it right here with my own eyes."

I wondered if my mother was referring to the day we had met a small crowd on the road on our way back from the grocery store. Me, Diana, and my mother were all carrying bags. Women circled a couple of policemen who stood in their vests and holsters. One officer gripped a skinny Black boy by the back of his coat collar and the other talked into his radio as the women berated them. *Where is this boy's mother? Shame on you!* I couldn't see the boy's face—it was tucked into his chin and his arms hung down loose—but fear prodded my ribs as Diana and I slowed to watch. My mother walked in front of us in her pumps, quickly veering over the curb toward the opposite sidewalk and tearing down the path home. Diana and I followed, leaving the policemen and the women and the boy to fend for themselves.

My father kissed his teeth. "If it was one of their girls, you'd see the difference in their behaviour."

"The police don't have no shame," my mother answered. "They should pay for not caring."

"Oh God," sighed my aunt, "our girls."

Sometimes the triangle of mother, father, and aunt would hop down the hill like that for hours. I would lie under my covers behind the pages of my book and listen to them, air slipping in and out of my pinched lungs. *Do you know what you did to us?* I imagined my family would say to Diana when she finally decided to come back home. *Do you know how we couldn't sleep and worried the whole night for you?*

Better to stay awake for a triangle family on a hill, I would think, *than for a circle Ferris wheel in the sky.*

✿

Paula leaned over the table, reading my English assignment. "It's marvellous," she said. "You're a good writer, you know that?"

A blush rose to my cheeks. I had given the pages to her before I had to turn it into my teacher. Our class had finished *Little Women* and been instructed to write a short story inspired by it. I did mine on Wilbur, the Marchs' housecat. In the story he was obsessed with usurping Beth's place in the family.

Paula underlined a sentence with her fingertip. "I like how the cat plants false evidence here. It's smart and funny."

"Thanks."

"I think it's marvellous. That woman better give you an A."

Contented, I played with my fingers until she finished reading the last page and flipped all the papers over. *It's marvellous.* I treasured her praise, savouring it in my mind.

Just then, something went past the library window—a whizzing, angular movement. It was the man from the mall, his gait and baggy white shirt, blue jeans, and black cap. I whipped my head to catch sight of him but tree branches were the only thing on the other side of the pane.

I had let myself forget what I had done. I was bewitched by compliments on a stupid school assignment. *That was your sister?* the man had asked me. *You two look alike.*

"What's wrong?" Paula asked.

My mouth hung open. "Nothing."

"Are you kidding? Tell me."

"What are the chances my sister will come back?"

My family carried on like it was only a matter of time. Diana's bed was made and her clothes were folded in her drawers. My mother had brought out her winter jacket to hang with the rest of our winter jackets, in first place in the coat closet. She hovered around Diana's bedroom as if she expected her to walk through at any moment. My father's newspaper ads had become more insistent, more convinced. *Call now, cash reward, family waiting.*

Paula took a breath. "I don't know how to answer that."

"Can you try?"

I had heard my father talk with the police more than once about finding her. His voice was always solid on the phone, speaking in statements more than questions, and he often repeated the things Auntie Julie had said to him. *Victim services can give children counselling and help them feel normal after something like this, yes?* They were all so confident about Diana's return that I had to believe along with them.

"I guess it depends on what happened, yeah?" she said.

"What if she was abducted?"

"Why do you think she was abducted?"

"I don't know. Would she be able to come back from that?"

"Alisha, I can't—"

"Tell me!"

"It doesn't seem very promising."

My lips parted but no words came out. No one had dared to admit this reality to us. No family or friends or neighbours, not even the detective, who had asked a lot of questions and spoke of procedures and forms and was now mostly silent. My parents and aunt only mirrored each other as they bounced down the hill in their triangle, reinforcing each others' expectations of what would happen when Diana came home.

Paula shook her head. "Oh, Alisha. What do I know? Anything could've happened, yeah? Maybe she's on her way right now. Maybe she'll be there when you get back home."

We thought you were abducted, Diana! How could you have done this to us?

I closed my eyes and felt like I was falling. For the first time, I was tempted to speak the truth. *I didn't wait or watch or search for Diana that day,* I wanted to tell Paula. *I don't know why I talked to that man and left him with my sister and didn't tell my parents about him. I just couldn't do it and now it's too late.*

"Who is Ave?" I asked her instead.

She blinked and checked for her pendant with her fingers. "My sister."

"Older or younger?"

"Younger."

"Is she alive?"

She nodded and turned her head to the window. She squinted when a burst of sunlight passed through the glass.

"Do you see her anymore?"

"Not so much."

"Why?"

"She doesn't want me."

"But why?"

She pinched and massaged the bridge of her nose with her thumb and forefinger, making her glasses wiggle up and down on her face. "It's complicated."

What I wanted wasn't complicated. I wanted Diana to come home. I wanted her to do her stretches on the living room rug and I wanted to be on the couch behind her, both of us watching television. I wanted to feel her there.

Paula and I sat in the library, looking at each other. She soon eased my story aside to pick up her pen and return to her book inventory. I felt her strokes rattle over the table, the vibrations meeting my elbows and entering my bones.

CHAPTER 16

1945

PAULA WAS THE LAST IN THE CART. SHE CLIMBED ONTO IT AFTER THE TWELVE boys had already gotten in and sat at the very edge with her back to them, pulling the heels of her boots to her bottom. Her body quivered. It was a chilly early autumn morning and the sun was preparing to rise, brushing red and orange watercolours over a frosty, yellowing treeline as it did. The cart was hitched to a spotted brown mare with cloudy eyes and scars on its flank. It whinnied and sneezed, dipping its head and causing the cart to rock on its wheels.

"Behave, you old nag," said the farmhand in his tattered cowboy hat, reaching to smack its muzzle.

"Psst, psst!" Paula heard one of the boys say behind her head. It made the others snicker. She didn't turn to look at them.

The farmhand puffed on his cigarette and the sweet, heavy smoke blew back. Paula inhaled it. She hugged her knees. The cart was damp and the moisture was seeping through her pants.

The farmhand flicked his butt into the grass and mounted the mare. The creature coughed and formed jerky steps, causing the cart to lurch back.

Whoa! the boys exclaimed.

"Can't wait to eat your ice cream today, can you kids?" the farmhand called out. "Which flavour are you gonna pick? Vanilla, strawberry, pistachio, chocolate?" He chuckled. "I'm gonna try strawberry in a cone."

He drove his heel into the horse and it snorted before clomping forward. The cart jittered down the path.

"We're getting ice cream?" Paula heard a boy whisper.

"You soft in the head?" responded another, and all the boys sneered.

Paula listened to the laboured breathing of the old horse as it trotted and bumped along. The trip was short. She imagined the horse taking new turns to bring them down a different path, a hidden trail that cut through the backwoods. She imagined emerging at a secret city with glimmering lights and cars and stores and houses, the one in which her mother lived.

She's there, I found her! She would run back to tell Ave with a glow in her chest. *Follow me and I'll take you to her!*

Ave would squeal and throw her arms around Paula's neck.

But they arrived in the fields as they always did, the large acreage where the home grew crops to sell: bushels of peas, beets, carrots, turnips, and strawberries. The farmhand handed out canvas slings and Paula trod over to the potato patch with her boots feeling like they weighed ten pounds each.

The soil had developed an acidic smell that mixed with the stench of root rot and manure. She squatted to get at the nubs of potato hiding under a web of dying leaves and shoots. She tugged, twisted, and wiped each one with a rag before tucking it into her sling. *Tug, wipe, tuck; tug, wipe, tuck* until the sky brightened above and the night winds died off.

It was about noontime and Paula had already unearthed several bags of potatoes. She stood and surveyed the space around her. The farm-hand was working with his back to her, slicing a shovel into the ground and throwing the dirt behind him. The other boys were all spread out between the rows, doubled over to harvest their own potatoes, peas, and carrots. No one looked her way.

The air was tacky in her lungs and the sun sizzled at her neck. She became aware of the things in her pockets again, the items she always carried with her now: a stolen spoon, a ripped piece of cloth, a pencil, and the serrated lid of a tin can, jagged enough to cut. They were the supplies she had been quietly scrounging since she turned fourteen. She thought about tossing her sack of potatoes to the ground right then, and zigzagging through the crops to sneak back to her sister.

Shhh, she would say, gesturing for Ave to take her hand and descend the back steps, leading her into the bush.

We're going home? Ave would ask.

They would find their way to a road, she imagined, one they could walk down until they arrived at another road and another road. Then they would find a pathway into a forest where they could bob and weave amongst the trees and finally arrive at the house where they used to live.

Oh, dear Lord, their mother would wail when she met them at the door. She would gather her daughters up into her arms. *It's been so long and you've finally come back to me!*

Drops of sweat rolled down Paula's temples and she slid off her coat, tying its arms around her waist and struggling to swallow against her dry throat and sour stomach. She felt hollowed out. She kneeled down to dig through her sack, rooting around for the smallest potato and dragging her thumbs over its skin to clear away the excess dirt. She crunched down with a bite that left a slick on her teeth. *I only need to figure out which way to go,* she thought, chewing hastily, *and Ave and I will never have to come back to this place again.*

When she had filled another sack of potatoes, Paula walked it over to the cart, holding it at her left side and leaning her body to the right.

Sweat ringed her collar and her knuckles and knees were stiff. The horse had been freed of the cart and the cart's shafts were tipped forward to balance on the ground. She braced her belly against its side to hoist the sack over the edge and turn it upside down. The potatoes rolled out in a dusty tumble, joining the big pile.

Swoop.

A narrow rush of wind filled her ears and a node of light pierced her eye. Paula turned to see the tall woman who stood next to her, her head wrapped in a gleaming cloth that was as white as her dress. In one hand she held a rifle, its barrel aimed to the sky. In the other hand she held a stalk of raw sugar cane. She looked down at Paula, her eyes flashing.

Paula's heart raced. "Who are you?"

A breeze raised the hem of the woman's dress to reveal her bare toes and ankles, calloused and dusty from her long warrior's journey. Paula couldn't fathom how Queen Nanny of the Blue Mountain Maroons had journeyed all this way to find her, travelling over islands and sea and land, over the impossibilities of time and place.

"You came to get us home," she said to Queen Nanny, "didn't you?"

Paula felt the women's flaming eyes sear into her. Doubt rippled through Paula's body though she had envisioned the escape she and Ave would make countless times.

"But I'm not ready," Paula spoke, her voice starting to slip away from her. "I need a little more time. If Granny found out—"

A clanging noise sounded in her ears, followed by the piercing warning scream of a steam whistle. Paula felt her blood drain from her limbs. Her belly ached and she felt faint. She tried to tense her legs but they wobbled and she dropped to her knees. Her head hit the soil and she watched the plane of dirt tip and surround her. Then darkness encased her.

✿

Paula woke with a start. She was lying on top of the blankets on her bed with thirty empty cots around her, all of them perfectly made. Her toes were cold and bare. Her coat was still tied around her waist. The dusky sky was cloudy in the window above her head and she heard the chattering voices of the others downstairs. She could tell they were in the day rooms, waiting on their evening prayers, starving for another soup dinner. She tried to identify Ave's voice in the muddle but she couldn't sift it out.

She lay there, hoping Queen Nanny would meet her at the foot of her bed. But as she listened to the children, the banging pots and chinking cutlery, she realized that the appearance had been a dream of her exhausted mind, that she had only seen what she had wanted to see. She couldn't run away with Ave. She had no idea where they would go or how they would make their way back to their mother. She had no defense against being caught, dragged back, and beaten like the other children who tried to run away.

She pressed the heels of her hands to her eyes and felt the sting of her tears. She would fail to rescue her sister, again.

CHAPTER 17

WITH THE ARRIVAL OF WINTER, THE NEIGHBOURHOOD ASSOCIATION STOPPED surveying the wooded areas and postering the telephone poles. All that remained of our search attempts were ads in the local paper. *Missing. Call. Reward.* My family received many Christmas invitations from their Guyana friends and family, but Auntie Julie called them all back to decline.

"We're not doing anything this year," she explained quietly into the kitchen telephone. "You can understand why."

Auntie Julie carried the box of decorations into the living room. I sat on the couch and listened to her and my mother shush and argue with each other in the kitchen.

"Julie, I told you, I don't want this."

"Do it for 'Lisha, Sister Bea."

"We can't pretend everything's all right."

"But when Dee comes back, don't you think she'll want a tree?"

I'm so glad you're finally back! I would tell Diana. *Christmas was going to be so* weird *without you.*

My aunt won the quarrel. She and I draped tinsel and hooked baubles on the plastic pine tree. My mother stayed in her bedroom. When I reached to put the star on the top spoke, I realized I had grown almost as tall as our tree—just as Diana had done a few years back—but Auntie Julie didn't notice. She had her back to me, bent over the box to fold and store the empty bubble wrap.

On New Year's Eve we watched the television countdown and held champagne flutes in our hands. Sitting next to me on the couch, my aunt put her arm around my shoulders. "Happy new year, babe," she said, kissing my temple and taking a gulp of sparkling juice.

People were waving and blowing kisses to the camera. I imagined catching a glimpse of Diana in the crowd, how I would spring up and point at the screen. *Oh my gosh, it's her, don't you see? It's her!* I would scream. *What's she doing in New York?*

'Lisha, my father would say to me, *if you hadn't caught her on television, if you hadn't been paying attention, we might not have found her at all....*

On my other side on the couch my mother lifted her glass to her lips and took a small sip. My father rose from his chair and walked his untouched glass to the kitchen.

My sister's sixteenth birthday passed in January and we hid in our own corners of the apartment, not acknowledging the day, not knowing what to do with it. Diana kept not being there for things I didn't think it would be possible for her to miss.

By the time March break came a couple of months later, the weather had changed from blowing snow to a messy mix of freezing rain and overcast skies. Our street was marred by muddy old snowbanks and the wind gusted against my bedroom window. Crows rocked on the telephone lines below, perching flush against each other like black pearls on a string. I worked on the essay our English teacher had assigned before the break and which had caused the kids in my class to kiss their teeth at her. She had hollered at them to stop acting like Jamaicans. Unlike them I was relieved to have an assignment to occupy my time.

It was raining hard. The wind howled so loudly that I hardly noticed the telephone ringing beyond my bedroom door.

"Oh, my God," my father said from the kitchen.

I had never heard him to appeal to God before.

❀

"It can't be her," said my father. "The dentist lost the x-rays so how could they even know what they have?"

"How can they call you, acting like they know?" my aunt responded. "It's not her."

He wore brown socks, grey suit pants, and a white undershirt. He was stalled in the hallway. "I need to see what they think they've found. You can't trust them. No, it's not her." He went into his bedroom and emerged again, wallet and keys in hand, his spine straight as ever.

I trailed him as he walked to the living room and stopped in the doorway.

My mother, holding a wad of tissues, sat on the couch. The hem of her skirt blanketed her feet. She dabbed her eye as my father walked past her to get into the kitchen. Auntie Julie sat down on the armrest in her T-shirt and pyjama pants and capped my mother's shoulders with her hands.

My father paused at the oven and turned to the silent phone on the counter. "I don't even know where this damn place is," he muttered to himself.

Auntie Julie stood and walked toward the kitchen. "I'll find the address, Brother Don."

But he retrieved a piece of paper from his pocket and began dialling.

As Auntie Julie turned back, I made eye contact with her and gestured toward my room. She followed me, her bare feet sticking to the parquet.

We went into my bedroom and I pushed the door shut. "I want to go with him."

"What? No, 'Lisha."

She tried to hold my cheeks in her palms but I yanked myself away.

She reached for me again. "You don't know what you're going to see there. You stay here with me and Mommy—"

I swatted her arm away. "Stop pretending I'm little and good. I'm not *good,* I was never *good.*"

"It's not even Dee, babe, I'm sure of it."

She tried to step back but I shifted toward her.

"You have to do it," I said, "please."

She tried to think of a response but when she couldn't, I saw her body deflate. "Oh my God." She checked her bun and adjusted the front of her T-shirt. "This is crazy."

I listened to her walk down the hallway.

"Brother Don," I heard her say, but then her voice snuck down low.

His response struck like a punch. "No. Absolutely not."

"But she says she needs to."

"Dear God," I heard my mother cut in from the couch, "what are you two entertaining?"

"She's begging to go, Sister Bea," my aunt answered, "and I think she needs a chance—"

"You're being crazy," my father said.

"It's not even Diana!" my mother exclaimed. "Why won't that girl listen?"

"Because you don't listen to her!" Auntie Julie yelled back. "You're not paying attention, Bea! It's her sister, her big sister! Can't you see?"

My breath lodged in my chest.

"I'm not letting her go anywhere," my mother said in return, "and you stay out of it."

"How can I stay out?"

My bouncing family triangle, Daddy and Mommy and Auntie, tumbling out of control.

"No more," my father said. "I don't want to hear no more crying from either of you, you understand?"

"I'm sorry," my aunt spurted, "I didn't mean to—"

"Donald," my mother pushed in, "don't you tell me what to do. You've done enough!"

"Beatrice, shut up!"

I whipped my door open and ran out.

"Don't fight!" I stood in the living room doorway, tears splashing down my face.

My parents and aunt stared at me.

"I need to see for myself! I won't ask for anything again, I just need to see it with my own eyes! Please!"

My mother began to weep on the couch and my father put his palm on his chest, unable to look at me anymore. Auntie Julie had her hands out toward him and toward my mother, unable to reach all three of us. She didn't have enough hands.

Circling over their heads, the spoked Ferris wheel wouldn't stop spinning. My sister was alone in one of the passenger cars, her back to me, her ponytail swinging.

✿

A woman in a lab coat led us down a hallway. Our steps reverberated on the linoleum floor. Rows of lockers lined both walls and severe fluorescent lights buzzed overhead.

My father held my hand. His spine was straight and stiff.

My aunt walked close behind us. I had been allowed to go—just barely—but my mother told Auntie Julie she had to serve as her stand-in. Auntie Julie couldn't argue.

The woman jutted down another corridor and we turned to trail her. Her hair was stuffed into a blue paper cap and a moulded white surgical mask hugged her throat.

We reached the end of that hall and the woman led us through a pair of swinging metal doors. The room was big and smelled of bleach.

The lights in there were even whiter and harsher and motors and fans hummed noisily. Nearly everything was made of scratched metal. The walls were lined with steel cabinets and shelves and doors with latches, and several small rolling stands stood in a line in the centre, each covered by a shroud.

We followed the woman to a table at the far corner of the room. A narrow shape lay covered by a large a blue cloth. My pulse and breathing came together in a single rhythm, as if my body had turned into a beating heart.

My aunt laid her fingers on my jacketed arm; I felt their heat through the material. *I know you fought for this and I fought for you,* they seemed to say, *but are you sure?*

I wasn't. But I couldn't turn back now. I nodded and her hand slipped away.

My father pointed at the table. "What is this?" I heard the tremor in his voice and knew he was wrestling with himself. *My Diana is not here and I don't know what they're talking about and they're wasting precious time, and I don't want to hear no crying from nobody!*

The woman looked at a clipboard, flipped up a few sheets, then placed it on a counter. She walked to the head of the table and nudged her hands into latex gloves, wiggling her fingers into the dips. We all stared at her hands. "I know this is difficult for you," she said, "and I'll remind you that you don't have to do anything you're not ready to do."

"No," he answered, "I want to see what you think you have."

Her weary eyes looked at mine before returning to the adults. I could see she thought it reckless of them to bring me here.

Sheer belligerence had allowed my father to distance himself from whatever they had told him to come and look at. In the car, I had seen his steely eyes, the silent orders he directed at my aunt through the rear-view mirror. *It's not our Dee, they're mistaken, they're lying, I don't care what they say. Pull yourself together, Julie.*

My aunt only took my hand in hers and turned her head toward the window.

But now, affronted by a foreign object under a cloth, he couldn't stay aloof. Someone had folded the plane of our existence in half and he and whatever was under the cloth were suddenly face to face. One would have to prevail over the other.

The woman pinched the top edges of the blue sheet. "Take your time and look carefully." She flicked a disapproving chin my way. "You're certain about your child?"

My father nodded. His grip tightened on my hand.

She lifted the sheet and walked it down, peeling it off. Hard things, rusted and blackened things, were laid on the table. At the foot of the table was a clear plastic bag with soiled, shredded pieces of black and white fabric and a single grimy shoe.

I turned my face up to my father's. I could see that he wasn't sure of what he was looking at, but only for a moment. Confusion exploded into horror in the black of his pupils.

His mouth broke open. "Oh my God."

I looked down again.

The human skeletal system is a wonder of strength and coordination, read one of my sister's medical books, *made up of 270 separate bones that grow into 206 as infant matures to adult.* That skull, that grin, a caricature of my mother's and aunt's lovely smiles, had the same overlapping canine as Diana's on the top, the same tiny spaces between the incisors on the bottom.

My father let go of my hand and I wished he hadn't. I couldn't look away from my sister's bones. I traced the long arm and leg bones with my eyes, thinking of Diana as she stretched in front of the television and ran relays on the track.

Out of the corner of my eye, my father's blurry shape shrank to the ground and coolness washed the side of my body where he had been standing. My aunt crouched over him and I heard a peculiar sound, an undulating bass.

Is that how my father sounds when he cries?

I took a clumsy step back with my left foot and my right followed. I heard a raspy cat-mewl. *Who's making that sound,* I wondered, *that ridiculous screech?*

My hip bumped a small cart and flipped over its covered tray. The contents crashed and scattered over the floor, scissors and knives and picks. I realized that I was the one screaming like a wounded animal.

Diana? Dirty bones on a table?

The sound of a horn pierced my ears and white dots sprayed across my vision like fireworks. They kept bursting until my knees buckled like two spilling pans of water.

So many implements I had knocked to the floor, so many things I would have to clean up for the lab woman, so many things were strewn around the spot where my head bashed against the tile.

And then, nothing.

I am roused by light, a bright blob that contracts into ovals and narrows into stripes inside a rectangle. I don't know where I am. My body feels like it's burning from the inside, from the muscles and tendons outward, but then I am suddenly shivering and overwhelmingly cold. I pat around in search of a blanket but all I find is the denim of my coarse jeans over my own thighs. Something catches my hand. Another hand. I try to tug mine away but my reflexes don't work. It's just like in my dreams. I am swimming in molasses.

But I wasn't dreaming. Auntie Julie was the one who took my hand. She stood over me with her eyes cloaked by tears, her eyelashes dripping watery black mascara. Part of her hair had freed itself from the bun and a lock dangled at my chin, tickling me.

She attempted a smile. How I hated a sad smile.

Her touch on my head triggered pain across my scalp. "You had a fall, babe."

"Daddy." My voice sounded far-off, like it had emerged not from my voice box but from somewhere behind her head.

"He's here, he'll be back right away." Her lips quavered and she bit them in.

I opened my mouth but a groan was the only thing to come out.

"No, don't speak."

Protest rose in my belly, the urge to fight. *They show me a table of bones and tell me it's my sister? Bullshit!* The anger quickly bulldozed through my insides, leaving me empty. My eyelids felt weighed down.

"Rest, 'Lisha-babe, rest."

The coffin was lacquered oak, embellished by brass bars and handles that my mother had selected. I studied it from the front pew of the Anglican church. Light streamed through a stained-glass window that portrayed a man being crucified upside down so that coloured squares and triangles, yellows and reds and purples, printed the lid of the coffin. He wore a loincloth and grimaced in a way that looked like he was laughing.

I heard rustlings behind me, coughs and cleared throats, sniffling noses and gasps and heaves. Many guests had come to the church that day, all of our family and friends, my father's coworkers, people who lived in our apartment block and the neighbourhood association, my sister's friends and teachers. Her coach and teammates wore their high-school tracksuits. But I was most aware of the people to my immediate right and left. My father and mother on one side of me and my aunt on the other.

My aunt had taken the lead in the funeral preparations, calling in help from her and my mother's cousins. She thought it best that the rituals be compressed into a single day. "Brother Don," she said at the living room table, "you think so too, right?"

He nodded, staring at his cooling tea. He didn't even confirm it with my mother, her own withered frame sitting across from him. He had been avoiding her ever since we had seen the remains.

My father and Auntie Julie seemed to be afraid of the same thing. If too much time was dedicated to funeral rites, my mother would act against their warnings and find an opportunity to peek inside the casket. I knew the triangle wouldn't be able to handle the consequences of that.

Standing at the podium behind the casket, the priest instructed everyone to say the Lord's Prayer. We staggered through the stanzas. *Thy kingdom come, thy will be done....*

My father had told me that, back home in Guyana, Sundays were for climbing sapodilla trees and splashing in lakes with his friends. He never took my family to any church or temple or mosque and probably hadn't had to recite the prayer since he was a rowdy boy in grade school. He closed his eyes and said nothing.

My mother only twitched her lips, looking to her shoes. My aunt had to speak for her.

I didn't try to say it either. I studied the crucified man instead, wondering why they didn't make it so that he was on the cross high above the onlookers, the weeping women and stoic soldiers. Instead they all stood right next him, yet no one was brave enough to reach over and rescue him.

Earlier that day the viewing at the funeral home had been packed with people. We stood beside the casket to greet a long line of visitors. My parents and aunt knew how to accept sympathies and sad smiles but I didn't raise my head to the faces. All I saw were pantyhose and pumps and belt buckles, passing in front of me like images on a filmstrip.

"Mister and Missus Sookermany, and you must be Alisha's aunt." Paula squeezed their hands in hers, one after the other. "You don't know me, but I volunteer at the school. When I heard what happened…oh God, I just feel sick about your loss. I can't imagine what you're going through."

It was the first time I had seen Paula in a dress. It was a long black velvet one that brushed over her square-heeled dress shoes. She wore her spectacles, her bun, and her leaf necklace. The same gold bracelets jingled over her long sleeves.

"Thank you," my aunt answered, "it's very kind of you to come."

Paula squatted close to me, taking both of my hands and looking me in the face. Tears welled in her eyes. "This is a horrible thing, Alisha. I don't know what to say except that."

"Thank you," I answered from somewhere at the bottom of my throat.

"How are you keeping?"

"Okay."

Her head slowly rocked up and down. "You will get through this. It's impossible to see right now. But I promise you will."

You don't understand, I thought. "Okay."

More shoes and pantyhose, more hugs and kisses. *I will not get through,* I thought, *because this is my fault.*

Funeral recitations were soon over and my father's cousins lined up to hoist that regal casket by its bronze beams. Our box of bones.

We followed, shambling down the centre aisle, my aunt holding my hand and my father holding my mother's. It was the last time I would see them touch. Paula was near the back row. Her fingers were woven together and she watched the wooden pocket of the pew in front of hers, where the hymnals and bibles were stored. Her mouth moved, maybe whispering some kind of prayer.

The sanctuary was so dim inside that the scene beyond the double doors, all that sunlight rebounding on the concrete steps, seemed like an ambush.

The wake was held at Auntie Julie's townhouse that evening. I left the swarming kitchen and living room, went upstairs, and pushed open the door to my aunt's bedroom. A purple-blue sky was spread out beyond the window. I felt the coarse carpet under my stocking feet as I shut the door.

The things in Auntie Julie's bedroom had always been peach-coloured, her rug, her bedspread, her lacy curtains. Even the knick-knacks on her dresser had a peachy tint. I sat on her bed and the mattress creaked. For the first time, I realized my aunt owned as many pots and tubes of pigment, as many makeup brushes and pieces of jewelry, as my mother. The two of them, the favoured near-twin sisters.

Even with the hint of perfume in the air, the room smelled stale. Months had passed since Auntie Julie had slept in her own home. She had been too occupied by our needs to take care of anything else.

A picture frame was on the night table next to her clock. It held a photo of me and Auntie Julie with my mother and Diana. We stood on Auntie Julie's patio, smiling. Diana and I seemed to be around five and seven years old. We wore shorts and T-shirts. My aunt and mother were in slinky shoulder-strap dresses. It had been taken on a summer day I couldn't remember, probably a Saturday and probably an afternoon the way the sunlight slashed the brick wall behind our heads. To the right of us my aunt's barbeque smoked. My father must have taken the picture. I recognized his old burgundy jacket slung over one of the chairs.

I turned the photo face down on the bedside table. Its cardboard kickstand cocked up in the air.

Back then, when we got together with family and friends, the adults would eventually get into boring stories about their lives back home and Diana and I would get fed up playing with their kids. When the party was hosted at my aunt's townhouse, my sister and I would always find an opportunity to escape up to her bedroom. We would bounce on her bed, rummage through her drawers, and hunt for her bras and slips. We felt entitled to her home and her belongings.

I saw a shadow on the ground outside the door, in the slice of free space between the door and the carpet. My mother came in and quietly closed the door behind her, returning the voices outside to a grumble.

She sat next to me on the bed. Her eye makeup had been wiped away and there were pink bags under her eyes. She had somehow prevented her tears during the viewing and the funeral, but she succumbed to them when the first shovel of soil, the one carried by my father, chunked against the oak. She had braced herself against my aunt and her wail had cut me from throat to intestines. My father passed the shovel to another brown man in a black suit like a baton, but I hadn't missed how his arm shook.

"'Lisha," my mother said, her voice tucked low, "you okay?"

"Yeah."

"You miss your sister?"

"Yeah."

A pause. "I do too. Very much."

Minutes passed. The fibres of the carpet began to wiggle and flash in my gaze, multiplying, dividing, and subtracting like atoms.

"She didn't like me, did she?" asked my mother. "Girls hurt their mothers, I know that. Me and Julie did it to our own mommy. We ran around with anyone we wanted to and we didn't think of how it would reflect on her. We were ungrateful children. But I loved my Dee, 'Lisha. I loved her more and more every day, with all my heart and soul. She was my special girl."

I felt a swelling inside of my chest. I imagined it as a tumour like the ones I had seen depicted in my sister's books, a penetrating growth that touched everything and couldn't be teased apart from my other organs. How could I have been so empowered to hurt Diana and so helpless to save her?

"What did she look like in the morgue? Did she seem afraid?"

I shook my head, slowly. "It just seemed was like she was thinking to herself. She was quiet and her hands were on her tummy and it was like she'd fallen asleep. Like it was nighttime and she was asleep in her bed and she'd combed her hair out."

My mother's fingertips reached for the ends of my hair and found a place to rest on my cheek. They felt cold on my skin. "You and your sister always had pretty hair."

I shifted, easing her forehead toward my chest, my arms encircling her neck. I cupped a palm around her bun and stroked the other down her spine, bump after bump.

She accepted my embrace and the invitation to cry on me, her only remaining daughter.

That was the moment I decided I would have to transform myself. I would take my sister's place. It was a position I had so desperately coveted when she was alive. I couldn't have imagined how terrible the path toward it would be.

CHAPTER 18

1946

WHEN PAULA REFUSED TO TELL THE MATRONS WHO HAD STOLEN TWO bottles of strawberry preserves from the kitchen, Granny banished her from mealtimes.

"No one'll foster a girl who doesn't tell the truth," Granny told her, "but you'll learn your lesson now."

Paula was not allowed to eat anything that Wednesday and Thursday, and on Friday, Ave had only been able to sneak a handful of Corn Flakes to her after breakfast.

"Tell her you're sorry," Ave whispered, pain on her face. "Do you even know who did it?" At ten years old she was short and skinny as she stood next to Paula, who sat on the side of her bed.

Paula barely chewed the cereal before swallowing it. "No, but I'm not sorry."

"Can't you just say you are?"

"What did I tell you? You can't give into them like that."

Paula remained defiant in front of Ave, in front of Granny and the farmhands and the other matrons and children, setting her jaw. She tried to persuade herself that plucked clovers and chokecherries between the hours of potato picking, leaf raking, and barn tending were enough. That she could go for days fuelled on nothing but air and fury as Queen Nanny and her warriors had in the mountains.

But by Sunday night, the hunger had coiled her stomach into a stabbing mass. She snuck out of bed and out the back door, crouching and creeping into the woods in her nightdress.

The midnight moon was hidden behind a barrier of cloud. Paula kneeled in the dark at a tree trunk, one of the two distinctive maples she had always fancied to be a couple—husband and wife. In summer, their canopies interlocked in radiant and undulating green, but it was October and they were going bald. She shivered, straining to claw at the rotting leaves cupped in an indentation between the roots.

She found the cloth bundle of navy beans she had buried a few weeks before. She had learned to steal and hide food from some of the other children. Even some of the matrons did it. She felt around to get at the fistfuls of slick shells, fingering and pelting down chunks of dirt and maggots.

"Hungry, are you?"

Paula jumped to her feet and hugged the beans to her chest. She couldn't see the farmhand's face but she made out his hunch and knew that he was the one with a deep and open gouge-scar on his cheek. She had never spoken to him directly but she had seen that scar day after day, how it opened and closed like a second mouth when he chewed and talked and laughed.

"You kids are always in trouble for stealing food, aren't you? Granny'll get you good."

She gulped a surge of nausea.

"But I won't say anything to her. I got bread in the shed. It's too good for swine. Want some?"

Paula didn't make a sound.

"You gotta do something for me, though," he said, "just you and me. What's your name? Paula?"

The chill of the autumn night didn't bother her anymore.

"How old are you?"

Above his head, Paula saw the flit of a bat's wings dashing from the branches of the husband maple to the wife beside it. She wondered when they would turn into a family of trees, when she would come to them and discover their new saplings poking out of the soil.

She heard the rustle of fabric and the clink of a belt buckle. She shut her eyes. Her legs felt stiff, as if her feet had sprouted their own roots and been planted into the dirt.

✿

Days later, Paula was still afflicted with diarrhea from eating the uncooked beans. It made her buttocks feel raw. Doing her nightly rounds in the girls' dormitory, Granny arrived at Paula's bed and bent close to her face, her eyes narrowed behind the scratched-up lenses of her spectacles.

Paula held her blankets up over her neck and shuddered, certain that Granny would sense the cramping in her guts. But instead of yanking the covers down, Granny whipped them up from the bottom of the bed. The flick of her nightdress made Paula wince.

"What's wrong with you?" Granny asked.

Paula's mouth opened but the word *nothing* didn't come out. She blinked into tears. "I—I don't know."

Granny's brows wrinkled into a single hairy earthworm and in that moment she seemed to know everything about what the farmhand had done. "When? This week?"

Paula nodded, unable to stop the tears. They slid down into her ears one after the other, warm and stinging.

Granny slipped her cold, rough hand under Paula's nightdress, over her narrow thigh and into the pit between her legs. "Where?" Granny frowned. "Here?"

Paula sucked in her breath and her whole body tensed like a plank of wood. Her view skidded to Granny's hairline, that brown wave greased across her forehead. Granny's exhales overtook her nostrils with its smell of eggs. Eggs and liquor.

Granny squinted. "You've been bleeding yet? Tell me the truth."

No, Paula mouthed, voice gone. She thought of her sister in a bed at the other end of the dormitory and hoped she was already asleep.

"Good," Granny answered in the spit of a whisper. "Better watch yourself." She pulled her hand away and covered Paula's legs with the blanket, tucking it hard under Paula's thighs, sealing everything in and making her bottom burn.

Through her pain Paula thought of the anxiety in all the girls, the shame dragging at the boys' shoulders. She thought of how the matrons stared and whispered to one another as the girls stripped down to bathe in a gritty bucket of water and how Granny's protective doting on Ave could easily go rancid, saving her from nothing. Paula thought about leaping out of her bed, ripping the curtains open and cursing bloody murder at Granny and the matrons and the farmhands—at all the people she and her sister had had to endure for eight years.

But she couldn't do it, not as she lay there famished and aching and utterly wrung out. There was no hope of returning to her mother. There was no hope in the legacy of a mighty warrior ancestor. She had nothing of her own left.

The tremors of Granny's footsteps rattled the mattress as she walked away. Paula counted the steps, weighty and slow, *one, two, three, four.* Granny stopped at the bed next to hers. Paula was a gouged plank of wood.

CHAPTER 19

THE LAST PHOTO MY FATHER TOOK UNDER THE CRABAPPLE TREE OUTSIDE OUR building was snapped a couple of months after we had buried my sister. The framing of this photograph is close, even claustrophobic, with only the ends of branches and their clustered blossoms to show at the top. It's difficult to guess where this picture has been taken, which street or neighbourhood. It could be any suburb in any city.

I'm in the middle. My mother is on my left and Auntie Julie is on my right. Neither releases her hair for the camera to record thickness or blackness or length. They wear ordinary buns. My mother is in a long dark skirt and my aunt is in khaki pants. Both wear unmemorable white blouses. There are no high heels and there is no one foot set in front of the other just so. There are no sashaying skirts. There are only three terse smiles, no teeth. I'm in jeans and a crumpled sweatshirt, now nearly as tall as the women on either side of me. My arms circle their waists loosely and I aim empty black pupils at the lens.

The problem in this picture is as obvious as the pink blooms above our heads: the core of our family is gone.

After the burial, we returned to our regular lives. The pitying gazes of neighbours, friends, and family eventually receded, and soon no one came to our door with food or called for updates. It taught me that grieving is only tolerated for so long.

To outsiders, we probably seemed reserved. We didn't talk about the shifting tectonic plates of Diana's death, nor the mile-deep gorge that had since cracked open under our feet. There was just the hushed awareness in our apartment that we had lost everything.

My father returned to his administration job at the brokerage and my aunt to her paralegal job by day and legal studies at night. Even my mother interviewed for a receptionist position at a nearby dental office.

"They made an offer," I heard her say in the kitchen between the crisp sound of a blade cutting into an onion. "The salary isn't bad."

The refrigerator opened. I heard a clinking glass and liquid being poured. My father was preparing himself a drink. "All right," he replied, as if my mother had simply asked him to add something to the grocery list.

Those old arguments about my mother getting a job, the ones I had dreaded when I was younger, ended as plainly as that.

I finished grade eight with no problems and, in fact, my grades had gotten better. High Achiever of the Week certificates and A+ quizzes bulged in my desk drawer.

"Alisha, can I borrow your French book?" my classmate asked, turning away from her friend and poking her head past her open locker door. Her lips were broad and slick with gloss and carried the tail end of a laugh. She had rainbow-coloured rubber bands on her braces. "I forgot to bring mine. I just need to see it for a second."

I looked into the shadowed cavity of my locker. "No."

"Huh?"

"I said no."

"But I just want to—"

"Take care of your own problems."

"Selfish bitch," she hissed through the metal tracks in her mouth. "I don't care how smart you think you are. That's the way to get your ass kicked."

I rammed in my locker door, pushing the hook of the padlock into the hole and clicking it shut. I hoisted my knapsack and walked away, hoping she and the other kids would forget my name by the time we all went to high school.

At my grade eight graduation ceremony I stepped onto the gymnasium stage in the hard-heeled dress shoes and knee-length skirt I had picked out of my mother's closet. It was similar to the outfit Diana had worn to her graduation. The principal, a man with wispy strands of hair combed over the top of his bald head and two bushy brown eyebrows, shook my hand and handed me a plaque.

Alisha Sookermany. For Highest Scholastic Excellence.

I had achieved the top mark in my grade. Diana had been given the same award when she left middle school. Mrs. Wilson had even decided to send me to be tested for entry to a gifted high school program and I had passed, just like Diana had.

My parents and aunt applauded along with the other adults in suits and skirts, *salwar kameez* and hosiery. They smiled politely.

Paula was out there too, applauding for me in her volunteer vest even though I hadn't been at the library to accept her book recommendations since before the funeral.

You're wrong, Paula, I thought, standing with the plaque over my chest, waiting for my father to thread himself through the row of attendees and snap an obligatory Polaroid. *I will not get through.*

On the final day of grade eight, I didn't visit the library to say goodbye to Paula. I went straight home and stood in the kitchen, sliding my finger under the envelope flap of my final report card. We'd been ordered to deliver it to our parents but my mother was noiseless behind her closed bedroom door.

I skimmed the grid on the paper in front of me as if I were reading a receipt: seven *A*+s, two *A*s, and a few exclamation marks. *Alisha has become the best student in her grade! What a triumph!*

I chucked the report card on the counter and walked to my bedroom.

"It might be time," I heard Auntie Julie say in the kitchen when summer heat swaddled our neighbourhood again. "What do you think, Sister Bea?"

Her voice had awoken me from the misty beginnings of a nap on the living room couch. The history textbook I had borrowed from the public library lay open on my lap. She and my mother were in the kitchen where they were frying kingfish in crackling oil. On the television screen in front of me a camera panned over a white vase.

King Augustus, the narrator spoke, *desperate to uncover the secret of Chinese porcelain, learned of Johann Friedrich Böttger's talents with alchemy. The king sentenced Böttger to house arrest, even though he had committed no crime....*

"You're right," my mother answered. "The grass must need cutting by now. It's been a rainy spring."

"And the hedges. Maybe I should dig them out and be done."

"Do what you have to do, Julie-girl."

A spatula scraped the bottom of the pan and tapped the rim a few times. My mother was also cooking chicken fried rice with onion, all-spice, curry powder, and vegetables. She cleared her throat. "You've done so much for us. I don't know how we would've—"

"It's nothing."

"You didn't have to—"

"I wanted to—"

"We imposed on you and—"

"No, I had to."

"You didn't have to, but you did."

Böttger laboured night and day to create this "white gold" all of Germany coveted, firing new formulas in his kiln. Under the critical surveillance of Augustus, he feared his labour would be in vain.

My father sat at the living room table. He sniffed and made sure his reading glasses were in their proper spot on his straight nose. He hadn't looked up from his folders in what seemed like hours. Since Diana's death he had even more of them and his carrying case had gotten fat. Most nights he would come home late after sorting through microfiche and newspapers at the reference library, searching for some kind of link between what happened to her and someone else. He seemed to have many threads and theories to pursue. My mother didn't do her own research but she supported him. My parents both seemed to believe they could find out what happened to Diana if only they worked hard enough.

"You'll manage, though?" asked my aunt. "I mean, you'll be okay?"

There was a lull in the looping tapestry of their conversation.

"It'll feel empty in here," came my mother's reply, "that's all."

In 1708, Böttger chanced upon a remarkable breakthrough. He mixed clay with ground kaolin and alabaster and discovered the formula for porcelain. The king's wrath would be abated, after all.

Ball bearings rolled about my stomach when I thought about Diana's empty bed and eating at a table with only three place settings. Even though I had gotten as good at school as my sister had been, I hadn't discovered the formula for turning one daughter into two.

✿

Seeking pertinent information and eyewitnesses, read the new advertisement in the local paper, though they had stopped charging us to place it. *Significant cash reward offered by family. Call right away.*

The police told us that they found Diana's remains in a crevice. As summer changed to winter, the skies above turned grey and the ground froze. In that place she had lain for months alone, in the soil amongst black trunk trees where the rumbling of city streets diminished to a hum.

Cause of Death: Inconclusive.

Location of Discovery: Crothers Woods, a pocket of green in the Don River Valley that cuts through the city, miles away from the mall and the job fair. The temperature, soil, and interfering coyotes and hawks had created the conditions for rapid decomposition that ran its course before the winter, and in that manner nature conspired against my family and obliterated the physical evidence that would've revealed the true end my sister had come to.

She was buried under shallow dirt and brush. Her bones and scraps of clothing were strewn over a radius of several metres, the centre of which was marked by three protruding boulders. For those months, she had been in the rain and sleet and wind and snow, unable to see the sky as it darkened and lightened, the city crows as they circled above her.

Scarcely a week after Auntie Julie returned to her townhouse, a story broke.

> *The body discovered on Tuesday in the Lower Don Parklands has been identified as seventeen-year-old Kaila Hedgebrook, reported missing on the twelfth of February. Experts say her body bore injuries consistent with sexual assault and strangulation. She was last seen leaving a Richmond Hill warehouse rave, reportedly under the influence of ecstasy. This is the second body of a teenage girl to be discovered in the Don River Valley this year, but no official connections have been made. Police are asking eyewitnesses to come forward and support investigative efforts.*

Our phone rang and rang as it had when Diana first disappeared. "The police didn't call to tell us a damn thing about this one," I heard my mother rail into the kitchen receiver. "We had to learn about it from the TV like everyone else."

I was in my bedroom at my desk, doing math homework for my summer high school prep course.

"They didn't search for my Dee properly and they made up their minds that she ran away. If she was a white girl, you think they'd behave this way? You heard what they do to us, to the Natives and the Blacks and the immigrants. You know they don't care. But my child's life is on their heads!"

I pictured the person on the other line, probably one of my mother's cousins, saying only *uh-uh* and *um-hm, no girl* and *yes girl* to my mother's assessments.

"But this Kaila girl was nothing like my Dee. My Dee was a good girl. She didn't run all over and talk to boys and drink. This girl? She didn't have a proper home and parents. No. My Dee was doing her job search like they told all the children to do at her school."

I waited, I watched, I searched.

The pencil in my hand rattled. I squeezed it so hard that it pierced a hole through the page of my notebook on the desk. *Mommy doesn't deserve to deal with what you did,* I told myself. *She deserves a good girl who is the best student in her class. She deserves Diana.*

"They don't care about brown girls, I'm telling you. It's the white girls who get their attention. It's a sin and a crime and they should burn in hell for how they treat people!"

That weekend Auntie Julie came back to our apartment to eat dinner. I could tell by the way she and my parents sat at the table like three brittle sticks that they were waiting on me to go to bed. I claimed sleepiness as soon as it was plausible.

"There was even a third girl," I heard my father say in the living room, "an eighteen-year-old Native girl they found almost ten years ago in the Don Valley. They didn't even say much about her in the newspapers."

"You see?" my mother said. "Damn police!"

"You told the detective about it, Brother Don?" Auntie Julie asked.

"As soon as I found the old article. He played like he was aware of it, but they're full of lies when they speak to you. They don't know how hard I've been searching this whole time. They don't know what I've found."

"They didn't look for Dee properly," my mother said, "and they know it, I'm telling you. Did they offer a reward? Did they really help the neighbourhood group or put up posters? Tell her what the lawyer told you, Don."

"You can hire a private detective. They're quicker and better than police detectives. And you can sue the police if they didn't do the things they should've done."

"You see?"

"All right, a private detective, then," my aunt replied. I don't think either of my parents was attuned to the hesitation in her voice. "The girl they found ten years ago," Auntie Julie asked so gently that I had to strain to hear, "was it the same as this Kaila girl? Were there signs of...."

She didn't say it because none of them had the heart to say it.

"Yes," my father answered.

My mother exhaled. "Oh, God...."

"I don't know," my father said, "but I don't think—"

"No, I don't think—" my mother echoed.

Auntie Julie didn't dare respond.

That night, the Ferris wheel reappeared in my dreams. I stood on the pavement and looked up to where my sister sat in one of its spinning seats with her back to me, her hair swinging back and forth. Hundreds of crashed vehicles steamed between us.

It's a sin and a crime, I thought. As I held those words, they amplified and distorted like feedback in a speaker, and the broken cars began to evaporate into smoke. The ground cleared in front of me.

I started forward. With every step, the Ferris wheel shifted closer to me; a mile away, then a block, then a few yards. But the man at the mall cut me off, stealing my path to charge toward the Ferris wheel himself. He spun on his heel and watched me with his muddy eyes under a baseball cap.

The sisters are angry at each other, his expression seemed to say. *The sisters are fighting. The sisters are separating.*

I wanted to scream but all that came out of my mouth was a useless spray of water.

A rattling sounded behind me, and I knew what had splattered like jacks at my heels.

The bones. *Don't make me look at the bones.*

I woke with a start. I kicked the blankets off. My nightdress was bunched at my hips, my underwear so twisted that pubic hair stuck out. In the moonlight, my legs were goosebumped and sallow.

I slid out of my bed and took unsteady steps to the hallway. Diana's door was half open. I placed a hand on the chalky wall.

Auntie Julie's sleep-breathing came from Diana's room. She had stayed over. I knew I could go in and wake her up, but I didn't know what I would I say. Would I tell her I'd had a bad dream? That I felt afraid and alone and wanted to be free of the secrets I carried? I would only blather things I knew I shouldn't and my parents would find out. I was supposed to keep doing well in school, not destroy them with what I had done to my sister. But could I really trust myself to do the right things?

I watched Auntie Julie's back through the open door, the spill of her black hair over the pillow and sheets. *That girl was right,* I thought. *You are a selfish bitch.*

I retreated to my room, quietly closing the door behind me.

CHAPTER 20

1947

LIGHT BORE THROUGH THE WINDOW AND FELL ACROSS THE FLOOR OF THE DAY room. It stung Paula's eyes. She had been ordered to change out of her stained trousers into a new-looking blouse and skirt she had never seen before. She could hear the children shouting in the yard. Ave was out there with her friends, the group of ten- and eleven-year-old girls who liked to boss each other around as they played make-believe wedding and house.

"Go in," the young matron said behind Paula's head, prodding her shoulder. She had only been around for a few months. "Don't haunt the doorway."

Paula walked into the room and sat at the table, the coolness of the chair on the backs of her thighs.

Her mother was seated across from her. She wore a tattered black overcoat that was too big for her shoulders, buttoned right up to her throat. Her lips were pressed tightly together and she looked at Paula with huge eyes.

The young matron, short and round-faced with hair that was flat on top and curled perkily about the white collar of her uniform, walked around the table to stand behind Paula's mother. With the window to her back she folded her arms. "What do you say when you meet someone, young lady?" The matrons always stayed near when family came to visit.

"Hello," Paula answered, quietly.

Her mother's hands were on the table, fingers woven around each other. They were weathered, each joint a bony knob. She sat with her spine a rigid line. She was skinnier and shorter than Paula remembered, a plain, shrunken woman. Her hair was tied into a roll and streaked with silver clumps that battled against the black. Dark wrinkles ringed her neck. Today was the first visit to the home she had ever made.

"Hello," Paula's mother said. "How have you been?" A sudden smile came to her lips to expose a row of small, chipped upper teeth, but it melted away just as quickly as it had come.

Paw! Paw! Paw!

Paula remembered Ave's cries from the night they had last seen their mother.

"Paula," spoke the matron, "didn't you hear the question? Show your manners."

"I'm fine." Paula felt as if her lips had hardly moved. She couldn't be certain she was even the resident of her own body anymore. She hovered somewhere above everyone's heads, an apparition passing through the rafters and out through the roof, possibly floating away from the earth for good.

"And your sister?"

"Fine."

"I asked them if I could talk to you alone first." Her mother searched her face, her eyes scanning Paula like the crows that flew two-by-two in concert above the home. *Ears, eyes, nose, mouth... everything that was there is still there, isn't it?* "You've grown so tall. Sweet sixteen." That smile of hers tried to escape again but she caught it and reeled it back. "I've missed so much of you and your sister growing up. Ave's already eleven and you're such a pretty young lady."

"Thank you."

She retrieved an orange and a few wrapped hard candies from her lap, holding them out over the table. "These are for you."

A truce of treats. Paula took them and held them in a mass in front of her chest. They made her palms prickle.

"Do you remember me?" her mother asked. "Do you remember that you and Ave used to be mine?"

Ave, she thought, and for some reason, she heard her sister's sweet voice singing a Christmas solo. *Behold, your King! Before him lowly bend!* It was a sabre penetrating her memory.

Her mother untangled her hands and lay them flat on the table. "You sister was so little, and maybe you don't remember that much about me either—"

"Nonsense," the young matron interjected, sunny as ever.

Paula's mother turned to her, wrenching her skinny neck.

"Children have better memories than we know, you know? I don't think they could ever forget their mothers."

Paula's mother turned back to her daughter. "I hope you understand I never wanted any of this. They didn't let you stay with me and I wanted to come to you many times." She was hardly able to voice the words between gulps. "Did they tell you any of it? That I wanted to see you so badly?"

"Are you taking us home?" asked Paula.

"Oh, God. I wish I could, sweetheart. I thought about you and your sister every day. When they took you, it was like my whole body froze solid, like I just turned into ice right there. Then you were gone, and I finally melted again. I melted and turned into fire. But when I tried to get you, they wouldn't let me. They wouldn't even let me visit—"

"Are you taking us home now?"

Her mother reached out to touch her daughter's arm. Their skin made contact and, even after all that time, it was familiar to Paula. Her body remembered all the hugs and clinging and caresses it had lost. It hurt in her bones like grief.

Her mother shook her head. "I can't."

Paula felt a massive collision inside of her. It was like the ground coming together, smashing and peaking into a mountain, shooting miles up into the sky. "I don't remember you," she whispered, "and neither does Ave."

"What?"

"We don't remember who you are."

"Please, just talk with me," her mother said, leaning closer. "I know you're upset but I need you to know how much I love you and your sister, how badly I wanted you to come back, but it isn't in my hands."

Her touch was still warm on Paula's arm, but Paula only glared, feeling the wildness of her own eyes. Her mother had finally come but Paula didn't believe in her old fantasies anymore. *I can't let her leave us again.*

"Do you remember how we used to talk," Paula's mother said, "how you used to call out to me and fall asleep on my shoulder? You girls were my pride and joy, but they told me I wasn't taking care of you right and took you away."

Paula's throat felt like a tube of rusty metal. "I don't know who you are and you are not allowed to talk to my sister."

"You can't understand what happened but—"

"Leave me and my sister alone. We don't know who you are and we don't want to see you again."

"But—"

"Don't ever come back."

Paula could tell that her mother saw it inside of her too, that looming mountain that had sprung up to block her out, and there was no sense arguing with her daughter to change her mind. Nothing had the power to do that. Her mother's hand shrank away and silence descended over the room.

"May I go back outside, miss?" Paula asked the matron, still holding her mother's orange and candies in front of her.

"Paula," the young woman answered, arms loosened to her sides. She looked to the back of Paula's mother's head.

"I want to go outside now. Please."

The woman shook her head. "Fine, then. Do what you want."

"Thank you."

Paula stood and her chair scraped the floor. She walked out of the room and down the hallway, leaving her mother sitting there with her face collapsed in her hands.

Granny met Paula in the front waiting room. She stood there as if she'd been waiting for her to come out, and blocked her path to the door that would take her back to her sister.

"How was it, Paula? Happy to finally see your long-lost mother?"

Granny had a small smile on her lips. Her spectacle lenses were all reflection and Paula couldn't see the eyes behind them. Granny scratched at the back of her pressed curls and pointed to Paula's gifts. "And what'd you get there? Maybe I should keep them locked up so the others won't get at them."

Paula wasn't going to behave like the other children when their families, their mothers, came to visit them. She had seen them shriek and cry to hold onto their gifts, certain they would never be allowed to touch them again. She placed the treats into Granny's open palms.

Granny had expected an argument. She frowned at the gifts; frowned at Paula.

Paula saw her own stony, flat face reflected in the glasses. "Promise you won't tell Ave," she said, watching herself speak.

"What?"

"You want her to keep singing and stay happy for you? You have to promise nobody will tell her our mother was here."

Granny stuffed the orange and candies into the two large front pockets of her white collared dress. Her expression hardened. This behaviour—this child demanding an adult to make a pledge—

was unprecedented. But Granny relented, sighing. "All right. For Ave, tough girl. No one'll say anything if I have anything to do with it."

It was a small mercy, the only one Granny had ever shown to Paula, but it was enough for Paula to feel rinsed by relief. At least Ave would be spared.

Granny stepped aside to let her pass. Paula made her way to the door at the far end of the corridor. Its window allowed a breeze to ripple the curtain, and it beckoned her into the afternoon sunshine.

CHAPTER 21

IN AUGUST OF 1999, A MONTH BEFORE I WOULD GO TO A DIFFERENT HIGH SCHOOL than Diana had gone to, my father and I went to collect the contents of her locker.

"I am so sorry, sir," said the teacher who coached her track team, passing my father a banker's box of Diana's things as we stood in the main office with a small gathering of teachers. "As a father myself...." He bowed, baring his bald spot, and the other teachers shook their heads.

My father fixed his eyes on the lid of the box, his chin jutting out. I'd never seen him so furious. My breath dammed up in my chest. I had to rush to keep up with him as he stormed down the hall and stairway and into the parking lot.

I stood behind him as he jammed the box into the trunk of our sedan and thumped the door shut. He braced his hand on the spoiler and dropped his head. His black *W*-shaped hairline lengthened.

I inhaled the smell of the dandelions that infested the schoolyard and understood he didn't want to be touched. *You let her go to the mall,* I thought, *but I abandoned her there.*

My father had started checking out true crime books from the library. He signed out more than he could possibly read before the due dates, stacking them on the floor in the corner of the living room next to his cases of manila folders. He sat at the dining table, scribbling notes in the margins, circling words, and dog-earing pages as if the books were his own.

The books attracted me with their stormy art and shocking red titles but I kept my distance as I had done with his folders, too afraid of the notes I thought I might find scrawled between the lines. *She waited, watched, searched? Unlikely. Coward. Liar.*

My mother would often skip meals, blaming headaches for her lack of appetite. One evening after she had brought out dinner and steeped tea but left for bed without having any of it herself, I decided to ask my father about his books. "Why do you read that stuff?"

He lifted his eyes from the pages of the book he was reading. "What?"

"Do you learn anything?"

His jaw flexed and he kept his thumb in place as he turned to the book's cover. It showed a photograph of a smiling family with two parents and three children—except the girl at the bottom corner of the picture, petite and wearing an orange headband in her mousy brown hair, was ripped off from the rest, askew on her own scrap.

I picked at a cube of curried potato on my plate. "What are they about?"

"Theories. Investigations." He reached for his tea and slurped.

"What else?"

"Court cases."

"What else?"

"'Lisha." My father set the book on the table. "I don't want you thinking about these things. They're terrible."

"But I want to know."

"I know you do."

"So tell me."

"No." He flipped through the pages, trying to find the place where he had left off. "You've seen enough bad things."

I thought of the bones we had seen together, how we had never spoken of them. "Can't you tell me anything?"

His cheekbones transformed into sharp angles when he crimped his mouth. "The private detective. When he gets deeper into it, he'll be able to tell us more."

But he doesn't know everything, I thought. *I'm the only one who does.*

I flattened the potato with the root of my fork, imprinting on it like a shovel on soil.

I began the gifted program at Don Mills Collegiate Institute, a flat-roofed brick and blue metal building I reached by taking two busses away from my neighbourhood, in September. Only a few kids from my middle school had transferred there for high school and I didn't introduce myself to anyone. I wore unassuming clothes, and I didn't venture into trying new makeup and hairstyles like the other girls. To keep up Diana's honour roll marks I had to study all the time. I dug into assignments in the free time between classes, squatting in the corners of the hallways and gravitating to the back of the study hall.

"Sookermany, right?" asked a Filipino girl I hadn't talked to before in English class. "Isn't that like the brown chick they found in the woods?" She braced her bottom on the edge of the desk of the girl sitting next to me. Both of them chomped gum, played with their hoop earrings, and stared at me.

"That was my sister," I answered.

The girls released a cascade of gasps.

"Holy *shit,*" she said. "I had no idea."

I returned to my notes and dragged a pink highlighter over a paragraph. "She was older than me. She got raped and everything."

"Oh my God," the one sitting at the desk said. "Are you, like, okay?"

"The body was just a skeleton when they found it. There was hardly anything to bury." I capped the highlighter and shrugged. "It could happen to you anytime, really. All it takes is one psycho. Do you think you'd have a chance? I mean, even with all the girl-power shit people talk about, do you really think you could fight a man off if he wanted to hurt you?"

They both stopped chewing. The Filipino girl left for her own seat and neither of them nor anyone else at my school dared to start conversations with me again. I was glad to be relieved of the responsibility of making friends.

Weirdo, psycho, freak, loner. This is what my classmates must have called me when I couldn't hear them. *Coolie girl with a dead sister.*

The phone rang and I waited for someone to pick up.

"Hello," answered a woman's flat voice.

I pressed my glove against my free ear as a garbage truck roared by. "Yes," I said, my heart pounding under my coat. "Is Mark home?"

She coughed a few times and the phlegm rattled deep. "Hold on, I gotta see."

There were rustles, a few pops, and muffled words I couldn't make out. I heard her set down the receiver. I exhaled breath into the only payphone booth in my neighbourhood, the one I walked by every day to and from the bus stop and only now had a reason to use. It was banged up, graffitied, and smelled of stale marijuana.

"Yeah?" a boy answered. His voice was thin and young and nothing like I remembered.

"Are you Mark Barrington?"

"Who is this?"

"A friend of Diana's."

"Who?"

"Do you remember Dee? The girl you met camping last summer?"

I heard the chatter of a television and what sounded like metal pots banging about. *Put it down,* I heard a woman scream in the background, *right now!*

"We haven't talked in a long time," he answered. "Who is this?"

"Did she visit you?"

"Huh? No."

"Are you lying?"

"No! I stopped talking to that chick months ago. Where'd you get this number?"

"You didn't see her again after the trip?"

He grunted. "Listen, if she's been saying stuff about me and her going out, she's a liar. I didn't do *nothing* with that girl and I barely even knew her. She doesn't even live around here. She was the one who kept calling me. You can't just phone my house and—"

I smacked the receiver onto the latch and it bounced off, spinning on its chord around the phone book. I felt the wetness in my armpits and at my hairline, the sweltering of my skin under my scarf.

She didn't leave us, I thought, *she didn't do anything at all.*

I rattled the accordion door to get it to fold open and tumbled out of the booth, gulping cold air.

✿

"Why didn't you tell me?"

I raised my head from the assignment on my desk. My mother stood in the doorway of my bedroom in her bathrobe holding my mid-term report card. Her hair was combed down her back and her skin was free of makeup, rinsed clean.

"You're doing so well, 'Lisha."

"Thanks."

She placed the report card next to my hand and rested her warm palm on my shoulder. "Your sister would be proud of you. She always knew you could do as well as she did."

Alisha is an exceptional student, read the teacher's comment at the top of the page, *already the best in her grade!*

That night, I dreamed of the amusement park and the crashed cars again. The man at the mall sneered and closed in on me. My shoes fused to the pavement. *This is it.* I bent my arms over my head, useless as an umbrella upturned by wind. He grabbed them and swung me around again and again like he was the centre and I was a spoke. My body stretched like a rubber band and my joints popped. The world blurred around me.

My eyes opened and I sat up in bed, overcome by nausea. My body didn't feel like it belonged to me. I jerked out of my blankets and tugged on my pants and socks and shirt. I only became conscious of my plan when I stood panting in the elevator.

I darted down the sidewalk. The buildings tossed behind me one after the other and sweat collected on my scalp and grew cold in the chilly nighttime air. The sky above had no moon or stars; there were only yellow street lamps and orange security lights. The road was black and quiet.

In the fifth building down the street from mine, three teenage boys loitered in the vestibule. Even with the security camera screwed to the ceiling, they didn't bother hiding their beer cans. I yanked the front door open and was greeted by their catcalls.

One boy had his foot jammed between the second security door and its frame. "In a hurry for a booty call, aren't you?" he said to me without a smile. His cheek was branded by a scar that was a thin pink line on his brown skin.

He saw me look at it and he looked down to the floor. He hadn't moved but didn't block my way so I swung open the security door and rushed through the lobby to get into the elevator.

I pounded on Paula's door until I heard her unlocking the bolt and chain. The air in my lungs felt hot.

"What the hell?" she exclaimed, swaddling herself in her robe. Her glasses were wonky on her face. Her hair was combed out of her usual bun and strands poked out around her ears. "It's two o'clock in the morning, Alisha!"

But she stepped aside and shut the door behind me. In the dark, the books on her shelves were large, uneven shapes. The only lighted lamp shone on a partial painting on her easel, two hovering sparrows with iridescent wings under the spotlight from the bulb.

"Did she get raped?" I asked.

"What?"

"Did my sister get raped?"

Her fingertips were at her jaw.

"They can't even say the word to each other but I need to know."

Her face was pained. "Dear God, I don't know."

"But do you think she was?"

"What does it matter what I think?"

"It just does!"

In the weak light, I saw her soft nod.

My eyes became foggy with tears. "What was it like?"

Paula exhaled. "Not sure. But awful. Terrible."

"Did it hurt?"

"In all kinds of ways."

"Was she afraid? Was she scared she'd die?"

"Yeah, I imagine so."

I started to cry.

I felt a brushing on my face, delicate flicks. Paula tended to my tears with a tissue, wiping them from my cheeks and chin. "There you go."

My arms and legs began to tremble. I couldn't control it. "I did something wrong," I said through my clattering teeth.

"What?"

I thought I might swallow my own tongue. I couldn't fish out the words. I couldn't tell her.

The clock radio on the shelf flicked forward, measuring time with slashed red digits. Paula cupped my jaw with her palms and somehow steadied my body. I pressed my palms to the backs of her hands to buttress myself.

"You need to know that you didn't cause your sister's death, Alisha."

"I just wish I could sleep," I managed to say.

"Bad dreams?"

I nodded at her leaf pendant, now flat against her brown skin.

"You haven't told your parents?"

No, my mouth said without the help of my voice. My eyes were weighted with tears again.

She pulled me in and hugged me tight. "Why wouldn't you?" I felt her breath on my scalp.

"They'll hate me."

"That can't be true." Her head shook against mine. "Poor girl. You need to tell them how you feel."

All the effort I had been heaving into my schoolwork, into transfiguring myself into the smart, capable, and strong daughter my family deserved. I now understood they were the actions of the gutless.

By the time I was on the street again, floating in the night of the neighbourhood, I was so numb that I didn't feel my heart thumping in my chest. I could see our living room light, blazing high and lonely on the twenty-third floor. It was like a lighthouse. The curtains were splayed as wide as they would go.

Inside the apartment, my father was on the phone in the kitchen and my mother was on the couch. Auntie Julie sat next to her with tousled hair, a jacket pulled over her pyjamas, and her car keys in her hand.

We stared at each other as if we were strangers. Then recognition swiftly set in, and so did the memory of the dirty bones. *We've gone this way before, haven't we?*

Auntie Julie was the first to move. She captured me in her arms, wrapping her body around mine and wailing in my ear. But my parents were weary. My father set the phone softly on its cradle and my mother smoothed her nightgown down over her legs before standing.

"How could you do this to us?" she said behind Auntie Julie's moans. "Where were you?"

She hadn't asked in a harsh tone. They were just questions. I had come to recognize that tired, just-a-question voice too well. My mother's ability to feel anger had faded. How much more her ability to feel joy?

My father placed a hand on my back. His eyes were closed and he seemed to have no desire to talk. It was like how he was at the funeral, refusing to recite the Lord's Prayer.

I let my arms go loose. My aunt pulled her head away. She looked at my father, my mother, and back to me, suddenly confused.

I slanted my head past my aunt's wild hair to find my mother. "I'm sorry. I couldn't sleep and went for a walk."

"I can't believe you," my father said. "Do you know how you hurt your mother? Why would you put her through this?"

But it had come over him again, the same exhaustion of failure that welled in him when we had picked up my sister's belongings from her locker. *Bea, she's getting older and you need to let her do things. She's a smart girl.*

My aunt watched him. I think she noticed it too.

I had to protect them from the truth. "I'm sorry, Daddy. I was just worried about a test and went for a walk. I won't do it again."

Soon enough, the apologies and admonitions were over. Only my aunt seemed to have more questions, but she held them back. She left our apartment, pulling the dented door behind her, and we returned to our bedrooms, drained and silent. Marooned in that apartment together. The three who couldn't forget they had been four.

CHAPTER 22

1947

SUN POURED INTO THE CLEARING IN THE FOREST. IT WAS A PARCHED PATCH where grass didn't grow and tree branches didn't cover. Insects flew high, battling each other with their hisses and clicks.

"Go ahead, get him good, tough girl," Granny called out to Paula. She always egged on the one she believed would win. "Show him what's right!"

Granny was the loudest in the messy ring, and everyone yelled and pressed in. That morning, Jerry had shoved Paula in the yard and Paula had surprised him by pelting her rake to the dirt and shoving him back. When they were both hauled to the office, Granny told them they would fight each other in the afternoon. What novelty this match would be. A boy getting beat by a girl!

Paula threw her fist and Jerry tumbled to his bottom. He had spindly limbs and a long scar on the side of his head where hair didn't grow. His threadbare T-shirt was streaked with grass stains. He cupped his nose and mouth with his hand. Blood leaked to his chin and dripped down in globs.

Paula thought he would stay where he was—she prayed he would. Granny hadn't broken up the last fight until the loser was knocked out cold, a jagged scarlet gash over his eyebrow.

You pussy, you wimpy little girl! Jerry glared up at Paula with new energy as he heard the insults of the roaring boys. He braced himself on an elbow, bent his knees, and planted both feet on the grass.

The matrons and children cheered. Paula saw the farmhand with the scar watching on from the edge of the crowd. She couldn't hear his voice but she saw his moving mouth and doubling gouge. *Get him, Paula, go on!*

She felt a red-hot spark at the base of her brain. She couldn't show them her weakness. She stomped the flat of her boot into the middle of Jerry's chest and felt a crack—a horrible shift—under her heel. His limbs lost all rigour and he collapsed, hugging himself in, curled and sweaty and writhing, turning his head to give Paula a full view of the scar on his scalp. It was a perfect straight line that started behind his ear and reached the back of his neck.

The boy's mouth distorted into the shape of a cry but Paula couldn't hear him. The screaming and jeering deafened her. She threw her fists into the sky and looked up because she couldn't stand to watch him or Granny or the farmhand. The reverberation of the boy's breaking rib, a memory now inscribed into the marrow of her leg, made her feel she might double over and vomit.

Paula's vision shot beyond the shrieking faces to a place deep in the woods where she wanted to run off and hide, far from this spot as well as the cluster of evergreens where the farmhand would often force her to meet him. *If you don't come,* he would threaten, *I'll tell Granny you've been stealing food. You don't want that.* Where she wanted to go now was the place where she and Ave sometimes went at night, sneaking out of the girls' dormitory together. They had been there a few nights ago, when a large moon hung so low it seemed like it might unhinge and plunge to the earth.

"We'll go to Toronto and I'll get a job," Paula told Ave as they sat on the ground side by side, their backs against a trunk, their heads touching. "You'll be able to sing. They have concerts in the city every night, you know." In that special pocket of trees, the scent of wildflowers prevailed over the odour of dung.

"But how will Mommy find us?" answered Ave. "You think she'll be in Toronto?"

"Maybe. Everyone goes there."

"We can buy a big house and the three of us can live together, right?" Her fingers went to her head, feeling about to make sure her pressed curls were still in place. Granny had done her hair to match her own that afternoon.

"We can visit a new place in the city every day, never the same place twice. Can you imagine?" Paula's hair was tied in the same two braids as always. She shivered and focused on the toes of her tattered shoes. She listened to her sister distractedly humming a radio chorus in that pretty pitch of hers, a song she had probably picked up while she was doing chores with her friends.

Paula didn't have friends. She held out her fists in a ten-and-two position. "I'll buy a car," she said. "I'll teach you how to drive. It's not so hard." But Paula didn't know a thing about automobiles, and she knew that neither of them knew much of anything beyond the home, the hunger, the weeding and toil, the scrapping chickens and the farting pigs.

"I don't think I could!" Ave giggled into her hand, tickled at the notion of holding a steering wheel. "Lucy says ladies don't drive."

"Where'd she learn that?"

"Minnie says so too."

"Those girls are stupid."

"You think Mommy drives?"

"I don't know."

"Maybe she can take us around the city when we get there."

"Don't bother with her," answered Paula.

Ave recoiled, shaking her head. "What do you mean?"

"You and me will do it on our own."

"But what about Mommy?"

"In the city, we'll be able to do and buy anything we want by ourselves. You'll see."

Paula wanted to make more and more claims about the things they would do, about the skills she would teach Ave and the gifts she would buy for her. She didn't mean to be a deceiver, but she couldn't help herself. It was only in their shared fantasies that she could protect her sister, that she could feel herself loved. With Ave, Paula had been a boaster from the start.

The audience walked off from the halted fight; the scarred farmhand and Granny and the matrons and children, still prattling to each other and laughing. They left Paula standing over Jerry, her shirt ripped and soiled and skewed off her shoulder. She panted and he wheezed on the grass. Drops of sweat fell from the tip of her nose.

Paula raised her head and saw Ave standing alone, gaping at the boy and looking at Paula like she didn't know who she was. Her eyes were as wide as plates in her head and her mouth was open.

Paula's arms hung down, weighty as stone pillars. The crown of her head felt like it had caught on fire. What sort of claims would she be able to make to her sister now?

CHAPTER 23

WE COMMEMORATED THE ANNIVERSARY OF DIANA'S SEVENTEENTH BIRTHDAY with a quiet Saturday dinner. Auntie Julie helped my mother cook the foods my sister most loved: rice and *chana, dhal puri,* curried lamb, fried plantain. Icy January winds blew outside, and from the way the smell of spice hung heavy in our apartment, it was as if we were celebrating Christmas all over again.

We sat at the table and nibbled at the meal. After dinner, we drank tea from my mother's gold-rimmed yellow posy tea set.

My aunt pulled a small box out of her purse. "I wanted to do something special this time." She opened the lid and peeled back tissue paper. "With the turn of the century, it only seems right."

My mother narrowed her brows. "What did you do?"

Auntie Julie extracted a delicate little cherub figurine, pearlized as our teapot, painted with translucent hints of blue and green and pink. It sat cross-legged on a cloud. One wing was engraved with cursive letters. *Our Guardian Angel, Diana.*

My aunt held it out across the plate of digestive biscuits. "For you, Sister Bea."

My mother took the cherub in her narrow hands, one curled below and one curled above. Her eyes were glossy. "It's very pretty. Every day, I feel her next to me like when she was a baby at my hip." She looked to me with that sad smile and a couple of tears fell, brushing the peaks of her cheekbones before getting lost on her lap. "I had my two babies with me at my hip."

"What do you think, Brother Don?"

He could only nod at the figurine. It was a rare moment that he wasn't distracted by manila folders and true-crime books.

My father, my aunt, and my mother sat at the dining table, each of them with tears in their eyes.

I leaned over to take the cherub from my mother and walk it to the bookcase by the couch. The middle shelf was dedicated to the same school portrait of Diana that my father had used in the newspaper ad. White candles stood like pillars on either side of the frame, and my mother lit them every evening. I placed the cherub next to the candle on the right.

"It's really for you, 'Lisha," my mother said behind me. "Dee's *your* guardian angel. She takes care of you and she's helping you do so well in school, you know. You're making her proud."

I looked at the cherub's rosy cheeks and puckered cherry lips, the way its pupils were set to the side to shrewdly watch everything and nothing at the same time. I returned to the table, giving my mother's and aunt's shoulders a squeeze on the way to my chair. I tried to catch my father's attention but all I could see was the bridge of his nose pointed to his placemat.

My mother's fingers inched toward my elbow. I took her hand and cupped it like she had cupped the angel.

Paula had a brush in one hand and her palette in the other. She wore a splotched New York Knicks jersey, suitable only for painting. "A cherub? One of the naked ones?" She had raised the brush toward her canvas but lowered it again.

"Yeah." I sat on a stool behind her easel, facing the canvas's frayed edges and blanched wooden frame.

On Wednesday afternoons, instead of going straight home from school, I would tell my mother I was going to the library and walk over to Paula's building instead. Her apartment always had the leftover aroma of a cooked meal and she would usually be at the living room window, working on a canvas. This was the first time she had asked to paint me.

She pointed the bristles of her brush to a high shelf where a pastel porcelain bowl had been inserted between the books. "My friend two doors down made me go to an antiques show with her. The subway was shut down that day, so we had to bus it all the way down to the convention centre. I had to buy something."

"You picked that?"

She bent her nose to inspect her painting over her tipped-down lenses. "Of all the butt-ugly things that were there, it was the least offensive."

She peered at me, peered at her painting, and plucked a brush with fanned bristles from a jar on the floor. She dabbed it in a dollop of indigo paint and added a flurry of light wisps to the canvas. "I'll be done soon."

"Can I see?"

"Jeeze Louise. These things take time."

"But you go so *slow.*"

She did a few more flicks. "All right. Take a look."

I got up to stand behind her stool. She had painted a close-up of my earring.

Alisha's Jewel, read her signature calligraphy at the bottom. It was one of two dangling silver dice my aunt had given me for my birthday. She had led me up to her bedroom, leaving my parents in her living room to watch a sitcom. I had worn them every day after that.

"What do you think, Miss Sookermany?"

"It's nice."

She turned halfway to see me in the margin between her lens and eyeglass frame. "Don't be so enthusiastic, dammit."

"I mean, I love it and you're an amazing artist. What are you going to do with it?"

"Sell it for a million bucks and move to a mansion in Forest Hill. Black ladies on fixed incomes live there, don't they?"

My eyes went to the wall beside the window where a painting of teenage Ave in side profile hung. Wavy brown hair, round oval eyes, light skin with a sprinkle of freckles, plump, pink lips. "And when do you plan to show Ave her portrait?"

Paula's shoulders rose and dropped in an exhale. She looked at the palette in her hand, the overlapping smears of colour. "Stop the pushing. I told you, I'm too old for it."

My neck flushed hot. "Don't jump down my throat. I just think it's your best work, that's all."

I couldn't stand to have her upset with me, but I couldn't shake off the thought of their fallout either. What would cause Paula to never want to talk about her sister, let alone *to* her?

In spite of what Paula said, I knew Ave's absence wounded her. There were times I would be on her couch, thumbing through her old *National Geographic*s or softcover romances, and I would catch her, frozen like a mannequin with glassy eyes, as she sat working at her easel. Who else would she be so distracted by the thought of if not her sister?

She rubbed her brush in a circle over the paint on her palette, mixing all the colours into a murky blob. "Listen, I might need you to read a manuscript I'm working on, yeah? I still have a ways to go before I finish typing it out, but I think I'd like your thoughts when I'm done. Can you do that for me?"

I thought I would eventually read all the books on her shelves, but I had no idea she was writing things of her own too. "What's it about?"

"You have to learn some patience, Miss Sookermany. You'll find out soon enough."

The lettering on her back—EWING 33—stretched as she bent to dip her brush into the jar and churned the water into a cloudy grey-blue.

Auntie Julie bought us all tickets to see a stage production of *Saint Joan*. She wouldn't admit that she had bought them for my parents' wedding anniversary, since she knew they wouldn't want to go out alone, certainly not the way they used to when Diana and I were little and were dropped off at her townhouse for sleepovers.

The theatre's curved seats angled down to a minimalist set onstage. Several square platforms that I imagined would be broken apart and rolled back together were clumped there. When the show started overhead lights surged and flickered and effects pumped from the speakers, sounding like thunder and warring armies and angry mobs.

> *You think that life is nothing but not being stone dead. It is not the bread and water I fear: I can live on bread: when have I asked for more? It is no hardship to drink water if the water be clean. Bread has no sorrow for me, and water no affliction. But to shut me from the light of the sky and the sight of the fields and flowers; to chain my feet so that I can never again ride with the soldiers nor climb the hills; to make me breathe foul damp darkness, and keep from me everything that brings me back to the love of God [...] without these things I cannot live.*

My eyes wandered the theatre. Auntie Julie sat in a blouse and dress pants on one side of me, fixed on the action onstage. My father and mother had never really been interested in theatre. They sat on my other side in polite boredom, their attention wandering to the flashing lights, the black ceiling, and the backs of fellow audience members' heads.

At least they were making an effort. My father wore a suit and my mother wore a striped dress. Her hand was on the armrest next to his, so close they almost touched. My father's wedding band caught a point of light for a brief moment. It brightened and suddenly went out, triggering a strange throb in my chest. I held my breath to will the feeling away, looking down to the buttons on the front of my blouse.

A strike of lightning from above jolted us. The audience twitched and gasped and my father's hand shifted in reflex, swiping my mother's baby finger. A slight, accidental touch. My mother's hand retracted into her lap and I didn't see her use the armrest for the remainder of the night.

At intermission, my parents stepped up opposite staircases to get to the men's and women's washrooms. They left me and my aunt standing in the lobby, with other audience members who drank wine and jabbered in their heels and shawls.

"You want a snack?" asked my aunt. "Chips? Ice cream bar?"

"Um, ice cream, I guess." I let her lead me to the back of a line that snaked up to the refreshment stands.

She whistled. "Oooh, look at that. Want to try the chocolate caramel almond? I'm going to get that one."

"Sure."

"Do you think your mom and dad want one?"

The memory of the strawberry ice cream they had once shared at the parking lot fair entered my mind, my father holding the cone for my mother to lick. Pink tongue on pink sugar. "I don't think they're into sweets."

My aunt curled her hand around mine as it hung at the side of my body. "Your mom told me you have a lot of homework these days. She wasn't sure you'd be able to come with us. I'm glad you made it."

Her hair was tacked above her ears by slender tortoiseshell combs. The rest floated down her back. She was so beautiful, embodying the radiance my mother used to have. I missed it in my mother and wished I could accept my aunt's as substitute. *Sister beauty queens blossoming by the Essequibo River in Guyana, the land of the mighty Mount Roraima.*

I intertwined my fingers with hers. "I'm glad I came too."

When the play was over, we drove back to our apartment. My mother padded into the kitchen in her stocking feet and filled the kettle with tap water as the stovetop clicked and popped. My father removed his suit jacket and slung it over his arm, untangling the knot of his tie as he walked to their bedroom. The sky beyond the living room window was black and the city lights shined sharp like flakes of diamond.

I took my time taking off my dress shoes, extracting my arms from my windbreaker and threading it over a hanger. When my sister was alive, things had been strewn in that closet every which way. Now the three of us somehow kept it in good order. Our shoes were lined on the racks with heels and toes set together, mittens and scarves and hats were neatly stored in baskets on the top shelf, and our jackets hung straight. Diana's things were still mixed in with the rest.

I passed my mother who was unhooking her earrings and laying them on the kitchen counter. I went down the hallway and into the bathroom, shutting the door and breathing air still damp from the three showers taken earlier. I pressed my ear to the wall that separated the bathroom from my parents' bedroom.

"We were out," my father said. "I'm sorry I'm calling so late."

It was the same call he made every day to the private detective, the one I often listened in on through the wall.

"Okay," he said, quieter, "I see."

A pause, some rustling.

"But they didn't ask me those things. They have to, don't they? Due diligence?" He waited for the answer but I could hear him drawing breaths, battling the impulse to interject. "No. I want you to keep looking. They didn't do what they were supposed to. They botched it." The discussion ended almost as quickly as it had begun.

Months back I had eavesdropped on longer conversations. I heard my father speak of the records the private detective accessed, the leads and suspects the police pursued and abandoned, the clashing opinions of the coroner's office over the hyoid bone, intact but fused in a way that was inconsistent with my sister's age, and the lack of soft tissue that had made any conclusions about the cause of death so difficult. He referred to the place in Crothers Woods where my sister's remains had been found, buried under thin soil to be disturbed by the elements and wildlife. The other girls, the unidentified one who was discovered a decade ago, and Kaila Hedgebrook, the one found more recently, hadn't been buried. They had both been tossed into the Don Valley, their arms and legs askew.

With my ear still to the wall, I looked at the mirror above the sink and connected with my own eyes. *They don't know about the man,* I thought. I reached to flush the toilet before walking across the hall to my bedroom to change into my pyjamas, conscious of my sister's diary still hidden in my closet.

I returned to the living room. My mother and father were at the table drinking tea. My mother stared into the night beyond the apartment window, her hands curled around her mug on the table. My father sat across from her and read the yellowing paperback pages of *Suburban Slaughter: The John J. Millman Files.*

I thought of how my father had once been the young man who wooed a tropical beauty queen. It was difficult to imagine how my parents used to be, the touching and hugging and linking arms, the uncomplicated romance of their daily lives. I eased a chair back from the table and joined their silence. I poured tea into the empty mug my mother had set out for me. I drank it black, strong as the yearning I felt inside.

✿

Years back, Auntie Julie had told me and Diana the mythology of my parents' first meeting.

> *Your father borrowed his friend's old motorcycle to ride into the city of Georgetown on a bright blue June day. He made it to the windy seawall before the engine started smoking, but he was young, cocky, and too proud to stop.*

Your mother and me were crossing the road on our way out of Stabroek Market when Donald turned down and barrelled toward us, struggling to get his brakes to work. I froze on my feet! Sister Bea pushed me out of the way and your father swerved to miss us both. He was hurled into the long grass and the bike crashed into a barrel-trunked palm tree.

Your mother rushed over to see if he was still alive. She knelt beside him and placed her hand on his beating heart. It was the first time they saw each other—the most beautiful woman in Guyana gazing into the eyes of Guyana's most handsome man.

When I returned to school on Monday, my civics teacher marked the start of ten minutes and my classmates began scribbling through the career quiz.

Of the following assignments, which do you prefer?
a. Math problems. b. Writing a book review.
c. Sketching a nature scene.

How do you type a sentence?
a. I plan it out and then write it down. b. I put words on the page and go back to add and take out. c. I don't type at all.

How would you prepare for your ideal vacation?
a. Spin a globe and go where my finger lands.
b. Consider the places I want to go, count my money, and select an affordable destination. c. I hate travelling.

I was certain that I wasn't like the other students at my school. I couldn't trust my instincts. I worked through the quiz as I'd done everything since Diana disappeared: by making myself into someone else. When the teacher returned our printed results, my career fortunes were exactly as I had anticipated. *Engineer. Accountant or actuary. Computer programmer. Lawyer.*

The criminal code my father had given to me was still on my dresser, now covered in dust, but I knew what I had to do. I would take the good marks I was imitating my sister to achieve and I would put them into getting into university and working to become a lawyer. I would not leave her case to police detectives or the private investigator my father dogged like a spurned lover. I would discover what happened to her and exactly how the police had failed my family in their investigation. I would seek and find an answer and return to my parents and aunt some measure of the peace I had stolen.

CHAPTER 24

1949

PAULA NEARED THE END OF THE DRIVEWAY. *N.S. HOME FOR COLORED CHILDREN* read the lettering on the iron archway that opened out to the road.

Her legs stopped moving. She stood on the gravel with a small canvas bag in her hand, cracked, stained farm boots on her feet. Blood pulsed in her neck and her muscles felt weak.

She turned back to look at the home at the top of the slope, with its brown shingles and white-framed windows. The structure was backlit by the rising sun. Crows perched like black specks on the roof's highest peak. The surrounding trees were in limbo, caught between summer and fall. Half of the leaves were green; the other half had yellowed.

Granny had called Paula into her office a few weeks before, days from her eighteenth birthday. She had stood at the centre of the room and pulled a letter from the front pocket of her dress. "I asked them to track your mother," she said, her helmet hair freshly slicked. She had dabbed peachy-pink lipstick on her mouth that day and it made her speak with a pucker. "Do you understand what it says?"

Paula took and unfolded the paper. She couldn't read much but she did recognize three bolded words near the top. *Meredith Benton. Deceased.*

"It says your mother died. Happened a few months ago. She drank herself into oblivion, went to bed, and didn't wake up. You know, your mother didn't have a cent to her name so she made a habit of selling her body. Bet she didn't even know who your and Ave's fathers were. She was just another girl who became a drunkard and a whore."

Granny's eyes were like slits behind her glasses, but if she were awaiting a reaction, she didn't get one. Paula felt nothing. She was numb save for the sudden awesome mass of her legs and arms.

Paula passed the letter back to Granny and shoved her hands into the pockets of her overalls. "Anything else?"

"Stay and work the farm. Ave's gone to the foster home and your mother's gone for good. There's no one to run to. What are you going to do with yourself out there?"

"I'll figure it out."

"Jobs for a girl like you, they don't exist. Not on this side of the ocean. You can't cook or mind children and you don't look the part either. Who's going to hire you?" Granny shook her head. "You girls don't respond to sense. You get to this age and start dreaming silly things about romance. It's a man you're putting your hopes on, isn't it?"

"No," Paula answered.

She harrumphed. "Men like the one you're dreaming of don't exist. They don't have the stones to rescue anybody, let alone a woman." She tossed the letter onto her desk and inspected her fingernails, each one stubby and buffed to a shine. "Even if they were out there, I doubt they'd spend time barking up *your* tree."

✿

Paula watched as a crow on the home's rooftop woke to throw throaty squawks. They pealed over the morning's chilly silence. She tugged the collar of her coat together; the wool of it itched her neck. If her feet wouldn't find the gumption to take her away, she decided she shouldn't trust them. She waited at the gate until a bumbling pickup appeared in the distance, and hoped it would be willing to take her as far as it was going.

Paula crossed the Bay and then left Nova Scotia altogether to find work. She bunked in a tiny room in Saint John, New Brunswick, saving as much as she could from the odd jobs and manual labour, but it wasn't enough. She took a bus to Montreal and got a job at a dressmaker's shop doing hems and mending zippers and adjusting seams.

The foster home isn't easy, wrote Ave. *Things aren't much better than before. Did you hear from our mother?*

Paula asked an elderly neighbour to help her read the letters and write her sister back. *I haven't,* Paula responded, *but I promise I'll come for you.*

✿

Five years passed and Paula saved enough to go back to Nova Scotia. She was twenty-three. It was the very week of her sister's eighteenth birthday.

But Ave wasn't at the foster home—or any of the places Paula thought she might go—not anywhere around Dartmouth or Halifax. Paula scoured the lower part of the province for weeks, frantic to find her sister. *Pretty girl with a pretty voice; have you seen her? If you saw her, you would remember....*

Someone told Paula about the rooming houses in Sydney, a collection of narrow, dilapidated buildings with floors stacked upon floors.

Unmarried girls lived in them, all the young women who worked in the shops and eateries that clung to the steel plants like mussels on the hulls of ships. Breathing the ocean salt that blew over the city, Paula arrived at a crumbling redbrick house with a street door that hung loose on its hinges. She ascended five crooked flights.

A white woman greeted her at the apartment door, unsmiling and standing to block the way inside. Her damp hair had been handled into snake-like twists pinned tight to her scalp. A skeletal Medusa.

"I got a Black girl here that says she knows you," she said behind her, bracing her elbow on the doorknob and turning into the room to speak. Her ratty slip exposed two dark areolas and a triangle of pubic hair. "Wanna talk to her?"

She stepped aside and swung the door wide. Ave sat cross-legged on a blanket on the floor. Beside her was a short stack of magazines, a box of saltines, and a small pile of clothes, on top of which was the hairbrush Granny had given her—the one Paula used to work through her curls at night, sitting behind her on her dormitory bed.

"She telling the truth, sweetie pie?" Ave's roommate cooed strangely.

At first Ave looked at her sister blankly. Her body was thin under a blue knitted cardigan. Then she offered a bashful smile. She was more beautiful than Paula remembered with her almond eyes and apple cheeks. But Paula noticed an unfamiliar stoniness about her too.

She wanted to scoop Ave into her arms. *Where on God's green earth have you been?* she wanted to ask. *I've been searching everywhere. Don't you know what you did to me, leaving without a word like that?*

"Hello, Ave," Paula said instead, clasping her hands in front of her.

Ave tightened her sweater around her torso and hugged herself close. "Hi."

"How have you—you've been okay?"

She nodded.

"I came back to get you. I got worried when I couldn't find you."

"Sorry. I meant to write."

"That's okay. I'm just glad to see you now."

"Me too."

But Ave stayed where she sat so Paula stayed where she stood, nervous that even a twitch might somehow scare her sister off.

There was no hug or enthusiastic chatter, nothing like what Paula had imagined would happen when they found each other again. *Paw, Paw, Paw!* Why would things have changed between them? She couldn't believe that the time she and Ave had spent apart would mean anything compared to the time they'd been together. Faith in their bond was what had brought her back to Nova Scotia, what had always kept her going. She wanted them to start over again.

Ave bit the insides of her cheeks and looked to her pleated-skirt lap, contemplating something. The roommate stepped down the hallway away from the room, slapping her bare feet on the floorboards.

Paula realized that Ave hadn't left the foster home to travel here, to the northern edge of the province where rock nosedived into the sea, intending that her sister should find her. Perhaps Ave's faith in their bond was not what Paula had thought.

CHAPTER 25

THE STAIRS LEADING OUT OF THE QUEEN SUBWAY STATION REEKED OF URINE. I stepped up the tiled stairwell breathing through my mouth and met a cloudy, drizzling March sky. I yanked the hood of my jacket over my head and heard the water drops land on the fabric.

Afternoon classes for grade ten students had been cancelled because we were supposed to attend a special conference at another high school. After lunch, I followed the crowd of students on their way out of the door, but I breezed past the parked line of yellow busses, stealing away with my coat and bag.

I had overheard classmates telling each other tales of going downtown to sneak into bars and clubs, but this was the first time I was going into the heart of the city on my own. The roads were swamped with cars and taxis. A hatchback with a bright blue paint job and a shattered windshield was hooked to a tow truck decorated by Sikh *khandas*. The truck hissed and puffed to lift the car onto its rear tires and vehicles trapped behind honked and inched forward.

I walked east along Queen Street, retracing the path I had heard my father discuss with the police detective. *Two hikers?* my father had asked. *It was cold that week. Why were they hiking?* Whatever their reasons, the pair of hikers had walked from Queen Street into the Lower Don River Trail, working their way north through the icy Don Valley. They made it all the way to Crothers Woods where they spotted the tip of one of my sister's dress shoes protruding from a melting cover of snow, just enough gloss left on them to catch a streak of sun breaking through the sky.

I felt a shiver radiate down my spine and ribs. I clutched the printout of the map folded in my pocket. Glass buildings were fogged and skyscrapers were stained by long swaths of water. Two men sitting on the sidewalk held pieces of cardboard over their matted hair. They sat side by side but looked off in opposite directions. They didn't seem like companions.

A streetcar lumbered by and squealed to a stop ahead of me. People assembled around it, probably going home from their jobs. They were expressionless as they waited to board, edging up to the doors impatiently. I thought of my father commuting home from the insurance brokerage every weeknight for years. I pictured him in his overcoat, one hand on his briefcase and the other holding onto the streetcar's overhead pole.

I kept walking. Tall buildings made way for squat storefronts, thrift stores, and empty restaurants, then soup kitchens, shelters, and drop-ins. I passed a young man wearing a puffy parka and gripping a chain attached to a scarred pitbull. It panted and strove forward on its knobby brown paws, hardly concerned about the weather, tugging its owner along. An elderly woman with a heap of mismatched grocery bags sat on a park bench, holding a leopard-print umbrella over her head.

I waited at a crosswalk where sex workers stood around in small groups. They wore wool hats and scarves and miniskirts. One woman wore silver hot pants and a short, sequined jacket. She held a lipstick-stained cigarette between her fingers and she looked at me and looked away, bouncing her weight from one leg to the other to warm up. Everybody on this side of the city seemed tired, and in that weariness, I felt some camaraderie.

I passed a strip club decorated by larger-than-life posters of women in lingerie. They looked sleepy and bored and they wore bras over impossibly large breasts. I remembered my family driving by the same place years ago, my parents in front, me and Diana in the back. I had to turn away from those poster women because I knew my mother wouldn't approve of me studying them.

"Hello, ladies," I said under my breath this time, looking directly at the sun-faded images, "it's been too long."

I came to a bridge that passed over the highway and I pulled out my printed map of the trail, standing in front of a convenience store with an old barber pole mounted to the brick. The pole's ribbon was bright red and blue but its glass was cracked and its metal cap was almost entirely eaten by rust. The street carried on but I saw the turning point I was searching for: a steep, unmarked laneway that snaked down from the street. It would lead me to the maze of footpaths the hikers had taken through the Don Valley.

Going down the laneway my knees and ankles ached. At the entrance to the ravine a clump of knotted grocery bags had been dumped and gave off a sweet, putrefying odour. Next to them lay a smatter of dog feces and an unrolled condom.

The sky was darkening. The path, littered by cigarette stubs and shattered beer bottles, led me to an underpass where a pair of scraggly men were taking cover. They leaned against the concrete under a giant spray-painted skull with teeth that were rounded like tombstones. In the ravine, the graffiti wasn't intricate, colourful, and planned, like the murals up on street level. The tags were chaotic and hasty and they bled over each other, scrawled in single colours.

What a waste of a canvas, I imagined Paula would complain if she saw it. *You should see what I could paint with that kind of space, yeah?*

One of the men gave his joint to the other, even though it was burned down to a nub. The man who had handed over his weed scrutinized me as I approached, scratching his chin with his free hand. I could hear his stubble. The one who received the joint held it out to watch it smoke. He sniffed noisily and hacked and spit out at his feet whatever he had dislodged. I passed them, one man eyeing me and one man eyeing the ejected fluid on the ground.

I followed the trail as it snaked through the thicket in the direction of the river. I walked for over an hour to arrive at Crothers Woods. My jeans and runners were smeared with mud. I followed my map to take one of the smaller paths that branched off from the main one and all of a sudden I was closed in by bush and dense trees. The eerie whistle of a train sounded over the rumble of cars on the highway.

I stepped up onto a large, fallen tree trunk. Branches scratched at my arms. Through a clearing in the trees, I saw the grey outlines of downtown skyscrapers far off in the mist.

The smell of damp earth hung in the air. I could tell that people looking for a place to sleep didn't come out this far. The ground was clean, devoid of plastic bags and bottles and old clothes. A bird cried above my head and I spotted black feathers nestled between the branches of a pine tree. *My witnesses, the crows,* I thought. *Always with me.*

The ground in front of me sloped down into layers of brush and decaying trunks. Each descending step was perilous. I set my heel on something slippery and my foot skidded. I managed to grab onto a branch before I tumbled down. How had those hikers made it through?

The sound of my own exhalation was amplified within the bubble of my hood. My mother would never have allowed me to come to this place on my own. *Diana, go with your sister and stay close to her, understand? Don't fret. Don't you know the younger always has to be at the side of the older? I had to take care of Julie too.* But my mother and aunt never acted as if anyone had had to force them to stick together.

I worried about the dulling effect of the rain on my coat. Would I hear it if someone were to come up behind me? Would I notice if a man were to speak my name?

I had convinced myself I wanted to retrace the steps of the hikers and uncover clues the police hadn't found and my father couldn't find, even with his own private detective. Maybe they cared too little or too much to pay such close attention. But when I reached the scant clearing circled on my map, the only spot where three large rocks protruded out of the dirt, I understood the real reason for my expedition.

I had listened to my father as he talked with the detective about that loose triangle of boulders around which Diana's bones and clothes had been scattered.

I rested my hand on the biggest rock, black with grey flecks, and I felt its cold graininess.

Did it hurt? I had asked Paula.

In all kinds of ways, she had answered. And, somehow, I knew she understood a truth about what happened to my sister better than my mother or father or aunt did. That she understood more than I had the strength to contemplate myself.

My eyes curved around the big rock's surface. I lay my body over it, pressing my belly against the stone, and my knees gave away. The ground was all mud but Diana had been there and part of her was still there. I placed my palm on the ground and let my fingers curl in, digging into the wet soil, feeling it under my fingernails.

What did you think you'd find? I thought.

Decomposition had happened long ago; her body had already melted into the landscape. I still didn't understand how I could have lost someone so important so easily. I had expected more by coming here, maybe some small sensation in my body, a tingle or a quiver to prove Diana had been here.

But I felt nothing but the flat, meaningless stillness of the forest. It made me feel more alone than ever.

It should have been me.

I eased my body down to the ground. I tried to put myself in her place, my head lower on the slope than my feet, my limbs straight against the sides of my body and my eyes staring up at the sky. Falling rain wet my face. Drops of water rolled into my hood and chilled my neck and ears. Blood pooled in my skull and the cold penetrated my runners and socks and infected my toes and licked the back of my legs.

My guts gurgled. I was as close as I had ever been to what had happened to my sister, but I still couldn't truly understand what she had gone through. I realized I wouldn't discover it like this, by retracing old steps and surveying abandoned crime scenes.

A ripple of lightning skimmed the clouds and a rumble followed, as if the sky had a hungry belly. Crows shrieked in the branches above.

CHAPTER 26

1954

AVE SAT ACROSS FROM PAULA ON THE CAFÉ PATIO ON PLACE JACQUES-Cartier. A plate of coffee cake and an espresso sat untouched in front of each of them.

"I knew you would react like this," Ave said. Under her old blue cardigan she wore the white-and-pink dress with flared chiffon that Paula had sewn for her at the dressmaker's shop as an apprentice couturière and a pink velvet hat to match.

"You thought I'd be tickled to find out you're pregnant?" Paula answered. "I'm supposed to be thrilled that you're one of those women now?"

Neighbouring patrons lifted their heads from their teacups and tarts.

"Don't say that. *Those women*. It's demeaning." Ave picked up her fork and stabbed at the crumbling square of coffee cake, missing the mark one, two, three times before putting it back down.

Wind gusted. Paula slapped her hand to the top of her wide-brimmed hat to keep it in place. In Montreal, sunlight hit the shiny flecks in the pavement and twinkled on the hoods of parked cars. The city was so bustling and pretty that it drew Paula outside at every opportunity, attracting her down its cobblestone paths and along its riversides. But now the brightness of the afternoon and the streaming city sun on her skin seemed too sharp and hot.

"Why'd you wait this long?" She let out a hard exhale and shoved her plate of cake away. "*Shit*. This is the last thing you need."

Ave's back went straight. "How would *you* know what I need?"

More people turned to watch them. These looks were not the same as the stares that seemed to follow Ave through the city, lingering on her curls and soft caramel skin. Now that the only two Black women in Place Jacques-Cartier were creating a scene, the ogling had become glares accompanied by pointed harrumphs.

"So what?" Paula asked. "You're going to go through with it?"

"Yes."

"Then you've damn well ruined yourself."

"I don't look at it that way."

"You're a stupid girl."

Flustered, Ave brushed her hand over her tummy. Only then did Paula properly follow its curve underneath the cardigan. They had been living together in her apartment for two weeks, since they had left Cape Breton, but she hadn't let herself recognize the signs.

"I shouldn't have said a word to you," Ave huffed.

"I would have found out soon enough."

"I would have left by then."

But Paula had thought that her sister would stay with her. At least she wanted her to. Pride would not allow her to admit to it anymore. "Where do you plan on going? Back to Nova Scotia? You think you'll be satisfied as a waitress forever? Don't you want a better life? A career, even?"

She shrugged. "None of your business what I do."

But Paula knew exactly what Ave wanted. Her sister would sing in the apartment's slim bathroom, trilling under the flow of water from the showerhead. Ave would practice her notes every morning, her scales and runs with crescendos and cadences. Paula listened to the luminous tone as she fretted over greasy eggs and pancakes on the stovetop. Ave's voice was drenched in young hope. It travelled through the walls and took the breath right out of Paula.

Paula coughed a sour laugh. "You think you'll be a star, don't you? You think someone has a place waiting for you. Where? New York, Los Angeles? London? *Paris?* World tours with a newborn baby! You'll be the first unwed mother to make a breakthrough!"

Ave's cheeks blazed red. She was self-conscious, turning side to side to see people watching.

But a throb in Paula's brain egged her on, just like Granny's vengeful voice urging her to pummel that boy in the forest. *Teach 'em good!* She would shatter ribs, because she never did have the ability to soothe the ache she felt in her own bones. "Your appetite for attention. You fancy any horny bastard who shows you the slightest bit of interest, even those snakes and snails back home." She straightened in her chair with theatric verve. "I hate break it to you, but men like the one you're praying for don't exist."

"Paula! Keep your damned voice down!"

The balding waiter who had first led them to their table with a nervy, elongated face started weaving through the tables to get to theirs. That some brave soul was going to do something about the problem of Paula and Ave triggered a stir across the patio. The wind picked up, nearly claiming both of their hats.

"You think you'll become a sensation and the world will welcome you, rags to riches? It doesn't matter that you can sing. You're just a rat to them, a smear of brown shit under their heels—"

"Paula!"

"I didn't teach you to play the fool. I don't know who you are anymore."

Ave pushed out an angry chortle. "A girl with a jealous sister? Isn't that how it's always been?"

Paula laughed back. "Think that way if it makes you feel better. Just don't look to me when the dream doesn't come true. And while you're at it, rule your mother out too."

"What?"

"She put herself to death with the bottle."

Ave's face slackened with confusion. "How do you know that?"

"Granny told me. She didn't bother sharing the news with you. Wouldn't want to upset prissy Miss Ave."

"Are you making this up?"

"Not at all. In fact, when our mother came to see us a few years before, she looked half dead as it was. Can't be surprised she went to her grave a drunk." Paula turned her head to lock onto the alarmed eyes of a woman at the next table over. "Goes like that in some families, yeah?"

The woman stuffed her chin into a fussy fur collar and looked away.

"You're telling me that our mother came to see us," repeated Ave, this time to her belly, "and then she died, and you didn't tell me a thing about it? Why would you do that?"

Only then did Paula realize what she had done. All those years, all that hope and agony her sister had carried for their mother.

Ave pushed her chair back and it scraped loudly against the patio stones. She caught her balance with one hand on the table and Paula couldn't believe that she hadn't noticed her slow, deliberate motions before.

The waiter edged ever closer to their table, but it wasn't his disapproval or the irritation of the other patrons that caused dismay to wash through Paula's body. It was the glaze of tears in Ave's eyes.

Paula was suddenly sapped of energy. "Dear Lord, I didn't mean to... I don't know why—"

"How could you?"

"I just—"

"You're a damn bully. You kept it from me to control me. To keep me under your thumb."

"That's not true."

"You almost killed that boy Jerry and now you're killing me. You happy?"

"God, Ave, I'm sorry."

Paula watched her sister tuck the corners of her sweater across her body and grasp the handle of her handbag, then turn and push through the clattering metal gate and walk away, her shoes clicking on the cobblestone street. The layers of her pink-and-white skirt ruffled in the wind.

Paula covered her face with her hands.

"Madame, you have to leave now, too," the waiter whispered in unsteady English from beside her chair. "*Vous n'avez pas le choix*. Okay?"

Paula knew Ave would leave her and not look back. She would have her baby and become the mother she'd never had—that she had never been given the chance to know. Paula wouldn't fetter her sister anymore, and time would only wrench wider the fissure between them.

CHAPTER 27

BY THE MIDDLE OF GRADE ELEVEN, I HAD ALREADY BEGUN EXPLORING universities and asking for their promotional packages. I read through the course calendars and looked at the pre-law school options at the University of Toronto and York, Queens and UBC, even Yale and Cornell. When my mother noticed I was receiving mail from campuses outside the city, she confronted me.

"There are good universities right here, close to us," she said, opening and closing the drawers in her bedroom on a pretend-search for something. "And why are you worrying about this so early?"

I sat on my parents' bed in pyjamas and slippers with the latest mail I had received, a shiny red folder from McGill University. "I know I'll have a better chance at getting into a law program if I apply far away. There's less competition. I'll be eighteen by then anyway, and everyone at school is going away for university."

But I knew time didn't move for my mother as it did for me. And she didn't care about what other people did.

"Your grades are so good you'll be accepted somewhere right here. It's too far and you're too young for it."

"McGill's only a five-hour drive and it'll be cheaper than living downtown—"

"Downtown!" She had taken up the ends of her robe's sash for tying but dropped them both. One end dangled at her knee and the other swept the carpet. The whole robe drooped open, exposing her long black nightie underneath. "We're moving to a brand new house and you want to pay a pound and a crown to move downtown?" The knotted cords of her neck showed under her skin. "It's dirty and crowded."

Her words looped in my ear—*pound and a crown to move downtown, pound and a crown to move downtown.* Somewhere along the way my parents had transformed into motivated employees, my mother working full-time and replacing most of the young part-time receptionists at her dental office and my father working extra hours to get promoted to the role of office manager at his insurance company. He didn't complain about the brokerage boys anymore. My parents were nearer than ever to their goal of home ownership. They'd been squirrelling away a down payment for a duplex in Brampton, a suburb a half-hour drive west of our neighbourhood. Instead of blocks and blocks of mismatched apartment buildings and townhomes and houses, Brampton had roads that swirled through well-planned single-family housing developments, some too new to have names.

I extracted from the folder a spreadsheet of my projections. "I priced everything. If I live downtown, I'll have to get a part-time job and share a place with a roommate. If I go to McGill, almost everything would get covered by my student loan—food, dorm, and tuition—and I think I might even be eligible for a scholarship."

I aimed the paper her way but she refused to look.

"No, 'Lisha. You'll have a nice new room in our new house."

By now, my father stood in the doorway, his reading glasses still on his face, his robe pulled over his pyjamas and knotted at the waist. He probably hadn't heard the details of our conversation from the living room, but there'd been enough flutter and flux in our voices to attract his attention. "Bea, we should look into it."

Her lids lowered. "She's too young."

"A lot of students live at school. There'll be people around all the time."

"They aren't us." She returned to her drawer of makeup tubes and pots, plucking out a lipstick and squinting at the sticker. "Expired," she murmured to herself and kissed her teeth. But she still tossed it back into the drawer.

I watched her root around her makeup drawer and felt my father's eyes on me. He nodded, just a little and just once, his glasses alight with the reflection from the lamp on the dresser. *Leave it to me,* the gesture said.

I had to push my lips together and lower my head to mask my smile.

Since the beginning of grade eleven, my father came to my room most nights, where I studied at my desk while my mother cooked dinner. He asked if I could join them to eat at the table, his suit and tie turning the invitation into a formal one, and I said yes even though I was never hungry.

After dinner, the two of us cleared the dishes. He washed and I dried, and we both took care not to clang the plates to make my mother come back out of the bedroom. When my eyes felt too dry and sandy for homework he sat beside me on the couch, silent as I sifted through the channels with one of those books about the law I always borrowed from the library on my lap. When I asked what he wanted to watch, he shrugged and lifted his eyebrows, his lips arched downwards.

Whatever you want, I took it to mean.

His manila folders and true-crime books remained untouched for longer and longer spans until, one day, they disappeared from the living room altogether. I discovered them in a stack at the bottom of his bedroom closet while putting away clean laundry. As for the private detective, my father kept him on retainer but they now spoke to each other weekly, not every evening. The detective hadn't found any new leads and when I finally mustered the bravery to look in one my father's folders, I could see the disappointment that dripped from every page. *Serial killer, three murders, possibly more.... Known offender or single-instance? No reoffending? Imprisonment, institutionalization, deceased? Unclear. Uncertain. Lack of physical evidence.*

Reading his neat British West Indies cursive made my lungs feel punctured. I tucked his folders back into their place. All those hours he had spent reading through records and articles at the library, all those late nights highlighting and dog-earing books, had amounted to little more than suppositions.

I'll find a way to figure out what you couldn't, I thought. *I promise.*

❀

Auntie Julie came for dinner on Saturday evening. My mother had made pepperpot with egg bread to sop up the tangy cassareep sauce. After we ate, my mother put tea and biscuits on the coffee table and used a barbeque lighter to light the candles around Diana's portrait. There were many candles now. Most were melted too low to fish out their wicks, but my mother wouldn't throw them away. She just pushed the old ones to the back and the sides of the shelf and promoted the taller ones to stand close to my sister's face.

"Dim the lights, Sister Bea," my aunt said, kneeling at the stereo under the television. "I found something when I cleaned the garage this morning."

My mother complied and sat on the couch. Auntie Julie pushed a cassette tape into the deck and turned the volume up. The static sounded like rain. She took her place on the armrest next to my mother.

"Welcome, ladies and gentlemen," a young child spoke after a clunky pop.

"And what is your name?" my aunt's voice asked.

"Diana Maria Sookermany."

My mother closed her eyes and dropped her head, taking in every syllable.

"Such a pretty name. Who gave it to you?"

"Mommy-Daddy."

"And what age did you turn today?"

"Three and a half!"

"Just three, Dee," my mother's voice came from somewhere in the background, sounding clean and high. I heard the echoey gurgles of an infant and the skin at the back of my neck instantly heated.

My father was standing in the space between the living and dining rooms in his suit pants, dress shirt, and slippers. "I forgot you did this, Julie."

"You weren't home that day," my mother answered. She opened her eyes to watch the stereo.

"What will you be singing, Miss Diana Maria Sookermany who is three years old, almost three and a half?" Auntie Julie asked from the speakers.

"Jingle Bells, Batman Smells. Robin laid an egg."

"Oh, do something nicer."

"'Itsy Bitsy Spider.'"

Beside each other my mother and aunt, their hair in buns, listened to my sister's toneless toddler performance and both started to sniffle. I walked the plate of Fruit Crème Peek Freans from the coffee table to the kitchen and shuffled through the pantry for the box. On the cassette tape, Diana started singing another verse, and my far-off baby squeaks turned into squeals as my young mother and aunt hushed and clucked.

Why did I need all that attention? I thought. *Why couldn't I just let my sister sing?* I wanted to upend the shelves, pelt the cereal and malt powder and cream of wheat onto the floor, but I smelled my father's cologne coming closer.

"What's wrong?" he asked, standing next to me.

"Mom put these cookies out but she's not eating them." I found the box at the back of the pantry and undid its flaps, transferring my irritation to my mother. "She brings them out but only ever wants digestives, and no one even has dessert anyway so they just sit there and get stale. I'm going to put out the ones she likes and maybe she'll eat something tonight. She had two bites of pepperpot, *two bites*. I watched her the whole time. She gets mad when we aren't hungry but she hardly eats a thing herself." I began slotting the biscuits back into the tray, one by one. "Queen Bea doesn't eat sweet cookies."

I startled myself. I hadn't thought of my sister's nickname for our mother for a long time and I had never repeated it to anyone. I continued repackaging the cookies, hoping my father hadn't noticed.

His fingers prowled to the lip of the serving plate and stole a cookie. "Hmm," he replied under his breath, crunching, "that sounds about right."

The resurfacing of his old playfulness, just a glimmer of it, puzzled and thrilled me.

✿

A few weeks later, my mother called for me from her bedroom. "Bring the thing."

I knew exactly what she meant.

She was preparing to meet Auntie Julie for another tour of the new duplex—she wouldn't buy anything her sister didn't approve of. Through the dresser mirror, she watched me place the red folder on her nightstand.

"Why couldn't you go to law school here?" she asked in that tired, just-a-question way. "And you're thinking about all this too early. I don't understand." She wore a black slip I had forgotten about and bent toward the mirror to work mascara onto her eyelashes. For the first time in a long while she was dressing up the way she used to, though pressed powder and rouge couldn't revive the warm hue that once lived under her cheeks.

I stepped close to her and made her turn around, brushed a couple of stray hairs from her bare shoulder. "You're pretty."

She smiled, the pancake powder an uneven cover for her nose and chin. Her hands weren't as steady with the makeup as they used to be. "Answer me, *nah man*."

If I stayed with my parents, I knew I would take their lead as I had always done. I would build a new life as a good and obedient girl in a suburban home with fresh paint and brown bricks, far from my childhood and our cluster of apartments. But it wouldn't change what happened to Diana. It wouldn't help me undo the harm I had done to my family.

"It'll be all right," I said. "We'll talk on the phone every day."

"It's not the same." She said it as a fact, no pleading.

"I know."

I didn't want to struggle with tears so I left her bedroom to take refuge in mine.

✿

On the night my parents were to sign for the house, my father returned from work with the knot of his tie slackened. My mother was waiting on the couch with her jacket on, her eyelids heavy with liner and her knees pushed together under her skirt. He stood at the apartment door as she got up to put on her shoes. The two of them left for the real estate office without saying a word to each other.

I intended to work on my book report for *A Midsummer Night's Dream*, but a half-hour passed and the page was still on the desk in front of me, blank. My black tea sat untouched, losing steam and staining a ring on the inner curve of the mug. Cardboard boxes had sprung up all over the apartment, and I kept looking to the ones on my bedroom floor, taped tight and holding nearly everything I owned. *Alisha room, Alisha room, Alisha room,* each read in messy marker.

I pushed out of my chair and walked to Diana's bedroom. My parents hadn't said anything but I knew they needed me to pack her things the way I had packed my own room. I didn't resent them for it. I wanted them to be free of the task they had dreaded for over three years. I would throw away most of Diana's things and store the remainder in a box for the attic, a place we would hardly have to visit.

I pulled a drawer from the dresser and turned it over on the bed that was still made up with sheets and blankets and pillowcases. Costume jewelry, earrings and necklaces, and a bracelet of glossy, multicoloured beads spilled out.

The jellybean bracelet. Auntie Julie told us she had bought it when she and my mother took us to the Kmart—me teething and crying, and Diana a precocious toddler. They didn't notice Diana pulling the bracelet from the rack to chew on it like candy and coat it with her saliva. My aunt had no choice but to face the irritated clerk and buy it.

The sight of the bracelet burdened me. I stuffed it into the back pocket of my jeans. I knew we would uncover more relics, even after the packing was done, even after Diana's photos and favourite things were locked in a box. Diana was frozen in time. She would always be a self-assured fifteen-year-old dreaming of medical school, no matter where we lived or what objects we surrounded ourselves with or threw away.

I sat on her bed, wondering how it was that I had made it through, how I was the one growing into the new sensations inside of me. My grieved mother, my stunted father, my aunt who called me *babe*—none of them seemed to notice I was growing up. Even Paula tried to deny it, refusing to acknowledge the attention I got from the group of young men at the Jane and Finch Community Caribana Picnic she had asked me to volunteer at with her. Kids danced around in homemade headdresses, jumping and waving tea towels over their heads, and the men stood by the amplifiers, bare-chested and smirking my way as I helped Paula at the food tables.

Dogs sniffing for a bone, I heard her mutter under her breath as she rooted through the condiment bottles. She didn't know that my flushed face was an act. It was how adults expected me to respond. They didn't know me at all.

Walking to the mirror behind my sister's door, I felt the outline of her jellybean bracelet against my right buttock. Diana had been the real complement to my aunt and mother, already rivalling their beauty. *Pretty girls, slim and nice-nice and fair skin!* I didn't do much with my hair and my lips were flat, but I had still somehow attained what had been starting in my sister, a ripening I could deny all I wanted but men noticed.

I felt a scurry in my groin, a burrowing pain-pleasure, a kicking back of the layers. *What is this?* I thought. I put my palm on my stomach, pressed down to smooth it out and watched the growing grimace on my face.

I left my sister's bedroom, put my sneakers on, and left our apartment without locking the door behind me. I went to the ground floor and pushed past the front doors to walk into the night. It was cooler than it should have been at that time of year, and foggy. My breath steamed in front of me as I left my familiar block, my feet moving faster and faster. I slipped in and out of the orange street light beams along Jane Street feeling fuelled by something other than blood and air. I had been punched awake by that burrowing feeling in my groin that was now looping its way through me again and again like it never had before.

Fifteen, I thought, *same age as Diana. I need to know.*

I hadn't taken a jacket. My sweatshirt, grey and only ever worn indoors, felt heavy and cold on my body. The neighbourhood was unusually still. I kept thinking that there should have been more horn-honking, more parked cars, and more people hanging around the bus shelters and going in and out of plazas. That night, everything was lagging and dreamy, as if the whole city had been padded with cotton. The mall, the fire station, the shops, and the park. I walked south, into a nicer area with large houses, big front lawns, and flowerbeds. It was the kind of suburb my parents had always wanted to move to and now would.

I came to a supermarket with a glowing yellow sign out front. I headed into the parking lot, and turned the corner toward the last loading dock. Beside it were garbage bins and tall, scraggly bushes that grew through a chain-link fence. A solitary boy stood there, resting his shoulder blades on the dock's ledge, which trucks would slap their ramps over. He looked as if he were lost in the swaggering saxophone melody that the store pumped from outdoor speakers to deter loitering. He didn't see me at first, barrelling toward him in all my fury.

"Want something?" he said when he noticed me standing there.

I didn't say a word when I pushed my hand into his open jacket.

He jerked back. "What the hell?"

I shoved my hips onto his and they seemed to stack, one over the other, like plastic lawn chairs. He was a little taller than me, a teenager with a light brown face and acne-scarred cheeks, pink and raw. Moonlight shone on his shaved-low hair. He had a tiny black leaf tattoo in the dip of his collarbone.

I smelled the odour of his body under the cover of aftershave and put my mouth on his. He tasted of cigarettes. "If you want me," I said against his lips, shoving my body harder onto his, "do it."

His belt buckle dug into the flesh under my belly button. He curled his arms around the small of my back.

"Make it hurt."

After messing with the security settings of a computer in the school library, I had scrolled through newsgroups when the other students had returned to class and the librarians had left for lunch. I had clicked through a stream of warped fantasies—ripped underwear and exaggerated screams, spread limbs and bleeding mascara. The shock of those images quickly dribbled away. I knew I wouldn't find what I wanted in rape pornography. It was theatre. It didn't show the blankness of wondering why this was happening, the instinct to save your own breath in your chest and try to survive. I suspected real violence would be plainer, so much quieter.

He had to pull his chin back to find enough space to answer. "You like it rough, do you?" He spoke harshly but I heard shakiness underneath, a tremor in his breast that I felt in my own.

Anger frothed in my throat. I hadn't expected him to be afraid of me. "No, you don't care what I like. I'm a good girl and you want to hurt me."

You know what they call it when it's so rough you can't walk after? a teenage boy had asked me in the elevator as I gawked at the numbers lighting and dinging on the panel. I could hear his sneer. His hair was covered in a *patka* knot at the crown of his head. *Wanna try with me?*

I rushed out of the elevator and heard him laughing as the doors closed, thinking he had frightened me the way most boys could frighten most girls.

Now I slipped my hand past his beltline, pushing my fist into the curve of his spine. "Do it *dagger*. I'm a bad girl and you're a dagger."

"You're a whore." He closed his eyes and tried to kiss me.

I sucked in air, a whole lung's worth of his sharp scent, and I turned so his mouth landed at the side of my cheek. "No kissing."

He cocked his head and I tilted mine to let him reach my neck. I thought of his body like a concrete block ready to crash and I braced for the bite, the vice-grip of fingers and blinding pain, but his teeth found my jaw instead, with a soft scrape of incisors over bone. Gentle and intentional.

I smacked both palms on his chest and shoved him away. "That's not how I want it!" I screamed.

He held both palms up and his eyes were wide. "What's your problem, bitch?" He sounded afraid. He cast his eyes to the pavement and shrank behind his raised hands as if I were pointing a gun at his face.

This terrorized boy had no desire to harm me. I was suddenly bowled over by fatigue. "Why don't you want to?" I heard my mother's just-a-question tone inside my own mouth.

"I don't know what you want," he spoke to the ground. "Just leave me alone."

His pockmarked face reddened and the same shame that seemed to swell in him swelled up in me.

✿

When I returned to our apartment, my parents still hadn't come home. I walked into the kitchen without removing my sneakers. I pulled the drawer open for the big knife my father had used to stab into watermelon on summer afternoons at Downsview Park when Diana and I were little.

I can spit further than you, she would tease, slurping watermelon flesh and collecting the seeds in her cheeks, proving her boasts by winning every time.

I folded the cuff of my sweatshirt up to my forearm and dragged the tip of the blade across my skin, cutting a long line between my left wrist and my elbow. I watched as the red edge sparked and stung and oozed into a wave. Blood pooled and dripped onto the floor, one, two, three times over. It was an impermanent fix, I understood that. But the pain enveloped my whole body and settled the rage in my stomach.

I bent to wipe the floor and used the same raggedly ripped paper towels to blot the wound. I went back to my sister's bedroom with the paper against my pulsing arm, which I cradled between my breasts.

That's right. You should hurt.

Diana's bracelet was still in my back pocket. I had felt it the whole time, rubbing and rolling as I walked. I would drop it into her box of things and tape it shut soon enough, but I couldn't imagine ever forgetting the sensation of those candy beads through my pants.

✿

"Will you help me decorate too?" Paula asked. "Nothing too fancy."

I helped her bake for the elementary school's parent–teacher night. I pressed the mouth of a glass onto rolled-out sugar cookie dough and Paula, beside me at the counter with an apron over her sports jersey, lay my cut-outs on a baking sheet. We had already finished a few dozen and her apartment was fragrant and warm.

The oven beeped. She wiped her fingers on the corner of her apron before pulling on oven mitts and retrieving the batch from the oven, placing the hot sheet on the burners. She poked at a cookie, inspecting it over the rim of her glasses, and her lenses fogged with steam.

I wiped my forehead with the back of my hand, feeling the grit of flour on my perspiring skin. "Do I have to run down to the store for decoration stuff?"

She stretched up over her fridge and pulled down a wicker basket, holding it out for me to take stock of the sprinkles and icing tubes and sanding sugars, the bags of opulent edible jewels in every colour. She grinned down at her collection. "Impressive, yeah?"

Sadness bolted through me. *Was this what you're supposed to do with your life after your sister is gone?* I thought about Paula's library and neighbourhood volunteering, her books and paintings, even her indulgence of my weekly visits to her apartment. *This is how you try to make yourself forget her?*

I returned to my task, scraping at the leftover edges of dough and mashing them into one big wad I could work over with the rolling pin. I knew I didn't have the capacity to help Paula and Ave. I was too young and needy myself, and Paula would never allow it.

The wound on my arm, wrapped in bandages underneath my sweatshirt, started to throb. *Damn you, Paula,* I thought, smacking the rolling pin against the dough and pushing. *If I had another chance with my sister, I wouldn't do what you do. I wouldn't waste my time painting pictures I'll never give to her. You're just like everybody else in the world. You're just a coward.*

It was a judgment so abrupt and caustic that it shocked me. I knew it was wrong to think such a thing, but I felt as if a screw was piercing into me, winding its helix into my heart.

CHAPTER 28

1968

PAULA WALKED PAST A CRACKLING BONFIRE IN THE MIDDLE OF EAST 71ST Street on the Upper East Side. It was circled by teenage boys with sweaty, ash-stained cheeks and unzipped winter coats that hung too big from their shoulders. They watched the blaze as it unleashed a plume of colours, odours, and soot into the sky.

The city was on the fifth day of a garbage workers' strike and the whole place reeked. Trash burst into the roads and blew along the curbs, accumulating in mounds between the high-rises. Office workers flooded the sidewalks at five o'clock, anxious to flee to the sweet-smelling suburbs. For those who lived on Manhattan Island, there was no escape from the chaos.

Paula walked up Lexington, block after block, finally reaching East Harlem. She only had to turn and go a few more blocks to get to her building, but she made the choice to keep going, her shoes clicking on the pavement. She stopped at the first bar she came to.

By the time she staggered to her apartment it was well past midnight. *What are you going to do about work tomorrow*? she asked herself at the bathroom mirror in her blue jeans and T-shirt, gripping both sides of the sink. *Why didn't you go home like a normal person?*

She hung her head, thinking about her four-thirty morning wake-up. She would have to bathe and dress and scoot through the subway before the sun even contemplated rising, making it to the hotel where she now worked in laundry service. She spent most of her days in this monotony of white towels, white tablecloths, white bedsheets.

The nausea that had come and gone for weeks started to rise in her again. *The stink,* she thought, *it's because the whole city stinks of garbage.*

She didn't look at her chipped bathroom mirror. She didn't want to catch her own reflection again. She turned to the window that faced the brick of the neighbouring building, so close that she could stick out her hand and touch it. Her dingy apartment was a cave no matter how sunny it was outside, and Paula avoided being there as much as possible. She would step inside and, the moment the door banged shut behind her, she would feel as if the walls were bowing in toward her head. It made her heart gallop.

There was a knock at the bathroom door and she watched the doorknob jiggle.

"Paula, open up, man, please," came the request from the other side, followed by a loud, watery belch. "I need to use the can, like, right away."

She felt as if her brain were a twirling top inside her skull, a wobbly whirl of red and white. She had already forgotten that she had let the man from the bar convince her to take him home.

She groaned, trying to remember his name over the nausea. Hanging onto the sink with one hand, she lowered her bottom onto the lid of the closed toilet. "Give me a minute."

He had approached her with orange-tinted skin, dirty blonde shoulder-length hair, and a wide-collared shirt. He was ugly from the start and looked just like the other young drug dealers who hung out in Harlem's dives, waiting for lonely people to talk to. He claimed the barstool next to hers, patted the pocket of his trousers, and leaned in close. "Have I got something for you, beautiful."

Paula smelled Granny's sour brand of tobacco on his clothes and flinched.

"Hey, hey, easy. I can calm those nerves for you."

She wasn't sure what he had handed to her. He'd just pressed a thick pill into her palm and slid his beer bottle over to her on the counter.

"Just what the doctor ordered, beautiful. They use it for horse surgery. My buddy was a grunt in 'Nam and swears by it."

"He made it out alive?"

"Not before emptying his machine gun into a bunch of women and children. It was, like, pitch black out there and he couldn't see nothin' and he fired off into the bush, *rat-tat-tat-tat-tat,* like they brainwashed him to do. This pill's the only thing that makes him forget the screams." He lifted his hands over his head. *"Dừng lại, dừng lại!* Imagine that in your head all night. Ludes keep him cool."

She hesitated but he clapped her cheeks between his hands and put his lips on hers. He pulled back and she smacked the pill into her mouth, gulping the beer. He laughed like a schoolboy.

Dừng lại, dừng lại!

Paula didn't understand why the amnesia wasn't working on her. She still remembered everything from the past. The hunger and the cold, the farmhand and Granny, and Ave's wounded face as she walked out of the café fourteen years back, all in technicolor detail.

The man pounded on Paula's bathroom door. "Come on, hurry up. Don't blame me if I go out here, okay?"

"Do what you want, just be quiet." She regretted everything. The bar, the pill, her present companion, even moving to America in the first place. There were no jobs for dressmakers and fewer apartments she could afford, but Paula had been so convinced that she needed to go there. She had accused her sister of chasing delusions, but after Montreal Ave had only made it as far as Toronto. Paula was the one who had stepped out of the bus onto New York City's streets like a dreamer, unsure of what exactly she was dreaming of. It turned out she would become just another body in an already body-infested town.

Paula pressed her fingertips to her temples, feeling as if a fever were growing in her. She slid off the toilet seat and lay on the floor, grateful for the coldness of the tile at her back.

Jack, she thought, *that's it. His name is Jack.*

She rested her hands, one on top of the other, on her belly and listened to new noises beyond the bathroom door. It seemed as if Jack was clanging about her kitchen, probably hunting for food after he had relieved himself in the kitchen sink.

Paula wondered what this self-destruction she had been flirting with would amount to, hunkered in a city hundreds of miles away from Ave. They had spoken on the phone only a few times since they had last seen each other in Montreal. Clipped, uneasy conversations. Ave's son would be thirteen by now but Paula had only ever seen a stamp-sized snapshot of him as a newborn, a photograph Ave had mailed to her, with *Gordon Benton* printed in her hand on the back. The envelope hadn't contained even a short note. Paula hid the photo in a drawer.

"Didn't expect to hear from you today," Ave told Paula on the other end of the line the last time they had spoken, two years back.

"I wouldn't forget your birthday," Paula answered. "Happy thirtieth. How have you been?"

"Very good."

"That's good."

Silence slid in between them.

Ave cleared her throat. "So, are you going to ask about him?"

"Yes, of course. How is Gordon doing?"

"Wonderful. Top of the class. He wants to go to the University of Toronto to become a surgeon, no less. Brilliant boy."

"Wow. And the grocery store?"

"I'm at Toronto General now. I help the nurses and distribute the medications. I've taken over shifts and done blood pressure rounds, bed checks, those kinds of things. I get on well with the patients."

"Is that so?"

"I'm going to start night school for nursing. How's the hotel industry?"

"Pays the bills. Night school, hmmm? Long way 'round. How many years'll that take?"

"Slow and steady wins the race."

"Well. Good for you."

Ave chuckled angrily. "He's a bit old for me to abort now, don't you think?"

"What?"

"That's what you mean, isn't it? Gordy's holding me back?"

"That's not what I said."

"You don't have to say it. What you don't seem to understand is that normal women don't give up their children when they become an inconvenience."

"Normal women don't have babies out of wedlock," Paula snapped, only to have wished she could snatch the words out of the phone before they belched out at her sister's ear.

"Lord, have mercy. Give it up. I don't care what you think of me."

"And you think I care?"

"You can't stand to know I'm doing well without you."

Paula didn't answer.

"You don't change," Ave said. "Like a damn rock." Ave breathed a long, loud exhale, as if she were ridding herself of her sister again. The pain of it brazed Paula afresh. "Listen. I've got friends on their way over tonight and I don't have no time for your nonsense today. Goodbye, Paula."

Paula opened her mouth but words didn't come before she heard the click of the receiver on the other end.

From the sounds of it, Jack had given up on finding food in her cupboards. Paula heard her apartment door squeak open and slam shut again. A few drops fell from the showerhead, reverberating when they hit the enamel.

Reconciliation with Ave seemed unimaginable because Paula had come to learn that there was no design behind what they had endured. She and Ave were simply abandoned sisters, probably only half-sisters, suffering together by chance and then split up for good. The past still tumbled on her at every turn, though Paula longed for it to leave her.

She prayed to be rid of Ave once and for all, no longer obligated to or pining for her.

Perhaps that was why Queen Nanny returned in her billowing white dress and headwrap, materializing at Paula's feet with rifle and sugar cane in her hand, bathed in sacred, otherworldly light. She stood and watched over her great-great-granddaughter with flames for eyes.

It's been so long, Paula said to her. *I waited for you, all this time. You never came back. You never loved me.*

Queen Nanny said nothing. Her face was a vision, smooth and brown and luminous as burnished bronze.

Is a life like this even worth it? Paula knew she shouldn't have asked such a question. If anyone knew how to live, it was Queen Nanny and her warriors.

But I'm not as strong as you. I'm nothing like you. I can't fight and I can't ask you to help me because you're not real. It's just the drugs. You know how much I always wished you were real. You know how much I loved you.

Queen Nanny remained without a word, waiting with Paula in that ramshackle apartment until she relented and committed all her pleading, all her questioning, all her wrecked logic and tears to silence.

She descended into a few hours of dreamless sleep on the bathroom floor, feeling Queen Nanny standing over her the whole time, patient. Her eyes opened from the black and her body resurrected the next morning, rising warm from the cold, unyielding tile, before the sun returned to the sky over the city.

CHAPTER 29

A FEW DAYS BEFORE MY PARENTS AND I WERE TO MOVE INTO OUR NEW HOUSE, I came home from school and left the house again, this time with my knapsack pulling heavy at my shoulders. I walked down the street in a burst of April warmth. Three children passed me on their bicycles, tailing each other so closely that they would've toppled each another with the slightest misjudgment.

A ball rolled onto the sidewalk, intercepting my path. I kicked it back to some little boys whose jackets were tossed in a pile on the grass as they played soccer in the middle of the street. Their sweatshirts were stained and askew and they scampered around each other, squealing. I thought of all those times Diana had taken me with her to meet the neighbourhood kids in the summer. We ran around in the same way, playing our games.

I'll find out what happened, I thought, *and I'll make them pay for not treating the case the way they should have.*

Crabapple buds were beginning to peek from the tree branches. I wasn't sure if there were any crabapple trees around the new duplex, or if the trees around there grew any fruit at all. Last time I had gone with my parents to see the place, the tenants were in the process of moving out and I was preoccupied with the clean siding and brickwork, the even sidewalk slabs beyond the front yard, free of cracks and penetrating weeds.

I boarded a bus and sat near the back, hugging my knapsack that contained Diana's medical books. I had to do something about them. I was the only one in the family who truly understood how important they were. I didn't want to trap them in the attic of the new house, but if I kept them inside my new bedroom I feared I wouldn't be able to resist pulling them out of the box and reading them. Without Diana sitting next to me on her bed, watching me turn the slick pages and explaining the medical procedures, it would just feel wrong.

I was out of breath by the time I walked onto Auntie Julie's street, marked by a tiny corner bungalow with a trio of wooden piglet lawn ornaments in the front yard. They wore blue fez hats and stood on their hind legs like humans. I had always assumed them to be the three little pigs, even if Diana hadn't been convinced.

So if they're the three little pigs, she had asked one time when my family drove past, *where's the wolf?*

He's right here! my father growled from behind the wheel, letting out a roar. We screamed happily and my mother laughed beside him. My mother had always insisted that the pigs should have painted-on clothes to make them more suitable to look at.

I inhaled the sweetness of the flowering bushes on the townhouse lawns, many of them untamed and threatening to take over, even in early spring. Newly planted white oaks along the road were budding, buttressed by twine and steel pegs. Through a nearby open window I heard the silly sound effects of a cartoon and the whines of a baby.

Auntie Julie's unit was at the very end of a row with its own side yard. Her car was parked in the driveway. I crept up in the hope she wouldn't poke her head from a window or around the backyard gate. I didn't want her to see me. I stepped up the porch stairs, arriving at her shoe mat and pots of lavender. Sweat collected under my nose and I tilted my head to wipe it on the shoulder of my T-shirt.

I felt mildly mischievous as I retrieved the books from my knapsack. I planned to ring the bell, drop the package on the stoop, and sprint off before my aunt could make it to the door. I raised my hand to knock on the door and the lacy curtain on the other side of the front window puffed away from the pane under a breeze. I saw a rhythmic motion on the inside wall by the window, a brown arm and a thin brown hand, an exposed breast and a square jaw. Black hair cascading.

My father and aunt.

The curtain deflated. It floated up again and we all looked at each other through the glass, two against one, frozen in time. My father and aunt cowered and skittered from the window, disappearing by the time the curtain fell again.

I looked at the door, at the chiselled bevels in the faux wood. I returned Diana's medical books to my knapsack and retreated as quickly as I could, the scent of those flower bushes turned to burning stink in my nostrils.

Sweat greased my back as I walked away. I reached the intersection and realized that my family's sedan had been parked on the street the whole time, the same vehicle my father was teaching me how to drive.

When I passed the yard with the wooden pigs, I plucked the card I had written out of my pocket.

Auntie Julie, I want you to have Diana's medical books. Mom and Dad gave them to her a long time ago and she loved them. She always looked up to you and I think she'd want you to have them.

I want to tell you that I look up to you too. You were always there for us. I'm not sure we would have survived without you. I don't say this enough, but I love you. Thank you for inspiring me. I promise things will get better for us all when I become a lawyer.

I ripped up the card, tossing the bits over the house's front fence. *This little piggy goes wee wee wee all the way home.* Paper wafted across the grass and fluttered against the piglets' hooves.

As I stepped out of the elevator, I could hear our kitchen telephone ringing and reverberating down the hallway. But I took my time unlocking the apartment door, dropping my bag, and untying my sneakers, and it stopped.

I flopped onto the couch and it started ringing again.

I turned on the television and stabbed at the remote, sifting through talk shows and soap operas my mother used to make me watch with her during summer breaks. The phone stopped for a few seconds before starting again. I stomped toward the kitchen.

"What do you want?" I blared into the mouthpiece.

"'Lisha, I—"

"I don't want to hear it."

"I need to explain."

"How long? A few months? Years? My whole life?"

"No," she responded quietly. "A year. Maybe a little more."

"How could you do this to your own sister?"

A heaving breath.

"Don't cry, answer me!"

"I'm sorry, I just felt so lost and I didn't know what to do to make it go away... after Diana died—"

"Don't even *think* about blaming my sister for what you've done!"

"No, no, babe—"

"I am not your babe!"

"Oh, God, please—I'm not blaming her. It's been so hard and your father and I fell into this mess, this *shit*, and...."

There was silence across the line. I heard her swallow a few times.

"'Lisha, I love you more than I can say. I'd do anything for you. I am so sorry."

In that moment, I could have admitted to my aunt that I understood, even in my anger. I knew what it was like to not know what to do about the bounty of heartache we had inherited. But to admit it would mean facing my own secrets. *I didn't wait, watch, or search. I just left Diana with that horrible man and didn't have the guts to tell anyone about it.*

"It doesn't work like that," I said instead. "What would Diana think? I can't talk to you about this anymore. Please, just hang up and leave me alone."

"But—"

"No. Don't call me again. I won't pick up. In fact, don't come here expecting me to talk to you again. I don't know who you are and I don't want anything to do with you from now on."

I put the receiver back on its dock, playing the righteous party in my family's four-way hell. I crossed my arms on the kitchen counter and bent my neck to rest my forehead beside the hushed phone. The yawning pit that had opened under me in the detective's office was still spiralling at my feet three years later.

I remembered the last time Diana and I had taken my father's camera. She was eleven and I was nine. She stretched to bat the camera down and I tumbled to catch it, only to get hit in the head by a shoebox. It fell open onto the floor and Polaroids scattered about our feet. We bent to look at them, all the images of my mother in lacy bras and slips, sitting crossed-legged with pointed toes and hair tossed over her shoulder. Diana gasped and started pelting the pictures back into the box. I wanted to see more, to ask my sister why my father had taken them, but I could tell Diana was not prepared to answer. I sat on the floor to cradle the camera in the nest of my crossed legs and pouted.

I stretched to retrieve a stray photo from under the bed, but it just was an image of Auntie Julie on our balcony, a plain T-shirt over her slender frame, looking the way she always did when she came to our apartment with kisses for our cheeks. *Diana-girl, 'Lisha-babe, you been good?*

My sister plucked the photo from my fingers. She seemed puzzled at first, then dumbfounded. "Let's get out of here," she said, rattled in a way I didn't understand. She tossed the unremarkable photo of our aunt into the box and returned the whole thing to the top shelf.

She freaks out about every little thing and can't handle the real world, Diana had written about me in her diary. I had always been too subsumed in childish adoration of my parents to notice something might have been amiss.

✿

The next Wednesday after school I went to Paula's. She was at her easel, leaning in to inspect a canvas and sketching light lines on it with a pencil.

I was on the couch with her copy of *No Longer at Ease*, reading the same line again and again, trying to blot out the image of my father and my aunt tangled against one another.

"What's all this here?" Paula straightened and prodded the air in my direction with her round-bristle Filbert brush. "You hurt yourself?"

I didn't realize I had been holding my injured left arm tight to my chest. I released it to my lap. "Oh, it's nothing. I sprained it or something."

"How does one sprain oneself doing homework? You enroll in ballpoint Olympics without telling me?"

"Don't know. Slept bad."

"Tossing and turning? Stressed?"

"Yeah. I guess so."

She picked up a dry brush, sweeping it over the canvas to plan out her strokes. "Well, I used to have my own issues with that, you know. I'd go days without being able to sleep. Maybe it was about Ave, I don't know. Probably."

I closed the book and placed it on the couch cushion beside me. "Oh?"

"That's when I learned that painting is the thing to calm me down. Gives me perspective. That's why I like it." She dragged dry bristles on a diagonal curve over the canvas—top right to bottom left. "Maybe you should think about what might give you perspective too, yeah?"

"Do you still get stressed? I mean, when you think about Ave?"

"Sometimes, I guess, yeah."

I had so many questions to ask. The words jumbled inside of me like a big prickly weed and I was aware of my gash again, wrapped in gauze and throbbing. It was taking weeks to heal. All I could do was return to the pages of my novel as Paula continued to pretend-paint her canvas.

In the end, I left her apartment without asking the questions I wanted to, *No Longer at Ease* inside my knapsack. But I did leave behind a bag of books and a note on her floor on the far side of the couch.

> *Paula, I'm sorry to stash these at your place like this. I don't mean to be dramatic, I just knew giving them away would be hard because they were Diana's favourite books. I would really appreciate it if you could to hold onto them now that my parents and I are moving away. I know you'll treat them well and, the truth is, you're the only person in the world I can really trust.*
>
> *Even though I won't be in the neighbourhood anymore, I still want to come by when you have time for me and read your books. There are a lot I haven't gotten to yet and I want to read them all.*
>
> *Hope that's okay.*
>
> *Alisha*
> *XO*

CHAPTER 30

1974

OTHER COMMUTERS DOZED AND READ THEIR NEWSPAPERS, BUT PAULA STOOD alert, scanning the advertisements in the subway car. She was teaching herself to read, taking in billboards and flyers anywhere she could. She had already read each *Thee* and *Thou* of the Gideons Bible, the whole diatribe of *Dianetics: The Modern Science of Mental Health*, and *The Book of Mormon*. On her days off, she would visit the Toronto Reference Library and hunt through the shelves. She found that reading material was readily available all over the city.

The subway poster that had caught her eye was for an event called The Annual Hospice Hullabaloo. She hadn't heard of the headliners but she did recognize one of the opening acts. Featuring The Daring Divas Quartet. The quartet's curlicue, big top–style logo had also been on the postcard Ave had sent Paula at Christmas, with its festive gold font on the front and a terse scribble on the back. *Season's Greetings. Ave.*

That was the level of interaction they had now: single-line messages written on stoic cards with boats and birds and trees; nothing too intimate or sentimental. They did not visit or call each other anymore.

Walking into Massey Hall, Paula felt like a vagabond in her blue pantsuit and flat shoes, surrounded by elegant women in black sequins and men in tuxedos. But it was the fanciest ensemble she owned.

After leaving New York for Toronto, Paula got a job as a hotel cleaner and took up residence in a low-ceilinged apartment near Spadina and Dundas above a Chinese grocer. It smelled of fruit and fish. It was the only place she could afford after walking away from a short-lived marriage. She had met John in East Harlem when she was thirty-eight. He worked for a mechanic just a few blocks from her apartment. She would pass the open garage every day on the way home from work and see him in his grey overalls, tucked under a car or fiddling with an engine, hunched awkwardly under the hood because he was so tall. She didn't think he noticed her until he started to wave when she passed, smiling shyly and shrugging when she would wave back. At the end of that summer he ran out of the shop, wiping his hands on an oily cloth before shaking her hand. He asked her to accompany him to dinner.

After six months, he proposed and Paula accepted. They got married at City Hall, but when they moved into his place and he started musing about starting a family she found she couldn't stay. It was the prospect of becoming a mother that was most troubling.

"You are a good man and you will be a wonderful father," she had told him, standing with her few packed bags around her legs in their apartment shortly after her fortieth birthday. "I can tell as much. I can't keep hanging around and keep you chained to me when you deserve everything you want. I'll hold you back. I do that, you know. It's like I can't help myself. I can't bear the thought of doing it to you too."

He sat on the end of their bed, still in his mechanic's uniform and boots. He was silent as she gathered her things and left.

Paula lowered the brim of her fedora, hoping she would blend into the fringes of the teeming crowd in the theatre lobby. A touch on her shoulder made her recoil.

"'Scuse me, honey," a silky bass voice spoke to her from behind, "didn't mean to spook you."

She stepped aside. "I'm sorry."

"No judgment." The drag queen was tall and had a red-lipstick smile and long eyelashes. Her blonde locks were pinned back by a feather, its edges in weightless flutter. "Love the hat." She sashayed off in a glittery flamenco dress.

Most Saturday nights Paula preferred to hang out in small cafés and community centres where she could find a secluded corner to pull out a book and read. Massey Hall was all brick and glass and red carpet. Waiters flitted about with trays of hors d'oeuvres and champagne. Paula scanned the people and looked up to the twinkling chandeliers.

"Give it a rest," she whispered to herself and turned toward the window at her back. Raindrops on the glass caught the lights of city street lamps and headlights, brightening and dimming like a million watery sparks.

She wondered if she would even recognize Gordon, if he was even here. He would be a full-grown man at twenty. She thought about his freckles and his striking almond eyes, the photograph she had of him as an infant. He wouldn't know her, but she knew she would recognize her sister's son anywhere.

When the auditorium doors opened most of the attendees rushed in to get to the centre seats, but Paula zipped to the far left, claiming a spot flush with the wall. She flipped up her jacket collar and sunk into her seat as the music and swiping spotlights swelled.

"Ladies and gentlemen," came the announcing voice from the speakers, "come one and all to witness the very finest in entertainment, designed to amaze and delight. Hold on to your hats and bow ties, spit out your gum, and prepare to be astounded!"

The show opened with a stand-up comedian, followed by a man juggling flaming batons. He tossed and twirled and the fire roared around him. Next, the flamenco beauty queen and two others dressed just like her glided around the stage, lip-syncing and doing choreography with huge feather fans.

Paula was restless. Her legs bounced in her seat. *You're crazy for coming here*, she thought. *What did you expect would come of it?*

She had purchased a bottle of wine to help her through the phone call she wanted to make to Ave, even though the smell of liquor these days made her gag. But the bottle remained corked on her kitchen counter, gathering dust for days, then weeks, and then months. Sometimes she got as far as holding the receiver to her ear, breathing deeply, washed in neon light that buzzed through her living room window. *Authentic Szechuan Massage. New girl every day.*

The phone would eventually cut to dead air, and in this way many opportunities came and passed. Paula finally gave up, setting the unopened bottle down on the floor mat fronting her landlord's door.

"Get ready to sing and dance and defy death! Without further ado, here's the Daring Divas Quartet!"

The house lights brightened and Ave pranced out onstage with three other women in glittery top hats and springing coattails, gold hot pants, and high heel boots. They sang in staccato acapella, stomping their feet and slapping their thighs, all grins and cheers. *He rocks in the tree tops all day long, hoppin' and a-boppin' and singing his song! All the little birdies on Jaybird Street love to hear the robin go tweet tweet tweet!*

"Put your hands together!" Ave called to the audience. She clapped her hands high over her head and everyone clapped along with her. She placed both palms over her mouth and fanned a big smacking air-kiss out to the audience. Paula trailed its trajectory—it landed in the centre of the auditorium, right on a clapping brown-skinned young man in a black suit. He was small from Paula's vantage point, yes, but she could see he was slim and handsome, with big brown eyes, and perched on the edge of his seat to watch his mother perform. His face was dazzling, bursting with potential; she could see it. Ave's boy was as special as his mother.

Paula couldn't take her eyes off her sister. Ave had thick rouge on her cheeks and her curls sprung from under the rim of her top hat. She was beautiful and lustrous and seemed stuffed to the brim with happiness. She had created the life she always wanted, the life they had whispered and fantasized about as little children. Paula felt a caress of gratitude slide over her. It soothed her. Ave had given her someone to protect, someone to live for, when living hadn't seemed possible.

Paula wanted to go home and paint the floors and walls of her shabby apartment every colour that sparkled off of Ave's top hat—reds and blues and greens and purples—she wanted to paint beyond the confines of the unit to the hallway and the brick and concrete and pavement, the buildings and busses, the trees and sky and water. Yonge Street to High Park to Lake Ontario—she wanted to paint the whole city like a rainbow and maybe her sister would see it. Maybe she would understand how much Paula adored her.

One diva kicked a leg in front of her and dropped into the splits. The other two jumped straight up in the air with their legs and arms out in front, their fingers touching their toes in mid-air. Ave lifted one knee like a dancer and twirled an impossible number of times, landing with her arms in a *V* above her head. The audience hollered for her.

Dear God, Ave, what a wonder you always were!

Paula considered the odds and hoped that, one day, she and her sister would find a way to come back together. She couldn't guess at how or when it would happen, but sitting in that concert hall, watching Ave perform, it didn't feel entirely hopeless anymore. The possibility would have to be enough, for now.

CHAPTER 31

WE MOVED TO BRAMPTON AND MY GRADE-TWELVE YEAR PASSED. EMBROILED in studies and assignments, I didn't tend to the sports playoffs, the pep rallies, the plays and proms, the cliques and boyfriend–girlfriend dramas. Those were not my domain. Instead I took on extra assignments in my law and society class, read unassigned books on the legal system, and attended public law lectures downtown.

"Aren't you a determined girl," said my law and society teacher, a thin man with deep wrinkles and wavy hair dyed black. He was always serious and taught in a suit. "In all my years, I've never taught such an active legal mind." For the first time since I had begun his course, he smiled at me.

Still, my days didn't feel very active. It felt like they were suspended, stuffed somewhere between the paragraphs of my textbooks.

I applied to undergraduate programs at several universities and received acceptance letters from them all. In the end, I decided to enroll at the University of Toronto.

"Why do you have to live on campus?" my mother asked me.

"At least I'll be in town."

"Then you'll come home on weekends, right?"

On the day of my high school graduation, in June 2003, both of my parents took the day off from work, but I curled up in my bed a few minutes before we were supposed to leave, pretending to have a migraine.

My mother lay a damp cloth on my forehead and pressed the back of her hand under my chin. "Do you want me to make you soup? A piece of toast?" Her bun and blouse and powdered face were all in place, ready to go.

"No, thanks. I think I need to sleep it off. I'm sorry about this."

She left my room and closed the door behind her. A stripe of sunlight blazed from atop my drawn curtains and I listened to the television in the living room as I watched the minutes pass on my bedside clock. Noon, the time the ceremony was scheduled to finish, finally came.

By the start of summer, I noticed my mother's cheeks were sunken and pale. Her office had hired me as her summer assistant to please her. She would sit with me in the kitchenette at lunchtime as I hurried through a sandwich before I forced her to stroll around the block with me, but she was still ghostly sallow and her flesh-and-bone body seemed breakable. Focusing on her frailness too closely made me feel unsteady on my feet.

My parents decided to imitate the neighbours and installed a gas grill on the backyard patio of our duplex. My mother bought four small steaks for us to attempt. She hunched behind me to watch the meat steam and pop.

"Mom, you have to move," I said, shifting my torso to block her from the heat. "You're going to get burned."

She stood up straight, salad tongs in one hand and a sweating bottle of dressing in the other. "But you're sure you know how to do it?"

"Of course."

She reached over to the little table beside the grill where colourful disposable cutlery, a tray of guacamole and chips, and a garden salad had been set out. She stuck the tongs into the bowl of lettuce, cucumbers, and tomatoes. "Your father should do it."

Juices bubbled when I prodded the steaks to check their texture. "He has no more experience than I do." I placed the spatula on the rack and moved to straighten the skew of her Guyana-gold earring, half of the pair she wore every day. She offered her ear, accepting the correction. "Go finish the rice."

"If you need your father, tell him." She stepped up the stoop in her flowered skirt, kicked off her flip-flops, and hauled open the sliding door. Her back was slender and rigid.

✿

I had gone to Paula's a few weeks back to plan more community volunteer hours and get her help with pre-law training program applications. I happened to mention my parents' new barbeque and she pushed me onto her tight balcony, a band of concrete that hardly seemed wide enough for standing. She kept a small charcoal grill and herb pots out there, thyme and basil and mint, planted into old yogurt containers. She insisted on giving me a demonstration.

Paula flipped a small steak on her grill and renewed its sizzle. "You have to give it the chance to stay moist, yeah? My ex-husband taught me that."

Angled in the space between the sliding door and the grill, I held a big plastic plate and enjoyed the smells of olive oil and charred meat. "You were married?"

She wrinkled her nose. "For a couple of years. Wasn't my finest hour."

"You didn't tell me."

She smirked. "There's a lot you don't know, Miss Sookermany."

What about Ave? I thought. *Tell me why you can't talk to her.* "Why'd you break up with him?"

"What's this here? It's my doing?"

"Bet you a million."

She giggled. "I suppose we wanted different things in life. Men are great to look at but tough to live with."

I thought of how my mother and father had always seemed to want the same things. Two girls, two loving parents, one happy home. How could they stand to stay together now?

Paula nudged aside the browning steak to make way for an uncooked one, oozing watery red onto a wood block on the balcony floor. "Say, aren't you at that age when girls and boys get awfully spirited with each other?"

"I don't care about boys."

"Hmmm. I like you. Girls these days. It's all low self-esteem and low-cut tank tops. Scary stuff. At least you're smarter than that."

✿

The steaks on my parents' barbeque were nearly done. I watched my mother through the sliding door. She was at the stove in the kitchen, rotating a spoon in the rice pot, her elbows bony in her sleeveless shirt. Standing solemnly at the kitchen table in cargo shorts, T-shirt, and reading glasses, my father used a cooking spoon to excavate frozen iced tea from a can, dropping it in chunks into a pitcher. It seemed like the grey hairs framing his ears and neck would soon take over his hair entirely. New lines at the corners of his eyes were matched by new creases on his forehead. These days, it seemed I only caught the features at the sides of his body since we spoke to each other in mid-strides, always pointing away, moving in opposite directions. We didn't lock eyes anymore.

It was the same way between my parents. They spoke of and for one another, but rarely to each other. I noticed my father avoided my mother, especially at dinners with my aunt. We all kept up the regular weekend routine, eating curry and dumplings and roti and rice together at the table, drinking our orange pekoe to finish it off, but my mother would always have to carry our stilted conversations, the clumsy questions and answers. Surely my mother noticed how my aunt, my father, and I could not properly look at each other. Perhaps she noticed my father's and aunt's cloaked glances, filled with messages, aimed in my direction.

That same day you saw us, they seemed to try to communicate in pointed sips and exaggerated flicks of forks, *it was over.*

I would pretend not to understand their cutlery choreography and forbid myself from too much analysis of my mother's expressions. At the least, I knew they understood that I wouldn't say anything about what I had seen.

I carried the steaks, whistling and steaming, to the patio table. The lime green umbrella above provided half-shade as the sun curled under it and drew a line over the tabletop.

"Done?" Auntie Julie asked. She sat at the table stirring spices, pieces of chives, and cubed radishes into a bowl of mayonnaise. She tasted a smear on her fingertip.

"Yeah. They're about medium right now."

A wobbly smile came to her lips. "You're really good at this."

"I'm learning."

Our backyard was surrounded on three sides by the backyards of our neighbours. Smoke and the noises of children drifted over the fences, along with a joyful Bollywood chorus that rang out in the distance. Everyone in the neighbourhood seemed to celebrate summer that afternoon.

I felt a brush at my wrist. My aunt's gaze had fallen around my chin and throat and her eyes were doleful. It seemed as if she wanted to say something to me but couldn't retrieve the words.

I retracted my hand and shooed a fly that circled the beef. "You guys can start without me. I'm going to lie down for a bit."

"'Lisha—"

"Just a headache. It'll go away soon."

I didn't look at her as I stepped away. I focused on the plastic lawn chair, bright white in the sun, the cracked patio stone, the barbeque's smudged chrome. I abandoned my sneakers on the stoop and walked past my parents in the kitchen, past Diana's living room shelf with the same grade-nine portrait now in a shinier gilded frame and Auntie Julie's cherub figurine. My mother added fresh candles and incense to the display, lighting the sticks and wicks after work and keeping them going all day on Saturdays and Sundays. The cloying scents of sandalwood, myrrh, and clove soaked every corner of the house.

I leaned my spine against the inside of my bedroom door to buttress it shut. The remorse in Auntie Julie's face, her need for forgiveness, was still an open wound after more than a year. I had told Paula about it at her apartment one day after carrying the two-ton secret for months. It was close to Christmas and snowflakes fell past her balcony door, white dots moving on a white sky.

"I had no idea until I caught them doing it in front of me," I said.

"Oh, *shit.*" She exhaled across the table. "That's bad. That's real bad."

"I'll never be able to get rid of that image in my mind."

"Which one? Where you see them as mere mortals?"

"What?"

But she shook her head almost imperceptibly. She pushed her glasses up the bridge of her nose and stood, wincing at her bad knee. "Your tea's cold. I'll make you more." She walked into the kitchen and clicked on the kettle, sorting through the drawer for a fresh spoon.

I waited, I watched, I searched, I thought. The only difference between me and my father and aunt is that they got caught.

I closed my eyes now to shut out my room, the window, the empty desk, even the bed I lay on. I still hadn't unpacked many things since we moved in. I had a plain beige bedspread, a lamp, and a functional taupe curtain. There were no books or stuffed animals or posters. Even Paula's hibiscus painting leaned against a wall on the floor.

I slid the top drawer of my desk open to find a thick clipped collection of papers under my stack of university acceptance letters. I sat over them as I had done many times—my own version of my father's manila folders—grouped by case summaries and articles. I would read and reread, highlight and underline and scrawl notes just like my father had done with his files. His were now in a box in the basement. He hadn't unpacked them.

My mother had long stopped doting on me but my father cooked pancakes and scrambled eggs on Saturday mornings, setting a plate out for me on the table beside a mug of black tea. He folded my laundry and left it in neat piles on my bed, and he hosed down my running shoes, letting them drip-dry on the patio. He was avoiding and admitting what he had done at the same time, and it left me disquieted. I didn't react. I showed no gratitude or irritation. But he persisted in these acts of devotion. To me, it seemed like a form of desperation. I couldn't imagine where it would take us now.

He had given up on finding Diana's killer, but I still went downtown to visit the legal archives at Osgoode Hall. Because my teachers awarded high-achieving students the benefit of the doubt I spent hours that I should have been at school in the stacks, reading and jotting, certain I could find what my father had missed. I scoured records of murders and rapes and kidnappings, searching for the men who stalked and hurt girls, and I called the private detective my parents kept on an ever-diminishing retainer.

No one knows about the man at the mall, I thought. I couldn't even bring myself to tell the private detective about him.

I watched my body in the full-length mirror of my closet door. I didn't like looking at myself. I seemed too small in my T-shirt and sweatpants, and my eyes were shadowed by blue-tinged bags when I didn't cover them with concealer. My hair was in a messy ponytail. I planned to crop it short before starting university. I knew my mother wouldn't be pleased, and it would be hard to disguise my haggardness without the veil of hair to comb over it—the early greys around my ears, my drooping features. But the luxurious black hair of my mother and aunt didn't suit me anymore.

My cellphone bleated in my pocket as I had expected. It was just past six o'clock.

"Hi," I answered in a low voice.

"Yeah, hi," the private detective said, tamping his own words as if he had secrets to keep, too. "I thought I wouldn't be able to find anyone, but I came across a buddy I used to work with on the force. He became a prison guard after he got injured on the job. He pulled a tendon in his calf arresting a schizo. What do they call it? Tendonitis?"

"What'd you find?"

"He's dead."

"What?"

"I know." He drew a noisy breath. "Millhaven Penitentiary. Couple of months ago."

"They should've given him parole. Sexual assault, right?"

"They did. But my buddy said he overdosed, like, the next day." He harrumphed. "He should've celebrated by romancing his boyfriend and calling it a night. These guys aren't famous for impulse control."

Outside my window, columns of light streamed through the blue-beech in the yard behind ours. Its leaves were thin and veined, like elderly hands spread to the sky.

"Sorry, kid. This perv fit the profile so well. Even if he was the one, we can't ask him."

I had no idea if the man who'd died in Millhaven was really the man with the baseball cap and sunburned face—so many of the mugshots the private detective had on file seemed to be him. White male, around thirty years old, 150 pounds, and five feet, five inches. As difficult as it was to place him, he was still the one I dreamed of and thought of constantly—struggling to recall his every detail, sentence, and quirk. It was as if I had developed a demented juvenile crush on him the day Diana disappeared.

"I have more names for you," I said, trying not to sound crestfallen. "Pull reports from the local units, even run-ins without arrests. Can you do that?"

"There are fees. Your father will see."

I had told my parents that I was saving my dental office earnings for tuition and had opened my own bank account. "Email me the invoices and don't say anything. Thanks for trying."

I folded my phone shut. The man at the mall always seemed to elude me. On a crowded bus or merging into a hallway of yapping students on my way to class, he would enter the edge of my vision. As soon I turned toward him, he would vaporize. It was his endless taunt. *Sisters as pretty as you should get along, okay? Just smile.* I wondered if he would haunt me forever.

I can't wait to get a real life, Diana had written. A blackness unfurled inside of me. What if I couldn't find the man even after I became a lawyer? What if he was simply gone? Panic slithered through me. The newest cuts on my arm had healed and only I could identify their paths, those needle-line scars that glistened when I held my arm to light at the right angle. I thought of the red ooze I would release again that night after my aunt was gone and my parents were asleep behind their bedroom door, maybe from an arm, maybe from a leg. Putting a knife to my skin was still the only thing that gave me some relief.

✿

I raised my hand to rap on Paula's apartment door the next day, a Sunday that conquered the whole city with sun. The door was ajar.

I nudged it open and saw heaps of books strewn across the floor. Her paintings had been cast from the walls, and even Ave's portrait had been displaced from its hallowed spot. The easel was bare and the soaking paintbrushes had been pitched from their Mason jars, discarded leakily about the easel's feet.

"Paula?"

I stepped into the ransacked apartment without taking off my shoes or tossing my jacket over the chair. Most of the plant pots on the windowsill had been bumped right over and dirt spilled out. I didn't smell brewing coffee or fried eggs and tomatoes, the scents I was used to in her place at that hour. There was only the stale odour of roused dust.

I heard movement from the bedroom and my body chilled. "Who's there?"

"Yeah, Alisha," Paula croaked. "In here."

I stepped over the mess and found Paula sitting at the bottom of her unmade bed, looking up at me. She was in her bathrobe and her body seemed as brittle as straw. One side of her hair was contained in a bun and the other spiked out. A band of light crashing through the window set one of her eyeglass lenses ablaze, along with the leaf pendant around her neck.

"Damn disaster in here." Her voice was an exhausted rasp.

I had never seen her eyes like that. The dark irises were contracted into dots and the whites were streaked red by exhaustion.

"What happened? Are you okay?" I had to fight my own alarm.

All around her were her blankets, on top of which were papers and folders. Bank statements, bills, newspapers and magazines, photocopies, scribbled notes on yellow-ruled paper. Cardboard boxes with open flaps littered the floor on both sides of her bed.

She blinked stiffly. "We're supposed to give them pictures... I looked and looked and couldn't find anything I wanted...." She surveyed the room as if she had just noticed the chaos that surrounded her. She pushed the papers next to her with an aimless, trembling hand.

Join us as we showcase the life and times of our illustrious longstanding community volunteers. Refreshments provided!

Paula was to be one of the honourees at the Jane and Finch Volunteer Awards ceremony at my old elementary school. She had given me the invitation weeks ago. "You're talking about your profile board?"

She nodded.

"You messed up your place for that?"

She raised her eyebrows before sliding them together in a frown.

"You were trying to find pictures of yourself in these boxes?" I could hear the odd high pitch of my own voice. I couldn't help but gape at the shadows tucked into the lines of Paula's forehead and in the hollow of her collarbones. It was as if she were a different woman entirely, a weather-worn shell of the woman I knew. She had never acted like an elderly person, not between her endless volunteering and painting, her library work with the children at the school.

What had made her so suddenly old? I could only stop staring by picking up and fanning through the muddle of papers on the bed.

She shook her head. "I already looked through those. There's nothing I can use anywhere. It's stupid. Why did they ask us for pictures? What if we don't have anything good? I can't do it. I have to tell them I can't do it. They expect too much."

Standing so close, I could hear her thin breathing. I knew the destruction wasn't really about the display boards. It had to do with the pain it demanded she excavate. This was the situation with Ave coming to a head, the resurfacing of an old distress. She had only ever let trickles of it dribble out to me. What could I possibly offer her?

I started piling and patting the corners of the loose papers. "You have to have pictures of yourself in here somewhere. I'll check through the boxes again. You missed them because you didn't take your time." But the only images I had ever seen in her apartment were the canvases she had painted. I had never seen any snapshots or albums, not even a single real photograph of her or her sister.

"How the hell am I going to clean this up?" She looked to her knees as if she had been scolded. The tendons in her neck were stretched like the ropes of a bridge.

That tension I knew well. I saw it in my father and my mother too. "Don't worry, Paula. I'll help you."

"It's too much."

"No, it's not."

Is that a shade of condescension I detect, Miss Sookermany? I waited on a snarky comeback to reassure me. *I'm not an invalid, you know.* But she sat there, slumped over. I could see past the fold of her robe's collar, down her bare back. All the way down the peaks and troughs of her hooked, aging backbone.

My belly flipped in dread that she might not go back to the way she was. The thought of losing her, someone I so loved and needed, swirled with the guilt of my own self-centredness.

I stacked the papers on her bed, trying to trick myself into believing that the faster I fixed her apartment the faster everything would rewind and resolve itself. I lifted a folder and found a printed cover page attached to a clump of papers. *Children of the Maroons. A True Story. By Paula Benton.*

Paula had told me that she wanted me to look at something she was working on, but she had never actually given me anything to read.

"Paula, I'm sorry. You'll have to move. I can't look through your stuff when you're sitting on it."

She combed her fingers through the messy side of her head with a rough scratch, but it did nothing to get that blast of hair in line. "Oh, yeah. Sorry."

I placed a hand on her back and cupped her elbow with the other, compelling her to stand up beside me. "That's it." I navigated the two of us into the living room, me still in my sneakers and Paula's wrinkled and shambling bare feet in slippers. "Watch where you're going now."

I buttressed her body beside mine and, at the side of my own leg, I felt the totter of her bad knee. I helped her into her armchair and tried to remember if she had always been the same height as me. She had always seemed taller.

Paula seized my hand, gripped it tight around the knuckles. "I know you understand, Alisha," she said, her eyes wide and locked onto mine. "I know you understand more than others."

She let go, tugged the collar of her robe, and sat back with neck collapsed against the headrest. Her fingers were restless, grasping at the armrests, clasping her kneecaps, and slipping flat under her thighs before threading into each other over her stomach.

I touched the back of her hand. "You just rest right there. I'll take care of everything. Okay?"

She nodded and closed her eyes.

I slid my knapsack from my shoulders, surveying the wreckage. It hurt to look at her, to think of how she must have agonized over years and years of Ave's absence. Her glasses dominated her aged and speckled face, all those youthful freckles somehow transformed into spots. I turned away.

CHAPTER 32

AFTER FIVE DAYS OF CLEAR SUMMER SKIES, THE NIGHT OF PAULA'S AWARD ceremony arrived. A mist had descended over the city and covered it with an unseasonable chill.

I stepped onto the concrete walkway leading up to my old elementary school. The building had shrunk since I had last been there. The front court was just a yard—hardly more than a strip of grass—and the main entrance a squat opening.

I eased the hood from my head and slowed my pace so my mother could walk next to me. We passed a cluster of teenagers shivering and puffing on cigarettes. Their hands were retracted into their coat sleeves and their ball caps were pulled down to their brows. A few little children chased after each other around their legs.

"Look how many people are here already," my mother said with a shade of worry in her voice. Her earrings glimmered as we came under the yellow-orange floodlights shining from the roof. Walking the distance from the parking lot to the school doors her bun had been completely coated with drizzle that made it glimmer.

I wove my arm around hers and pushed my hand into my pocket to lock it in place. She seemed to accept it as comfort. She wouldn't have come if I hadn't asked her to, and I had only made the request that afternoon, holding out the invitation and fumbling over my words because I couldn't imagine facing Paula by myself.

Wiping invisible crumbs from the stovetop, my mother had complained about not having enough time to get ready, but she came with me anyway. Not just as a favour to me, I knew, but also so she could evaluate Paula for herself. My mother never could hide her frown when I talked about Paula. She was still confused as to why I would continue to go back to our old neighbourhood and spend time with a strange lady. *Why would this girl want to remember that place, those people?* No matter what help with school I claimed Paula was giving to me, it was Paula who had gifted me *Jeanette's Hibiscuses*, breaking my mother's rule about what an adult should do for a child unconnected by blood.

Past the main office, the walls were as cluttered with student artwork as ever. This time, they had bedecked it with paintings of the seasons: blobby suns and beaches, Christmas trees, Easter bunnies, jack-o'-lanterns.

The gymnasium's painted cinder-block walls throbbed with voices. It sounded the same as it used to sound minutes before the start of a school assembly, when we children carried our excitement in our mouths and babbled and shrieked at each other until the teachers made us stop. The dividers were opened up and the retractable basketball nets folded against the ceiling. Blue mats were strung up along the walls and refreshment tables ran down the length of both sides of the gym.

The crowd bustled around us. Attendees were of all ages, dressed in sari and dashiki, hijab and jeans, running shoes and high heels. Nothing had changed in Jane and Finch since my family left. It was the same place Diana and I had known when we were little. We felt closer to our neighbourhood than our parents ever did and, at the time, I hadn't been able to imagine leaving.

My mother was reminded of the past too. I saw it in her inflexible spine. I grasped her hand and led her through the crowd, through the prattling and mirth in many languages.

We came to a little girl no older than five or six years old. She was standing at the yellow kanga-covered legs of an elderly woman: brown-skinned with braids that fell from a fuzzy woollen cap. Her eyes were bright and playful, and she returned my smile with one that was more precocious than friendly, poking at the cover of a picture book in her arms. It was the same kind of book the disapproving Italian librarian used to put aside for me to patch up on my lunch breaks in the school library.

Paula had told me she would be in the library until the awards ceremony began, leading a reading circle for kindergarteners and their parents. I was relieved that I wouldn't have to see her right away. I had been unable to bring myself to visit her apartment that whole week. It had taken me several days to work up the courage to phone her after she'd torn her place apart.

"Thank you for finding my pictures and cleaning up, Alisha." Her mouth was very close to the receiver. "I think you came here at the right time. I was a bit overwhelmed by it all, yeah?"

"I get it. No big deal. See you Saturday."

"Okay. Make sure you wear something nice. No sweats."

"I will." I was stuffed to bursting with the wad of pain in my chest.

My mother and I made our way to the base of the stage where a row of corkboards were lined up on easels and crowded with people. I got on my tiptoes to peek between the heads, to see how they had arranged the photographs I had given to them from Paula's chaos of boxes.

As I cleaned up her apartment I had studied each picture I found, collecting them in an envelope and listening for Paula's soft, steady snoring from the easy chair in the living room.

I found a photo of Paula that had been taken when she was in her twenties or early thirties. She wore an angled blue fedora and her arms were curled around the hips of two women, one on either side of her, dancers I guessed, with tight ponytails and black leotards. In another picture that looked like it had been taken in the seventies, Paula had a big afro and wore cat-eye spectacles, an eggplant-coloured pantsuit, and a gold clutch. She stood in the middle of a white archway with woven ivy and baby's breath. There were photos from the places she had worked before she'd retired and begun volunteering at the elementary school: a hotel, a bookstore, a place that looked like a community centre, a university-style library.

I found wedding photos in her boxes too. They were curled at the edges as if they'd been unpeeled from the pages of an album. They showed Paula in a lacy, sleeveless white dress hemmed above the knees, next to a tall Black man in a suit. In one photo, the couple faced each other at the bottom of a set of stone steps, thick stone pillars in the background, and it seemed clear to me that the pairing was doomed from the start. He looked down at the ground as Paula looked directly into the camera, beaming at the lens, dimples and freckles on her rouged cheeks.

In the end, there was only one childhood photo in the whole bunch, black and white and slightly out of focus. It showed two little girls in coats, holding hands in front of a shingled house on a hill with a field behind it and trees in the distance. Braids were drawn tightly along their scalps and past their ears. Wispy grass enveloped their legs. Paula was taller, skinnier, and darker in complexion than the other, probably under ten but still recognizable to me. Ave was just a toddler, with round cheeks and pouting baby lips. Their expressions were flat. They both stared past the camera's lens somewhere. Paula's hand was clenched over her sister's. Ave's hand was nestled inside.

That photograph I slipped into my pocket. It was still hidden in the breast pocket of my shirt the night of the awards.

❀

"Nice legs, hmm?"

I turned my head to find an old man with short dreadlocks standing next to me. "Pardon?"

He clucked his tongue at the photographs. "That right there is a special lady. Been friends with my dear Paula for many years. What a beautiful person. She deserves every award they want to give her."

I didn't reply. My whole life, I had always assumed I knew everything about the people who loved me. They formed a collage cut out of fancy paper and pasted in place, never allowed to move or grow, never allowed to reveal anything new, surprising, or trying about themselves. I had realized my error when instead of putting Paula's manuscript back into a box, I quietly zipped it inside my knapsack and brought it home. I read it overnight. I learned that I didn't know anybody as well as I had thought, least of all Paula. It had ripped a howling hole in my gut.

I wanted to throw my arms around the old man's neck and cry. Beg him to tell me more about the Paula he loved. But I only managed a nod without returning his smile. Who was this woman, really? How could I have spent all that time with her and not know any of the things she had written about in *Children of the Maroons*? An irrational upset overtook me. I was angry at Paula for not telling me what she and Ave had gone through, and I didn't know how to will the feeling away. More than anything I was ashamed of the years I had spent with her in oblivious, selfish ignorance.

I know you understand more than others, she had said to me.

I felt my mother brush my shoulder.

"I can't see anything," she said beside me, almost shouting to be heard over the racket as she tried to catch sight of the photos through the people.

I pulled her through a gap right to the board where they'd posted the photos of Jane and Finch volunteers at work. There they all were, cupping hands to shout across a field, marking chalkboards, sorting through leaflets, cleaning up litter. There were pictures of Paula sitting over open books with little girls and boys hugging her sides. It was how I had known her best, donning a sports jersey and spectacles and cocoa-coloured bun, wearing her volunteer vest.

My mother pointed at a photo. "Your friend does a lot. The teachers must be glad to have her." She surveyed the display, up and down and side to side. "You sure there isn't a picture with you?"

I knew what she really hoped for was a glimpse of Diana, and I couldn't blame her. For us, the school was drenched in her memory. "Why don't we check?"

We hunched and examined the images, pushing through the people waiting for the celebration to begin. I lifted my eyes at a burst of laughter. Three young women in cropped jackets leaned close to the flip-up screen of one girl's cellphone as she snapped a picture of a picture.

"Holy cow, Paula was hot back in the day!" one cackled, chewing a wad of gum that stained her lips purple.

That's when I noticed the woman close by. She looked at the same photograph of Paula as they did but with no acknowledgement of their amusement. She was no taller than me; her hair was the colour of milky tea, curled close to her scalp. Her skin was caramel and her jaw was tucked into her coat collar, its buttons done right up to the top. Her hands seemed fused in her pockets and her eyelids were low behind square-rimmed spectacles. It was the heart-shaped lips, the almond eyes, and the rounded-cherub face that gave Ave away.

I had found yellowed newspaper clippings in Paula's boxes, most of which dated from the early 1990s. *Abuse allegations and chronic underfunding at historic home*, a headline read. *Long road for former residents in class action*, read another, with a fuzzy black and white picture of small children sitting at attention against their pillows, their beds all in a row, a young matron with clipped-up hair and a button-down dress standing against the wall with her hands folded over her stomach. One article had even featured a photograph of the adult Paula, close-up and pixellated, with her gold leaf pendant threaded over a sports jersey.

There were legal documents too, and one had Paula Benton's signature. *The Plaintiff states she entered the home in 1938 and remained in the care of the state until eighteen years of age, but had never met her state-assigned social worker or been given an explanation as to why she and her sibling were institutionalized.* Upset as I was about *Children of the Maroons,* I understood why Paula couldn't tell me about it.

For a moment, Ave's stoic gaze collided with mine. Then she straightened and her body slunk away from the three giggling girls. She slid from my view, reabsorbed into the crowd.

Paula's folders contained a list of names. Most had addresses and phone numbers next to them and some had been highlighted and corrected a few times over. Others had checkmarks, and still others had been cut through by pen lines. I matched some of the names to some of the legal documents and understood it as an accounting of former residents, the ones who were and were not involved in the class action. A few names had been circled. The most important one was circled and highlighted and starred.

Ave Benton.

Paula had to have been the one to mail Ave the same invitation she had handed to me. Despite their estrangement, they were clearly not finished with one another. Why would Ave have come if she truly didn't want to be found? I stood tall, ready to slice through the crowd to get to her.

"Where are you going?" My mother's voice yanked at me and I looked to her, unsure of what to say. "I just saw someone I wanted to say hello to. I'll be back in a minute."

"But they're going to start."

In the sea of heads, Ave's had been swallowed up. The voices amplified, a clatter of white noise.

The city councillor stood at the podium, the honoured volunteers in a line on chairs behind him, grinning. The crowd bulged into the hallway and out of the gymnasium doors.

Paula's name was called. She stepped forward in her blocky heels, black dress pants, and bright white blouse. She was taller than the councillor and she bent her head to shake his hand. She accepted the framed certificate and held it over her chest, leaning close to the councillor as everyone cheered and the cameras flashed. She looked about the room with her bright smile.

The applause overwhelmed my ears. I clapped, straining to follow the path of her eyes as they moved from face to face. I imagined she was searching for her sister, and I was afraid she would be disappointed.

My only friend and her lost sister. The thought of them being so close to each other yet so unwilling to do anything about it distressed me. I couldn't change what had happened to Diana, but maybe I could do something for Paula and Ave.

Evergreen bushes encircled four gigantic weeping willows. Their spangled ribbon-leaves almost touched the ground, and they twisted in the breeze. Tall clusters of hollyhocks guarded the walkway and iron fences, looming over all the other flowers. Red and pink and yellow, battling one other for supremacy.

When we had come to this cemetery for Diana's burial, a pond with a boulder fountain and tinkling waterfall separated the mausoleum from the plots. Today, the pond was stagnant. There was no movement on the surface beyond minor ripples and the scuttling of insect feet. Lily pads and bulrushes had grown in, and I could see where the gardeners had laid new sod around the perimeter. The old and new shades of green hadn't blended.

I walked the rambling path through the plots, thinking how I might be the only one who could recognize the changes in the landscape since that day. Everybody else at the funeral had only circled around the plot in the ground. They had gazed at the black dirt there, blinkered by grief.

I had done the opposite—allowed my view to sweep the grounds, forcing an imprint of the cemetery's layout on my brain. It seemed important for at least one of us to remember exactly where my sister would have to live now, amongst the dead.

My parents and aunt had not visited the gravesite after the burial and none of them admitted to any desire to do so, at least not in my presence. It didn't bother me because Diana didn't belong in the ground. It seemed perverse to go to that place and pretend that she did.

Still, I knelt by the salmon granite marker with Diana's name, a dusty square embedded flat into the ground, and felt my knees grow cold. On the neighbouring plots fresh cut flowers had been laid. A few plots away another visitor used her finger to trace the engravings on a gravestone. She was white-haired and gaunt, swallowed by the collar of her trench coat. I couldn't see the marker she crouched over. I wondered who her loved one was.

My vision blurred. A light whiff of gasoline drifted from the highway that curled around the cemetery and cordoned it off from the rest of the city. I looked up beyond the plots, the wrought iron fencing, and the trees, to the distant horizon, the rotating Ferris wheel with Diana's pendulum ponytail ticking inside of it. For the first time, I wondered what it would be like to mourn my sister without feeling a crushing stone of guilt.

Leaving the cemetery, I took the bus and subway to Moss Park Arena to join the two hundred other hopeful test-takers also applying to a special pre-law program at the University of Toronto. They had travelled into the city from miles around, all anxious to make it past the LSAT and into the best law schools in the world. Many had arrived early to pay their fees, find their assigned desks, and pore through the study handbook one last time.

The countdown started on the large arena scoreboard. It wasn't long before I got distracted from the test papers on my desk. One hour and fifty-four seconds remained. I inspected the backs of the heads in front of me and started tapping both of my feet.

One of the proctors at the far end of the arena clasped her hands and stretched her arms straight out in front of her, yawning. Her shaggy blonde hair and fuchsia mouth stood out to me, even from that distance.

She began a meandering inspection, weaving though the desks in my general direction. She must have noticed my movement—nobody in that place should have been so fidgety this early in the test.

My driver's license was duct-taped to the upper right-hand side of the desk. My pen had leaked a pattern onto my thumb and index fingers and, pressed together, they formed an inky blue Rorschach. I listened to the pen scratches all around. They sounded alive, like beating insects' wings. There were scuffs of shoes, chair legs scraping against the floor, a cough that began at the back of the room and skipped all the way to the front. In a place where nobody was permitted to speak, other noises were contagious.

My desk was near the centre of the arena, on top of the red and white logo on the floor that would be covered by ice at hockey season. The scoreboard continued to wind down: one hour, forty-eight seconds left. *To ensure successful completion,* the study handbook read, *applicants should spend no longer than thirty seconds per multiple choice question, thereby enabling themselves to utilize the remaining time for the three assigned essay questions.*

The proctor was still making her way toward me, her lips now set in a stern pink oval.

"I hate to say it," the private detective had told me the night before, "it's just the way things work. You understand that, right?" For a few moments, his breathing into the phone filled my ear. "Things get hard fast, like, real fast, not like *Law and Order.* There's hardly such a thing as a solved cold case. The window shuts on you and it's over." He chuckled softly. The sound of it wilted my insides. "And the cops? Listen, I know how they work. They shift some things to the top and push others to the bottom. It's not right, but who can prove it from the outside looking in? There was nothing for months and when something did turn up, all you got were bones. Man. Bones are a bitch. I told your dad from the beginning. I had no intention of misleading him but the poor guy insisted. He told you what I told him, didn't he?"

My father and I had never uttered a word about the bones we'd seen together.

Bones are a bitch.

The proctor reached my desk. She seemed short now that she stood over me and I could see how young her face was. She was probably enrolled in law school herself, doing this job to pay off her tuition.

"Everything okay?" She had coffee on her breath and a fleshy sheen where some of her lipstick had worn off.

I nodded up at her.

"Keep your eyes on your own paper, okay?"

It wasn't too late for me to follow the proctor's orders, to barrel through the test and make up for my lost time. But I looked to the dots I had drawn on my scorecard and they seemed too deliberate, as if I had filled in circles to create a pattern. All make-believe, all for show. Did I know what I was doing? Exhaustion rippled through my muscles.

"Did you hear me? I need you to pay attention to your own test. You understand?"

I had sweated and prepared for law school all through high school, but my aspirations didn't have the power to give anybody any true relief. Not my parents and not my aunt, and least of all, myself. None of this had the power to change the shape of my family's loss. It had only been a distraction from what I really needed to do. *Diana the doctor and Alisha the lawyer, and everything, everything we've done from the day our girls were born, south to north, familiar certainties to unstable footings, will have been worth it.*

I flipped the booklet of questions to the first page and handed it and my scorecard to the proctor, along with my leaky pen.

Her face was alarmed. "What are you doing? You can't just leave."

But I stood and gathered my bag from under the chair. "I know," I whispered. "I'm really sorry."

I tore my license card off the desk with a grinding rip. It startled everyone around me and they looked at the both of us, glaring at the interruption.

Swinging my knapsack over my shoulder, I walked toward one of the auditorium's glowing exit signs, peeling the excess tape from my license and crumpling it into a ball. My desire to go into law for Diana's sake ended there.

I returned home to tell my parents what had happened the day of the job fair. They were silent as I spoke. My mother was in the kitchen doorway, in a long skirt and pullover, holding a towel in her damp hands. She had just started chopping onions on the cooking board for lunch. My father stood across from her in the living room, wearing the ratty shorts and sneakers he used for yardwork. I had caught him on the way out of the sliding door to trim the hedges around the fence.

I finished speaking and felt the weight of my coat on my shoulders. My father's mouth was open and I could see that the implications of what I had kept from them didn't make sense to him, not yet. *There was a man? There was a diary? What do you mean?*

My mother, on the other hand, had been lucid the whole way through. Her eyes were dark and she didn't let them leave me. I was the one to shrink and lower my head when tears turned her eyes to glass.

"You didn't tell us," she said. "Why?"

"I'm so sorry."

I barely got the words out before I choked on them. What could I say to her? That disappointing them had been the worst thing I could have imagined? "I know I should have said something. Right away. I have no excuse and there's nothing I can do to make up for it."

The three of us stood there until my father lay his palm across his stomach and crossed the living room, walking away from me and my mother. I heard the soft sound of my parents' bedroom door closing, then the click the kitchen phone made when the receiver in my parents' bedroom was raised.

My mother turned to the kitchen phone as if it had called her name.

"Yes, please, extension 4053," I heard my father say. "I need to talk to him right away." It was the first time he had called the police detective in over a year, almost two.

My mother didn't say anything else. She placed her towel on the counter and took measured slipper-steps toward the dining table. She pulled out a chair and sat down, placing her hands in her lap. Her black bun faced me and the tag of her pullover stuck up against her bony neck. I fought my inclination to push it back inside.

Let it be, I thought. *Imperfect will have to do.*

I looked past the sliding door, where our backyard was awash in noontime sunlight and the leaves and grass quivered in a breeze. I wondered if I would ever have the urge to take my jacket and shoes off in my parents' house again.

An ordinary speckled bird landed on the concrete stoop, picking at it with the needle-tip of its beak. The bird bent its legs and pressed down on its brown flank, sitting and covering its own feet in feathers.

CHAPTER 33

I DROVE THREE HOURS OUT OF THE CITY, FIRST DOWN THE HIGHWAY AND THEN onto two-lane roads, past farmland, churning wind turbines, and acres of hydroponic tents. The clouds spit and spun, and I met the town of Bracksbury in gloom, marked by an aging wooden sign on the right side of the road and a small, ancient graveyard on the left.

The town's main street had a jumble of giant maples and Victorian brick homes, a defunct gas station and strip malls with several empty units. I passed a series of boutiques with shutters and sloping shingled roofs dwarfed by neighbouring fast food joints.

Everything beyond the windshield of my parents' sedan was uniformly dreary and I missed the turn into the subdivision I was searching for. I drove into the parking lot of a liquor store where boys with skateboards and hoodies sat on wheel stops. Damp and morose, they watched as I swung into a self-conscious U-turn.

I turned down a residential street lined by bungalows and parked at the curb of the only low-rise in the area. *The Bracksbury Manor,* read the bronze letters nailed to the brick. It was fronted by squat, browning evergreen bushes and an uneven concrete walkway.

I only remembered to switch off my headlights when the alarm bleeped. I stepped onto the footpath with my knapsack, walking past a cacophony of chirping birds on the lawn. They were house sparrows, foraging for insects. They hopped around, undeterred by my presence.

In the airless vestibule beyond the first door, the name *Ave Benton* was posted close to the top of the residents' list. I didn't use the intercom to get in because the deadbolt that should have kept the inner door shut hadn't properly retracted. I realized that I had never been in an apartment building where the security door actually locked.

Ave lived on the ground floor, a short walk past the lobby down a hallway that smelled of cooking oil and cleaning products.

I rapped on her door. "Miss Benton? It's Alisha."

I heard the bolt unlatch and the chain unhook and the door slowly opened. Up close, Ave seemed older than I remembered from the awards celebration, but she still had her cherub face. She wore blue jeans and a pastel pink button-down shirt with untucked panels that reached her knees. Looking at her eyeshadow and lipstick, I decided she hadn't put on the makeup for my arrival alone.

"So," she said, "you made it."

We had spoken over the phone a few days back, but the conversation had not seemed to put her at ease. She sorted through my features as I stood in her doorway: a plain brown girl in sweats and a ponytail, a knapsack on her back, taller than she was but clearly intimidated. Perhaps she was trying to remember what she had seen in me that had caused her to scurry so quickly from the award ceremony.

She blinked behind her tortoiseshell glasses. "Welcome to Bracksbury. Come in."

She led me into her apartment with a limp, clutching her right hip as she walked. A little white terrier emerged and followed us with clicking paws. It wagged a clipped tail, its fur curled into half-moon tufts.

"She's an old fart now," Ave said over her dog's laboured panting. "Or else she'd be jumping and yapping all over you. She never liked strangers."

The hallway was narrow but it opened into a living room with a window as wide and high as the back wall. Out beyond the building was a rolling treeless field that extended all the way to a stretch of single-family homes in the distance.

The Manor has its charms after all, I thought to myself. I had never seen a Jane and Finch apartment with that kind of floor-to-ceiling view, grand enough to make even a gloomy day worth looking at. Light shellacked the wall above the couch and enlivened the floral patterns of her cushions.

Ave sat on the far end of the couch, close to the window wall. I took the rocking chair beside the television, my back to a square dining table, and placed my bag on the floor next to me. The terrier lingered at my foot to sniff it before lumbering off to climb onto the other side of the couch beside her owner. She circled the cushion a few times, crouched, then rested her jaw on her stumpy front legs and settled her view on an infomercial that had come on beside me. It garbled through a sales pitch, the volume too low for me to guess at the product.

"Cute dog," I said.

Ave only raised her eyebrows.

"Thank you for letting me come by. I know it's an inconvenience."

"It's okay." The suspicion I had heard over the phone still laced her tone. "I'm not the prime minister or anything."

Her voice resembled Paula's, but I could tell the sisters were as different as I expected they would be after reading Paula's manuscript, even down to Ave's preference for pastel porcelain vases and milky figurines of Victorian-looking gentlewomen that stood on the stand next to the television and graced the side tables.

Ave held the armrest with her wrinkled hand, trying to raise herself. Her fingernails were short, square, and polished with the same rose pink my mother often wore. "I didn't offer you a drink when you came in. How rude."

I shook my head. "No, thank you. I'm full of coffee. I'd really just like to talk with you, if that's all right."

It had been that easy for me to make her expression change from guarded to weathered. She settled herself back and tugged on the curls at the side of her head, causing her whole scalp to shift—she was wearing a wig that looked not unlike the hair of her younger days.

"What can I do to get you to consider joining the lawsuit, Miss Benton?"

"What are you, Paula's little lawyer? How old are you? Eleven?"

I had to smile. "Like I said, I'm a friend. She doesn't know I'm here."

One eyebrow rose. "So, you're meddling."

"She'd say so. But leave me to deal with her."

"I'll have to leave you to all this stuff too." She jostled the terrier's ears and it flinched and shut its eyes. "Court battles aren't for me. I'm old and it's a waste of time. After twenty years of trying, what do people think they're going to get from the fight? A million dollars each? And would that make up for anything? Listen, Paula knows this. I told her the same thing when she asked me. You're not the first to ask. I didn't change my tune with Paula and I won't do it with you now." She set her sight square to the television. With a growling voiceover and distorted electric guitars it sounded like a commercial for a monster truck rally.

"Paula would never say it to you directly, but I know it would mean the world to her to have her sister—"

A harrumph. "Other people were forced to live there too. They can take my place just fine."

The dog raised her head to watch as I shifted to retrieve the photograph from the back pocket of my jeans. I set it on the coffee table for Ave to see: the old black and white image of two little girls holding hands in a field, too laden to smile at the camera.

"Did you know she had this?"

Ave bent forward but only gave the photo a passing glance. "We haven't been in touch very much. We know it's best to keep contact to a minimum." She clucked her tongue, smoothed the cotton over her stomach. "You're too young to understand."

"I know, but—"

"She lied to me, you know. She didn't tell me that our mother died while we were in the orphanage. Do you know what it's like to wait on someone who will never show up? To think that you'd actually be able to go home when there's no chance? But there I was, like an idiot."

"You and your sister loved each other, though, didn't you?"

She offered the first smile I had seen on her, even if it was wry. "Didn't make me any less of a chump. The main thing is that Paula and I didn't agree on a whole lot of things as we got older. The two of us trying to get along now? It would be like trying to take a piss in the wind. I won't get into it."

"I wish you would. I want to understand."

Her lips flattened. I worried that I had pushed too far, that she would end the conversation and refuse to answer any more of my phone calls. I had used all my persuasive powers to get even this far.

She pushed her fingers into her dog's fur. The dog yawned and smacked its mouth.

"She wanted to be in charge of my life. It's why she didn't tell me. Knowledge is power and she had the power." She dragged her palm along the dog's spine, took her tail and gave it a soft yank. "Did she tell you about Gordon?"

"Not so much." I thought about the young man I had read about Paula seeing at the concert, beaming at his mother's performance.

"She didn't like the fact that I had him, right from the very start. No one did, really. Teenage moms weren't appreciated back then, I get it." She swiped the corners of her mouth with her thumb and index finger. "But I wasn't about to blame Gordy for my problems. He was an innocent baby. Paula was at my back about it for years."

The sun was strengthening and penetrating the window and the dog found herself favoured by a beam. She rolled on her side, her four sausage legs stretched straight, her fur a white aura in the light.

"Can you believe it? She didn't want to have anything to do with me and my son. She was ashamed of us and she wouldn't give it a rest. By the time she tried to come around, it was too late. He had passed. Leukaemia took him at forty-four."

I looked at the lamp on the table beside her, its lacy blue shade. A cast iron picture frame leaned up against its base, a portrait of a young man, no older than thirty, in a striped suit jacket and paisley tie. Ave's shrine to her lost child. There were no sticks of incense or props. Only his freckles, his wide brown eyes, and a tender smile I couldn't imagine Paula denying.

"He was young," I answered quietly, for the first time questioning my motivation in meeting her, in reading *Children of the Maroons* without telling Paula, in pushing my way into this. Maybe it was just selfish curiosity, after all. "I'm so sorry."

The hard edges of her face dissolved. "I know you care for Paula and you're trying to do something good for her. But there's too much the two of us can't work out. I don't mean to upset you. I just don't want to open those wounds again."

She scooted forward on the couch cushion. For a moment the dog tried to ignore the disturbance and stay in the warmth of the sunbeam, but too much had changed. She reached out her front paws and clacked to the foot of the couch, sitting on the parquet by Ave's slipper.

"Sorry you had to come all this way, little miss."

I reached into the pocket of my bag. Human and canine eyes were on me as I fished for the wad of papers inside, placing the pile on the table beside the photograph. "Let me just leave this with you, then."

I pushed the photocopy of Paula's book closer to her but she didn't look down to acknowledge it.

"I'll never understand the horrible things you two went through back then, I know that. But I did lose my sister. I know what that's like, at least. I know you can't get back what you lost."

She frowned and looked down.

"So I guess I'm here for a simple reason, in the end. I think it would be a shame for you not to read this because I think Paula really wrote it for you."

Ave's eyes fastened onto the title. For a moment I saw the recognition, the shimmer in her eyes. Even the dog had felt it, stiffening her neck and holding her nub-tail straight. Perhaps Ave still had faith that she and sister were joined together as great-great-granddaughters of Queen Nanny. She pointed at the pages. "Paula wrote this? She knows you're giving it to me?"

"No, and I'm completely out of line in doing it. Maybe she didn't even know who she was writing it for when she started into it, but after reading it, I know without a doubt that she wrote it for you. Please take a look at it. I promise this'll be the last thing I ask of you."

She sighed and her expression thawed. "Okay. What can I tell you? I'll try. I can't promise more than that."

"That's all I want."

I gathered my things and let Ave and her terrier walk me out of the apartment. As I returned to my parents' sedan, disbanding the army of birds at the curb, a small spark of hope flickered inside of me. I thought it must've been miniscule compared to what roared in Paula, but I considered it a bit of the Maroons' fire that flashed within me on the long drive back to the city.

EPILOGUE

MY WINDOW ON THE FIFTH FLOOR LOOKS OUT ONTO ST. GEORGE STREET AND the student centre. Tents and booths take the place of parallel-parked cars and herds of people weave and twist past each other on the road. Some wear yellow hard hats and others wear blue athletic jerseys and hold big foam fingers.

The sun and wind work in tandem over a blue April sky. Banners snap straight and the student centre's steps and railings gleam like new. Green buds dot trees across the campus, but I still find it difficult to put my finger on early spring without the appearance of crabapple blossoms.

My dorm room window doesn't open much beyond a sliver but it's enough for bouts of cool air to get in and skim my neck. As I type these pages at my desk, I'm listening to muddled orders being barked into a megaphone, floating over the buildings from King's College Circle. *Jump the gun! Just get one!* I can't decipher what the visiting high school students are being commanded to do.

Every year these University of Toronto tours seem to stretch out longer and longer. I suspect they're designed to fool hopeful entrants into thinking that they'll get to campus and the fun will carry on past frosh week, that everyone won't eventually have to fend for themselves. Now that I'm almost finished with my Bachelor of Arts in English Literature, the first-year lectures with hundreds of students have shrunk to rooms of less than forty students, and I spend most of my time by myself, typing on a laptop into the morning hours. It's a companionless pursuit.

My mother didn't say much when I switched majors and left home for my first year. In fact, she didn't say much of substance to anyone that whole summer. After I told my parents about what happened at the mall, I quit the student position at her dental office so she didn't have to spend all day with me. I missed her talking to me so much that I listened from my beige bedroom for her voice when she answered the phone or complained under her breath doing chores in other rooms of the duplex. Over those summer weeks, I mostly caught her presence in smells, in the moments when she fried curry paste on the stove or in the whiffs of her perfume mixed with the incense on Diana's shelf. I couldn't begrudge her for keeping her distance, but I inhaled deeply in an effort to store her in my nostrils. No matter how much air I pulled in, I could never hold her inside of me.

Still, I had noticed her perplexed sympathy-sniffles that evening as I stood on the phone and she stood in the kitchen doorway, watching me with her fingers at her lips and water in her eyes, her Guyana-gold earrings still in place though she had changed from her work clothes into her bathrobe. She saw my tears drop onto the counter next to the telephone as I spoke to Ave.

"God, it was like that between us," Ave said to me across the line, equal parts amazed and disturbed and giddy. The *tap-tap* of dog paws clacked in the background. "I don't know. I thought too much time had passed for anyone to remember anything, and I doubted myself too—am I Alzheimering? Did I make it up? Honest. I thought I was the only one who'd remembered us like that. I never could block things out the way you see some people doing it, you know? I remember too much." A swallow. "That hard-headed woman. But the two of us were really like that back then, back when we were little. We did meet in the night. I used to wait all day for it. I mean, she was the only one who made that hellhole bearable. I can't even tell you." She made a noise, the combination of a cleared throat and a guffaw. "And look at us. We're all elderly and bitchy now. Can you believe it?"

I used my sleeve to catch the spilling liquid at my nose. "Oh, I believe you."

"So, the ball's in my court, is it? Fine, I need a favour. You got her phone number on you? The one in my book's old."

I watched as my mother turned to leave, one hand on her stomach and the other clasping her robe at the chest. "Sure, give me a minute." She passed over squares of light on the hardwood floor on her way to her room. For the first time in a long time, I felt a balm of relief soothe my spine.

❀

In early August, I drove the sedan out of the city again, this time with Paula sitting next to me on the passenger's seat in her buttoned-up jacket. She laid both hands flat on the big brown handbag on her lap. I had never seen her carry a purse before. She snapped the visor down to check herself in the mirror—she had already done that a dozen times over the two hours we had been on the road.

"You all right?" I asked, looking at the sky beyond the highway. It was wax paper white. Sunlight was just about to tear through.

"See that truck up there? Be careful. It's too wobbly." She cranked the volume on the news station to make sure the conversation would end.

She followed me as we walked up to the Bracksbury Brew, a cottage converted into a café at the edge of the town. It had orange marigold flowerpots on each front step. *Open under renovation,* the sign said, and like any house, it had a storm door and a knob to turn. Inside, the place smelled of coffee, baked sweets, and latex paint.

Ave was the only patron at two o'clock on a weekday afternoon, sitting in a position to monitor the door from the third table in. She got to her feet when our eyes met, wearing blue jeans and a paisley blazer. Her curls were in place and she kept one of her hands on the back of her chair.

I stayed where I was and let Paula walk to her first, carrying her handbag at her side.

"Hello, Ave," Paula said.

Ave blinked at her a few times behind her glasses. "Hi."

They both stood there, watching one another and saying nothing more.

I claimed the seat across from Paula, my back to the window. I pulled my jacket from my arms. "I need something to eat. It's past lunchtime and I'm famished."

Paula took my cue and took her coat off. Ave sat only after the two of us were seated.

I busied myself with the menu. "What's good here? They make a decent Americano?"

I wasn't sure what I had expected by their meeting. A smash of hugs and tears and laughter? An explosive rekindling of a long-fractured relationship? *You won't believe how many paintings I've done for you, Ave! I can't wait to show them to you!* Surely I should have known that meeting in person is different than phone calls, that coming face-to-face after all those years wouldn't effortlessly repair anything.

"What'd you order?" I asked Ave.

She shrugged. "Nothing yet. But everybody raves about their pecan pie."

Paula cleared her throat. "You can't go wrong with pecan. Hard to screw up."

I flipped to the back of the menu. "I was thinking rhubarb."

"No way, they'll bring it out of the freezer," said Ave. "Trust me. Wrong season. See the little stars by the food names?" She tugged the top of my menu down to point at the page with a pink nail. "Those are baked fresh. Get a starred one."

"Rhubarb gets wacky when you freeze it," Paula said. "No amount of sugar can hide the texture. That's why I only eat the rhubarb I make, yeah? People don't know how to do it."

Ave picked at the curls at the back of her neck. "Baking's a lost art."

"People just buy everything. No one even tries anymore." Paula turned her head to the counter where a girl in a hairnet and apron, probably a high school student, bent to rearrange scones in the display case. "She comes here or we go there?"

"Go there." Ave looked to me. "Starred."

"Fine," I said, "I'll do pecan."

A half-smile came to Ave's mouth. "Live to our age, little miss, you'll learn a few truths about pie."

And that was the sign I needed to understand things would be okay between Paula and Ave, in time.

✿

My father drove me to the university soon after their reunion. I carried a gym bag and my knapsack out of the dormitory elevator and he followed me with two stacked cardboard boxes in his arms. We pushed to the sides of the hallway, making space for the other first-year students and their parents tramping in and out.

He set the boxes on the bare single mattress that dwarfed my new room and picked at the packing tape, a furrow on his forehead. I wondered if the room's narrowness, its grimy single window that faced the brick of the dormitory next door, was causing his unease. Perhaps he didn't like the sparseness of my luggage in comparison to the cases and cases the other girls had brought with them.

"Do you have to get back right away?" I asked him, standing at my nook of a closet and threading one of my sweatshirts onto a hanger. "They're doing a tour. You might want to see where everything is."

He yanked a strip of tape from one box with a noisy rip. "All right."

My father stayed with me for the tour as well as the student–parent dinner in the dining hall after that. By then, he had taken off his suit jacket and rolled his shirtsleeves up to his elbows. He sat across from me at the table and bent his head to slurp a spoon of carrot soup over his bowl, pressing his tie to his chest. I tried not eavesdrop on the enthused chatter of the families around us, all those eager university students and their enraptured parents.

Even with the information we had given to the police and the private investigator, there were no new discoveries about what had happened to my sister. It remained a cold case.

"I went down to speak with the police," my father said to me a few days after I had told him and my mother what really happened the day Diana disappeared. "He made a copy of her diary and recorded everything. He wants me to bring you to talk to him again."

I nodded. "Yes. Of course."

"He said there's no way of knowing what that man was really doing. He said we have to make sure we don't let it eat us up. Not at this stage. I know Diana wouldn't want it. She wouldn't want it for you."

I was sitting on the edge of my bed and my father stood in the doorway with his reading glasses on his face and his hands folded together in front of him.

"What the detective meant to say is that too much time has passed," I answered to my knees. "If they'd known about everything sooner, things might've been different...."

"He didn't say that."

I shook my head and found I couldn't look my father in the eyes. "Did you tell Auntie Julie?"

"No."

"Will you?"

"I don't have to. Neither does your mother." He pressed his lips together and pushed them back out. "They don't know that it would have changed the case. And I hope you know that even if you wanted us to tell her, your aunt wouldn't think anything...anything bad of you...."

But he left my room after the cushion of some silence, maybe because it was clear that the two of us were in the same situation. Not prepared to forgive ourselves for any of our wrongdoings, but consoled to forgive each other.

✿

During my first year of university I would sometimes spot the man at the mall rows over in the lecture hall or on my journeys to class—even across the seats of a subway car when it slid out of the tunnel to blinding sun streaming in its windows. The mirages became more vivid than they had been in grade school, and it was only around my third year that the man stopped stalking me with such persistence. I think the process of writing this account between my classes and all through my school breaks, alone in the bedroom my parents kept for me in their house, finally curbed the visions.

"It's strange to get it on paper, yeah?" Paula told me when I brought her the first draft of this manuscript, rough and without an ending. After reading and sharing her memoir without asking, I thought it only fair that she be first to read mine.

I used the house key she had given me to get into her apartment without disturbing her work. She was in the old Knicks jersey, sketching an outline on a fresh canvas, looking back and forth between it and the photograph she had taped on the easel above it: little Paula and Ave in the wide field, holding hands.

"Couldn't even do mine in first person," she said. "Too close for comfort."

"Yeah, it wasn't easy."

"I wouldn't tell everybody to attempt it. All this stuff they talk about you telling your story is utter bullshit. It's not a magic cure. And they don't tell you that you have to be prepared for how much it hurts."

I leaned the thick manila envelope against her easel, right next to her leg. "Don't feel like you have to read it all the way through. I'm not sure it's any good and it's not even done yet."

"Read something by Miss Sookermany only partway? Yeah, right."

I stood behind her as the curtain beside us undulated in the breeze. I placed my hand on her shoulder. "Try doing this painting in black and white. It fits."

"What's all this here?" She turned her head to watch me, the black of her pupils glinting. "You don't get a say in this one." Her freckles congregated on her cheeks when she smiled.

✿

It wasn't until I started my final year of my undergrad that my mother and I began to talk on the phone beyond basic updates about work and the house, my courses and when I would be able to come home and sleep over.

"I'm making a stew," she said on the other end of the line, "and you're supposed to use red curry. You know red curry? They call for coconut milk. Everything from Thailand needs coconut milk. And peanuts. You ever had that? Crushed peanuts on your noodles?"

"Yeah. There are a few Thai places around here."

"I have to tell you, it smells nice. Your father's helping. He can cook when he puts his mind to it."

I thought of him standing at the burner, stirring a steaming pot. He had started helping my mother cook more often. He'd even started attending a grief support group at the nearby community centre. But I couldn't envision this new version of my father properly, him in that suburban kitchen with salt and pepper hair. In my imagination, he was still in our old apartment, with his suit and his precise black haircut, and I was there too, listening for that cough-laugh of his that so thrilled me.

"I hope it turns out," said my mother. "I shouldn't have promised to make something so fancy but the lady who's retiring tomorrow came from Thailand. What else can I do? Everyone brings cold salads and samosas to these buffets. Somebody has to make something proper. She was a hygienist for over twenty years and the children love her. I don't know how we'll manage without her. She's such a nice person."

I heard rustling, a familiar clicking noise. I knew my mother was using the barbeque lighter to light the incense and candles around Diana's portrait.

I looked to the skinny crescent moon outside my dorm window. "Mom, did you buy a gift for Sunday?"

"A case with a strap. It's leather and has pockets. It's much nicer than a man's briefcase. Your aunt will need something like it." I heard a rush of water from the tap in their kitchen and knew my father was washing up at the kitchen sink. "I didn't write the card yet," she continued with a lower voice. "Put your name on it too?"

My mother, quietly rescuing us.

"Okay."

I never revealed anything about the affair to my mother, and I had never spoken of it again with Auntie Julie either. I was too afraid that naming it would undo the smiles and soft cheek-kisses my aunt and I had managed with each other again, bashful as they were. Things hadn't gone back to the way they had been between us, but between my mother and her sister things seemed the same. They continued to visit and call each other as they had done my whole life, never wasting an opportunity. Even for Paula and Ave—even after they'd been separated from each other for so many years—their relationship wasn't all that different. Neither could claim much space from the other. Are all sisters like that? Despite their plans and better judgments and life and death, are they only able to survive in reference to each other?

When I arrived at the café that Sunday afternoon before my aunt's law school graduation ceremony, I lingered at the front window and peered through to the table where my family sat together. The three of them were in work clothes, blouses and skirts and suit, but Auntie Julie had arranged her hair in a braid instead of the bun she usually wore. In the window, I saw the reflection of Roy Thomson Hall, its mirrored curve juxtaposed over their bodies. After lunch, we would all go there to watch Auntie Julie get called to the bar.

She blinked up from her menu, her eyes traced and shadowed with more makeup than usual. She said something in my mother's ear and her Guyana-gold Pisces necklace caught the light. My mother nodded and read the menu in her hands. She leaned over to inspect the print on Auntie Julie's menu as if they might be different from each other. I waited for my father to say something but he only brought his coffee mug to his mouth, blew into it, and took a lengthy sip. He put it down and slipped his fingers under the folds of his collar to adjust his tie.

A waiter arrived at the table in front of theirs and blocked my view. The back of his white shirt acted like a screen and, with the window glass over it, I saw the reflection of a passing streetcar and the chained bicycles on the street. In that brief margin of time, separated from my family, I realized that I didn't write this account for Paula or even for myself.

I wrote it for you, Auntie Julie.

I wondered what you would make of it when I printed it out for you, how my words might change your memories of all of us, of Diana and Don and Beatrice and Alisha. The possibilities made my heartbeat quicken and it still does, even as I type these last sentences. Still, I am confident that this book is really yours to read, that I need you to understand my story more than anyone else. It can't replace anything or reconfigure our pains, but it might allow you and I to reclaim what we meant to each other, if only partially. I have come to understand the possibility of reconciliation to be enough.

I stood, looking at the waiter's back and watching people eat and drink inside, the only seat available likely the one reserved for me. I waited for him to step out of the way, hoping to see my family one more time before my feet could find the energy to carry me inside. This was our life. My life for the three of them.

A cluster of seagulls crossed over the reflection of sky above my head, some fluttering, some gliding by on sturdy wings.

AUTHOR'S NOTE

THIS BOOK WAS INSPIRED BY THE REAL LIFE EXPERIENCES OF MY LATE FRIEND, Mr. Garnet Smith (1938–2017). Along with four of his siblings, Garnet was taken from his mother's home by Child Welfare Services and brought to the Nova Scotia Home for Colored Children in 1941. He was four years old at the time and he remained in the care of the home until approximately 1955, when he was eighteen.

I won't recount his story here. It is well addressed in Wanda Lauren Taylor's 2015 non-fiction book, *The Nova Scotia Home for Colored Children: The Hurt, the Hope, and the Healing*. In it Garnet shared the difficulties he and other children faced in the home, and the traumatic consequences of institutional abuse. He spoke of the challenges he faced growing up without full access to education, health care, and life skills that support a child's transition to adulthood.

Taylor's book provides useful history about the founding of the home in a time of racial segregation. It was opened in 1921 as a community response to the reality that mainstream child welfare facilities did not accept Black children. Even though child protection services apprehended Black children on behalf of the Government of Nova Scotia and relied on the home to house them, they provided much less funding for and oversight of these residents compared to what they offered to residents of other institutions. Feeble governmental funding of Black children was a reality for the majority of the home's sixty-eight-year history.

In this context, terrible things happened, and they happened almost entirely unimpeded. Underpaid, undertrained employees perpetrated a host of physical, sexual, and mental abuses against residents. They pitted children against each other and allowed bullying between residents to go on unchecked. Children experienced constant hunger and deprivation, lack of basic health care, forced labour, pressure to fundraise for the home's operations, and little access to education, programming, and opportunities to experience the world outside of the home.

Some of the things that happened at the Nova Scotia Home for Colored Children echo what happened in similar institutions across the country, including other orphanages, residential schools, and group home facilities. The removal of children from their homes and communities itself has followed a familiar pattern: children and families who face racism, poverty, ableism, and other forms of discrimination are most often subject to institutionalization. As a nation, we have to continue to confront and break from a colonial history of mistreating vulnerable young people and their families.

Garnet was forced to live in the home for fourteen years, in the earlier days of its operation. He was very open about his story. I am honoured that he chose to share it, and his subsequent struggle for justice, with me. I read the many documents, records, and articles he collected about the home and the class action lawsuit launched by former residents—an incredible group of survivors that included him. He was excited that I wanted to write something about his experiences. I told him that I didn't want to retell his story because he had already been so effective in the ways he'd told it himself. He was incredibly supportive of my efforts to fictionalize some of the things he experienced. He read an early draft of this manuscript and wrote suggestions in the margins of the pages, correcting my spelling and grammar. This was a man who had to teach himself to read, whose love of words and books was so hard won. I often think of his soft pencil marks on the pages, gently encouraging me to do better.

Garnet was nothing short of an inspiration. He was an avid community volunteer and a compassionate, God-fearing person who loved his family, friends, and neighbours. I realized early on that this novel could not possibly reflect how special he was, what he meant to me and the many other people he impacted. But I do hope that, in some small way, it honours him.

Proceeds of this novel go to VOICES, the Victims of Institutional Child Exploitation Society, and specifically toward the Garnet Smith Educational Bursary for young people connected to survivors of the Nova Scotia Home for Colored Children.

ACKNOWLEDGEMENTS

SINCEREST THANKS TO THE ORGANIZATIONS THAT ASSISTED ME IN THE writing process, namely: the Ontario Arts Council, Banff Centre for Arts and Creativity, and Hedgebrook. The two amazing community-based organizations where I was employed while writing, METRAC Action on Violence and Eva's Initiatives for Homeless Youth, were wonderfully supportive as well. I am thankful to them.

I am grateful to Stephanie Sinclair and Transatlantic Agency for believing in this manuscript and Whitney Moran and Vagrant Press for taking it up and publishing it. In addition, I worked with several mentors, editors, and generally gifted and kind people who were invaluable to the completion of this manuscript. They include Karim Alrawi, Dionne Brand, Bethany Gibson, Lawrence Hill, Greg Hollingshead, Tessa McWatt, Kate Juniper, Michael Schellenberg, Linda Spalding, Wanda Lauren Taylor, and Janice Zawerbny. On top of that, several people with talent and wisdom provided me guidance, feedback, encouragement, and endorsing words. Some talked me out of dark literary and non-literary corners. There are far too many to list here, but I am thankful for their generosity and for the ways they spoke with care so I could understand and listen.

I'd like to offer my deepest thanks to Garnet Smith, the man who shared his life experiences with me and gave me his patient blessing to write this book. He is sorely missed. To Tony Smith, Gerry Morrison, Tracey Dorrington-Skinner, and all members of VOICES, the Victims of Institutional Child Exploitation Society, your support has heartened me and your desire to make systems better for all young people is thrilling. Thank you for being the voices of lived experience that push hard to make change. I wish things were set up in such a way that you didn't have to push so hard to achieve your worthy goals.

And to David Hunter, my love, thank you and God bless you. This whole thing would frankly be impossible without you.